Classics of Modern Science Fiction

THE CLASSIC
PHILIP JOSÉ FARMER
1964–1973

Volume 5

Classics of Modern Science Fiction

THE CLASSIC
PHILIP JOSÉ FARMER
1964–1973

Volume 5

Introduction by Martin H. Greenberg
Foreword by Isaac Asimov

Series Editor: George Zebrowski

Crown Publishers, Inc.
New York

Library of Congress Cataloging in Publication Data
Farmer, Philip José.
The classic Philip José Farmer, 1964–1973.
(Classics of modern science fiction; v. 5)
1. Science fiction, American.   I. Greenberg,
Martin Harry.   II. Title.   III. Series.
PS3556.A72A6   1984b
813′.54   84-7081
ISBN 0-517-55545-X
10   9   8   7   6   5   4   3   2   1
First Edition

Contents

Retrieving the Lost

by Isaac Asimov

T HE HISTORY OF contemporary science fiction begins with the spring of 1926, when the first magazine ever to be devoted entirely to science fiction made its appearance. For a quarter-century thereafter science fiction continued to appear in magazines—and only in magazines.

They were wonderful days for those of us who lived through them, but there was a flaw. Magazines are, by their very nature, ephemeral. They are on the newsstands a month or two and are gone. A very few readers may save their issues, but they are fragile and do not stand much handling.

Beginning in 1950, science fiction in book form began to make its appearance, and some of the books retrieved the magazine short stories and serials in the form of collections, anthologies and novels. As time went on, however, it became clear that the vast majority of science-fiction books were in paperback form, and these, too, were ephemeral. Their stay on the newsstands is not entirely calendar-bound, and they can withstand a bit more handling than periodicals can—but paperbacks tend to be, like magazines, throwaway items.

That leaves the hardback book, which finds its way into public libraries as well as private homes, and which is durable. Even there, we have deficiencies. The relatively few science-fiction books that appear in hardback usually appear in small printings and few, if any, reprintings. Out-of-print is the usual fate, and often a not very long delayed one, at that.

Some science-fiction books have endured, remaining available in hardcover form for years, even decades, and appearing in repeated paperback reincarnations. We all know which these are because, by enduring, they have come to be read by millions, including you and me.

It is, of course, easy to argue that the test of time and popularity has succeeded in separating the gold from the dross, and that we have with us all the science-fiction books that have deserved to endure.

That, however, is too easy a dismissal. It is an interesting and convenient theory, but the world of human affairs is far too complex to fit into theories, especially convenient ones. It sometimes takes time to recognize quality, and the time required is sometimes longer than a visible existence of a particular book. That the quality of a book is not recognizable at once need not be a sign of deficiency, but rather a sign of subtlety. It is not being particularly paradoxical to point out that a book may be, in some cases, too good to be immediately popular. And then, thanks to the mechanics of literary ephemerality, realization of the fact may come too late.

Or must it?

Suppose there are dedicated and thoughtful writers and scholars like George Zebrowski and Martin H. Greenberg, who have been reading science fiction intensively, and with educated taste, for decades. And suppose there is a publisher such as Crown Publishers, Inc., that is interested in providing a second chance for quality science fiction which was undervalued the first time round.

In that case we end up with Crown's *Classics of Modern Science Fiction* in which the lost is retrieved, the unjustly forgotten is remembered, and the undervalued is resurrected. And you are holding a sample in your hand.

Naturally, the revival of these classics will benefit the publisher, the editors, and the writers, but that is almost by the way.

The real beneficiaries will be the readers, among whom the older are likely to taste again delicacies they had all but forgotten, while the younger will encounter delights of whose existence they were unaware.

Read—

And enjoy.

Introduction

by Martin H. Greenberg

un/con/ven/tion/al. Not adhering to convention
con/ven/tion. General usage or custom

PHILIP JOSÉ FARMER certainly did not and does not adhere to the thematic and stylistic conventions of science fiction; in fact, he was personally responsible for changing several of the most important and long-lasting conventions in the field. Science fiction had ignored one of the most important of all human concerns—sexuality—partly because pulp SF's audience was considered to be adolescent boys (a strange reason on the face of it) and partly because the men who controlled the field didn't think the readership wanted strong doses of it mixed in with the adventure and the technology.

Farmer proved them wrong with his first published work, "The Lovers," which appeared in the August 1952 issue of *Startling Stories*. It's gripping depiction of love and sex between a man and an alien insectlike creature had a tremendous impact on the field, broadening what was "acceptable" and opening up the market for others to explore. Largely because of this single story, he was voted a Hugo Award in 1953 as "The Best New Writer of 1952." It was the first of what to date constitutes a body of work totaling more than forty novels and collections, characterized by originality, inventiveness, and a use of symbolism that was yet to be equalled.

Philip José Farmer was born in Terre Haute, Indiana, in 1918 but was raised in Peoria, Illinois, where he spent the bulk of his life. He enrolled at Bradley University in 1941 but had to drop out due to lack of funds. He later returned to school as an evening student, earning a degree in 1950; he also worked in a steel mill for many years. Farmer began to write in the mid-1940s, and "The Lovers" was published when he was thirty-four, an advanced age by the standards of the science-fiction community. However, he quickly made up for lost time by an astounding prolificity, although he did not write for considerable portions of time during the first decade of his career.

His major literary themes and obsessions were clear from early on and have been noted by all who have written about him—a concern with sexuality and reproduction in all their variety; the good and evil that he seems to believe resides in all of us; an interest in religious beliefs and imagery, especially with matriarchal religions; parasitology, frequently coupled with sexuality; and a deep love of American popular culture and the books he read and adored as a child and as a young man, especially Burroughs, Baum, and Twain, but also including the characters and magazines of the pulp era. Indeed, he has reworked these stories and characters in his own writing to the extent that he has produced a whole body of work about parallel universes, parallel places, and parallel people, books in which Samuel Clemens, Tarzan, Odysseus, and Doc Savage all interact and most are even related to one another.

His writing is characterized by rapid pacing, some weakness of plot, a wonderful use of puns, protagonists who are deeply flawed—a quality especially true in his "heroic" figures—and a deep cynicism that pervades even his humorous work.

But most of all, Farmer (like the late Philip K. Dick) writes of the real, the unreal, and the maybe real, combining and integrating them into the same story in ways that have revolutionized one corner of modern science fiction. Few writers have been as daring so early as Farmer, few so willing to shock, in his case usually to good effect. One of his most important critics, Mary T. Brizzi, has commented that "he is certainly among the brightest stars in the science fiction sky," and that "his early works were beautifully crafted, exploring unconventional themes in a sensitive way." His work has also been called "nauseating," "filthy," and "obscene." John W. Campbell, Jr., said that one of his stories (which he didn't buy) made him "want to throw up." He notes that other, more admiring critics have noted the powerful influence of Freud and Jung in his work, but he rejects these references saying that "the term Farmerian should be good enough." Indeed it is.

This volume collects what I consider to be representative selections of his best work from the years 1965 to 1973, years that saw the publication of numerous important longer works and collections, including *The Maker of Universes* (1965), the first volume in his World of Tiers series of five novels; *To Your Scattered Bodies Go* (1971), the award-winning first novel in his best-selling Riverworld series; *Night of Light* (1966); *The Stone God Awakens* (1970); and *Down in the Black Gang, and Others* (1971).

We hope that outstanding examples of his best work since 1973 will be included in a future volume in this series. For now, we offer you such stunning stories as "The Shadow of Space," whose image of a gigantic woman floating in space and of entire planets the size of Ping-Pong balls passing through a spaceship are among the most vivid in the history of science fiction. This story gives new meaning to the words *point of view*.

The very short "Don't Wash the Carats" first appeared in the third volume of Damon Knight's late and lamented Orbit series of original anthologies. Farmer calls the story one of his "polytropical paramyths," which, he says, "came like a hot flash while reading a passage in Henry Miller's *Big Sur and the Oranges of Hieronymus Bosch*. This was, if I remember correctly, diamonds are sometimes born during violent storms. Damon Knight, who bought it . . . wasn't sure what it meant, and neither did, or do, I."

"The Jungle Rot Kid on the Nod" is pure Farmer and had an unusual publishing history. Thought by Farmer to be far too extreme for the regular science-fiction magazines, it first appeared in *Broadside*, one of the raunchiest "girlie" magazines of its era, and was then reprinted several years later in *New Worlds Science Fiction* in England. Phil asked himself a—to him—simple question: What would have happened if *William* Burroughs had written the Tarzan books instead of Edgar Rice Burroughs? The answer is the incredible "story" you will shortly read.

"The Sliced-Crosswise Only-on-Tuesday World" and "Sketches Among the Ruins of My Mind" are two very different stories about time and what time does to people. "Sliced" can be read as a tour de force or as a grim joke; either way it is one of his most unforgettable stories. The much longer "Sketches" is much better read than summarized and contains one of the increasingly rare and best examples in science fiction of a beautifully implemented *new* idea. The last story in the collection, "After King Kong Fell," is an outstanding example of what happens to one of the strongest myths in popular culture when Phil Farmer gets his hands on it.

"Riders of the Purple Wage" and "The Oogenesis of Bird City" (the latter was originally part of the former but was taken out and published alone in *Amazing Stories*) are two of Farmer's most famous works, and rightly so. "Riders" appeared in Harlan Ellison's now legendary collection of original stories, *Dangerous Visions*, in 1967. The collection was conceived by Ellison as a showcase for material that could not be published in the genre science-fiction magazines of the day because of existing language and thematic taboos. However, the book took a long time to assemble, and most of the barriers that Ellison was concerned with had actually fallen by the time the book appeared, or shortly thereafter. This in no way detracts from the book's excellence or impact, both of which are impressive. "Riders" was by far the longest story in that volume and the one that attracted the most notice. It is a powerful "utopia becomes dystopia" story about the impossibility of perfection in an imperfect world, and its use of slogans like "luxury is a necessity" reminds one of 1984. Philip José

Farmer is a man who clearly believes that everything in life has its costs as well as its benefits—and it is up to us to choose what is most important. "Riders" was nominated for a Nebula Award in 1967 and won the Hugo Award in 1968 as the best novella of 1967. "The Oogenesis of Bird City," while it won no awards, is in some ways even more interesting than "Riders," especially in its discussion of the city's politics.

These were productive and creative years for Philip José Farmer, and there were, and we hope still are, more to come.

Classics of Modern Science Fiction

THE CLASSIC
PHILIP JOSÉ FARMER
1964–1973

Volume 5

The Shadow of Space

1967

1

THE KLAXON CLEARED its plastic throat and began to whoop. Alternate yellows and reds pulsed on the consoles wrapped like bracelets around the wrists of the captain and the navigator. The huge auxiliary screens spaced on the bulkheads of the bridge also flashed red and yellow.

Captain Grettir, catapulted from his reverie, and from his chair, stood up. The letters and numerals 20-G-DZ-R hung burning on a sector of each screen and spurted up from the wrist-console, spread out before his eyes, then disappeared, only to rise from the wrist-console again and magnify themselves and thin into nothing. Over and over again. 20-G-DZ-R. The code letters indicating that the alarm originated from the corridor leading to the engine room.

He turned his wrist and raised his arm to place the lower half of the console at the correct viewing and speaking distance.

"20-G-DZ-R, report!"

The flaming, expanding, levitating letters died out, and the long high-cheekboned face of MacCool, chief engineer, appeared as a tiny image on the sector of the console. It was duplicated on the bridge bulkhead screens. It rose and grew larger, shooting towards Grettir, then winking out to be followed by a second ballooning face.

Also on the wrist-console's screen, behind MacCool, were Comas, a petty officer, and Grinker, a machinist's mate. Their faces did not float up because they were not in the central part of the screen. Behind them was a group of marines and an 88-K cannon on a floating sled.

"It's the Wellington woman," MacCool said. "She used a

1

photer, lowpower setting, to knock out the two guards stationed at the engine-room port. Then she herded us—me, Comas, Grinker—out. She said she'd shoot us if we resisted. And she welded the grille to the bulkhead so it can't be opened unless it's burned off."

"I don't know why she's doing this. But she's reconnected the drive wires to a zander bridge so she can control the acceleration herself. We can't do a thing to stop her unless we go in after her."

He paused, swallowed and said, "I could send men outside and have them try to get through the engine room airlock or else cut through the hull to get her. While she was distracted by this, we could make frontal attack down the corridor. But she says she'll shoot anybody that gets too close. We could lose some men. She means what she says."

"If you cut a hole in the hull, she'd be out of air, dead in a minute," Grettir said.

"She's in a spacesuit," MacCool replied. "That's why I didn't have this area sealed off and gas flooded in."

Grettir hoped his face was not betraying his shock. Hearing an exclamation from Wang, seated near him, Grettir turned his head. He said, "How in the hell did she get out of sick bay?"

He realized at the same time that Wang could not answer that question. MacCool said, "I don't know, sir. Ask Doctor Wills."

"Never mind that now!"

Grettir stared at the sequence of values appearing on the navigator's auxiliary bulkhead-screen. The 0.5 of light speed had already climbed to 0.96. It changed every 4 seconds. The 0.96 became 0.97, then 0.98, 0.99 and then 1.0. And then 1.1 and 1.2.

Grettir forced himself to sit back down. If anything was going to happen, it would have done so by now; the TSN-X cruiser *Sleipnir*, 280 million tons, would have been converted to pure energy.

A nova, bright but very brief, would have gouted in the heavens. And the orbiting telescopes of Earth would see the flare in 20.8 light-years.

"What's the state of the *emc* clamp and acceleration-dissipaters?" Grettir said.

"No strain—yet," Wang said. "But the power drain . . . if it continues . . . 5 megakilowatts per 2 seconds, and we're just beginning."

"I think," Grettir said slowly, "that we're going to find out what we intended to find out. But it isn't going to be under the carefully controlled conditions we had planned."

The Terran Space Navy experimental cruiser *Sleipnir* had left its base on Asgard, eighth planet of Altair (alpha Aquilae), 28 shipdays ago. It was under orders to make the first attempt of a manned ship to exceed the velocity of light. If its mission was successful, men could travel between Earth and the colonial planets in weeks instead of years. The entire galaxy might be opened to Earth.

Within the past two weeks, the *Sleipnir* had made several tests at 0.8 times the velocity of light, the tests lasting up to two hours at a time.

The *Sleipnir* was equipped with enormous motors and massive clamps, dissipaters, and space-time structure expanders ("hole-openers") required for near-lightspeeds and beyond. No ship in Terrestrial history had ever had such power or the means to handle such power.

The drive itself—the cubed amplification of energy produced by the controlled mixture of matter, antimatter and half-matter—gave an energy that could eat its way through the iron core of a planet. But part of that energy had to be diverted to power the energy-mass conversion "clamp" that kept the ship from being transformed into energy itself. The "hole-opener" also required vast power. This device—officially the Space-Time Structure Expander, or Neutralizer—"unbent" the local curvature of the universe and so furnished a "hole" through which the *Sleipnir* traveled. This hole nullified 99.3 per cent of the resistance the *Sleipnir* would normally have encountered.

Thus the effects of speeds approaching and even exceeding lightspeed would be modified, even if not entirely avoided. The *Sleipnir* should not contract along its length to zero nor attain infinite mass when it reached the speed of light. It contracted, and it swelled, yes, by only 1/777,777th what it should have. The ship would assume the shape of a disk—but much more slowly than it would without its openers, clamps and dissipaters.

Beyond the speed of light, who knew what would happen? It was the business of the *Sleipnir* to find out. But, Grettir thought, not under these conditions. Not willy-nilly.

"Sir!" MacCool said, "Wellington threatens to shoot anybody who comes near the engine room."

He hesitated, then said, "Except you. She wants to speak to you. But she doesn't want to do it over the intercom. She insists that you come down and talk to her face to face." Grettir bit his lower lip and made a sucking sound.

"Why me?" he said, but he knew why, and MacCool's expression showed that he also knew.

"I'll be down in a minute. Now, isn't there any way we can connect a bypass, route a circuit around her or beyond her and get control of the drive again?"

"No, sir!"

"Then she's cut through the engine-room deck and gotten to the redundant circuits also?"

MacCool said, "She's crazy, but she's clear-headed enough to take all precautions. She hasn't overlooked a thing."

Grettir said, "Wang! What's the velocity now?"

"2.3 sl/pm, sir!"

Grettir looked at the huge starscreen on the "forward" bulkhead of the bridge. Black except for a few glitters of white, blue, red, green, and the galaxy called XD-2 that lay dead ahead. The galaxy had been the size of an orange, and it still was. He stared at the screen for perhaps a minute, then said, "Wang, am I seeing right? The red light from XD-2 is shifting towards the blue, right?"

"Right, sir!"

"Then . . . why isn't XD-2 getting bigger? We're overhauling it like a fox after a rabbit."

Wang said, "I think it's getting closer, sir. But we're getting bigger."

2

Grettir rose from the chair. "Take over while I'm gone. Turn off the alarm; tell the crew to continue their normal duties. If anything comes up while I'm in the engine area, notify me at once."

The exec saluted. "Yes, sir!" she said huskily.

Grettir strode off the bridge. He was aware that the officers and crewmen seated in the ring of chairs in the bridge were looking covertly at him. He stopped for a minute to light up a cigar. He was glad that his hands were not shaking, and he hoped that his expression was confident. Slowly, repressing the impulse to run, he continued across the bridge and into the jump-shaft. He stepped off backward into the shaft and nonchalantly blew out smoke while he sank out of sight of the men in the bridge. He braced himself against the quick drop and then the thrusting deceleration. He had set the controls for Dock 14; the doors slid open; he walked into a corridor where a g-car and operator waited for him. Grettir climbed in, sat down and told the crewman where to drive.

Two minutes later, he was with MacCool. The chief engineer pointed down the corridor. Near its end, on the floor, were two still unconscious Marines. The door to the engine room was open. The secondary door, the grille, was shut. The lights within the engine room had been turned off. Something white on the other side of the grille moved. It was Donna Wellington's face, visible through the helmet.

"We can't keep this acceleration up," Grettir said. "We're already going far faster than even unmanned experimental ships have been allowed to go. There are all sorts of theories about what might happen to a ship at these speeds, all bad."

"We've disproved several by now," MacCool said. He spoke evenly, but his forehead was sweaty and shadows hung under his eyes.

MacCool continued, "I'm glad you got here, sir. She just threatened to cut the *emc* clamp wires if you didn't show up within the next two minutes."

He gestured with both hands to indicate a huge and expanding ball of light.

"I'll talk to her," Grettir said. "Although I can't imagine what she wants."

MacCool looked dubious. Grettir wanted to ask him what the hell he was thinking but thought better of it. He said, "Keep your men at this post. Don't even look as if you're coming after me."

"And what do we do, sir, if she shoots you?"

Grettir winced. "Use the cannon. And never mind hesitating if I happen to be in the way. Blast her! But make sure you use a beam short enough to get her but not long enough to touch the engines."

"May I ask why we don't do that before you put your life in danger?" MacCool said.

Grettir hesitated, then said, "My main responsibility is to the ship and its crew. But this woman is very sick; she doesn't realize the implications of her actions. Not fully anyway. I want to talk her out of this, if I can."

He unhooked the communicator from his belt and walked down the corridor toward the grille and the darkness behind it and the whiteness that moved. His back prickled. The men were watching him intently. God knew what they were saying, or at least thinking, about him. The whole crew had been amused for some time by Donna Wellington's passion for him and his inability to cope with her. They had said she was mad about him, not realizing that she really was mad. They had laughed. But they were not laughing now.

Even so, knowing that she was truly insane, some of them must be blaming him for this danger. Undoubtedly, they were thinking that if he had handled her differently, they would not now be so close to death.

He stopped just one step short of the grille. Now he could see Wellington's face, a checkerboard of blacks and whites. He waited for her to speak first. A full minute passed, then she said, "Robert!"

The voice, normally low-pitched and pleasant, was now thin and strained.

"Not Robert. Eric," he said into the communicator. "Captain Eric Grettir, Mrs. Wellington."

There was a silence. She moved closer to the grille. Light struck one eye, which gleamed bluely.

"Why do you hate me so, Robert?" she said plaintively. "You used to love me. What did I do to make you turn against me?"

"I am *not* your husband," Grettir said. "Look at me. Can't you see that I am not Robert Wellington? I am Captain Grettir of the *Sleipnir*. You *must* see who I *really* am, Mrs. Wellington. It is very important."

"You don't love me!" she screamed. "You are trying to get rid of me by pretending you're another man! But it won't work! I'd know you anywhere, you beast! You beast! I hate you, Robert!"

Involuntarily, Grettir stepped back under the intensity of her anger. He saw her hand come up from the shadows and the flash of light on a handgun. It was too late then; she fired; a beam of whiteness dazzled him.

Light was followed by darkness.

Ahead, or above, there was a disk of grayness in the black. Grettir traveled slowly and spasmodically towards it, as if he had been swallowed by a whale but was being ejected towards the open mouth, the muscles of the Leviathan's throat working him outwards.

Far behind him, deep in the bowels of the whale, Donna Wellington spoke.

"Robert?"

"Eric!" he shouted. "I'm *Eric*!"

The *Sleipnir*, barely on its way out from Asgard, dawdling at 6200 kilometers per second, had picked up the Mayday call. It came from a spaceship midway between the 12th and 13th planet of Altair. Although Grettir could have ignored the call without reprimand from his superiors, he altered course, and he found a ship wrecked by a meteorite. Inside the hull was half the body of a man. And a woman in deep shock.

Robert and Donna Wellington were second-generation Asgardians, Ph.D.'s in biotatology, holding master's papers in astro-

gation. They had been searching for specimens of "space plank-
ton" and "space hydras," forms of life born in the regions between Altair's outer planets.

The crash, the death of her husband and the shattering sense
of isolation, dissociation and hopelessness during the eighty-four
hours before rescue had twisted Mrs. Wellington. Perhaps twisted
was the wrong word. Fragmented was a better description.

From the beginning of what at first seemed recovery, she had
taken a superficial resemblance of Grettir to her husband for an
identity. Grettir had been gentle and kind with her at the beginning and had made frequent visits to sick bay. Later, advised by
Doctor Wills, he had been severe with her.

And so the unforeseen result.

Donna Wellington screamed behind him and, suddenly, the
twilight circle ahead became bright, and he was free. He opened
his eyes to see faces over him. Doctor Wills and MacCool. He
was in sick bay.

MacCool smiled and said, "For a moment, we thought . . ."

"What happened?" Grettir said. Then, "I know what she
did. I mean—"

"She fired full power at you," MacCool said. "But the bars of
the grille absorbed most of the energy. You got just enough to
crisp the skin off your face and to knock you out. Good thing you
closed your eyes in time."

Grettir sat up. He felt his face; it was covered with a greasy
ointment, pain-deadening and skin-growing *resec*.

"I got a hell of a headache."

Doctor Wills said, "It'll be gone in a minute."

"What's the situation?" Grettir said. "How'd you get me
away from her?"

MacCool said, "I had to do it, Captain. Otherwise, she'd
have taken another shot at you. The cannon blasted what was left
of the grille. Mrs. Wellington—"

"She's dead?"

"Yes. But the cannon didn't get her. Strange. She took her
suit off, stripped to the skin. Then she went out through the airlock in the engine room. Naked, as if she meant to be the bride of
Death. We almost got caught in the outrush of air, since she fixed

the controls so that the inner port remained open. It was close, but we got the port shut in time."

Grettir said, "I . . . never mind. Any damage to the engine room?"

"No. And the wires are reconnected for normal operation. Only—"

"Only what?"

MacCool's face was so long he looked like a frightened bloodhound.

"Just before I reconnected the wires, a funny . . . peculiar . . . thing happened. The whole ship, and everything inside the ship, went through a sort of distortion. Wavy, as if we'd all become wax and were dripping. Or flags flapping in a wind. The bridge reports that the fore of the ship seemed to expand like a balloon, then became ripply, and the entire effect passed through the ship. We all got nauseated while the waviness lasted."

There was silence, but their expressions indicated that there was more to be said.

"Well?"

MacCool and Wills looked at each other. MacCool swallowed and said, "Captain, we don't know where in hell we are!"

3

On the bridge, Grettir examined the forward EXT. screen. There were no stars. Space everywhere was filled with a light as gray and as dull as that of a false dawn on Earth. In the gray glow, at a distance as yet undetermined, were a number of spheres. They looked small, but if they were as large as the one immediately aft of the *Sleipnir*, they were huge.

The sphere behind them, estimated to be at a distance of fifty kilometers, was about the size of Earth's moon, relative to the ship. Its surface was as smooth and as gray as a ball of lead.

Darl spoke a binary code into her wrist-console, and the sphere on the starscreen seemed to shoot towards them. It filled the screen until Darl changed the line-of-sight. They were looking at about 20 degrees of arc of the limb of the sphere.

"There it is!" Darl said. A small object floated around the edge of the sphere and seemed to shoot towards them. She magnified it, and it became a small grey sphere.

"It orbits round the big one," she said.

Darl paused, then said, "We—the ship—came *out* of that small sphere. *Out* of it. *Through* its skin."

"You mean we had been inside it?" Grettir said. "And now we're outside it?"

"Yes, sir! Exactly!"

She gasped and said, "Oh, oh—sir!"

Around the large sphere, slightly above the plane of the orbit of the small sphere but within its sweep in an inner orbit, sped another object. At least fifty times as large as the small globe, it caught up with the globe, and the two disappeared together around the curve of the primary.

"Wellington's body!" Grettir said.

He turned away from the screen, took one step, and turned around again. "It's not right! She should be trailing along behind us or at least parallel with us, maybe shooting off at an angle but still moving in our direction.

"But she's been grabbed by the big sphere! She's in orbit! And her size, Gargantuan! It doesn't make sense! It shouldn't be!"

"Nothing should," Wang said.

"Take us back," Grettir said. "Establish an orbit around the primary, on the same plane as the secondary but further out, approximately a kilometer and a half from it."

Darl's expression said, "Then what?"

Grettir wondered if she had the same thought as he. The faces of the others on the bridge were doubtful. The fear was covered but leaking out. He could smell the rotten bubbles. Had they guessed, too?

"What attraction does the primary have on the ship?" he said to Wang.

"No detectable influence whatsoever, sir. The *Sleipnir* seems to have a neutral charge, neither positive nor negative in relation to any of the spheres. Or to Wellington's . . . body."

Grettir was slightly relieved. His thoughts had been so wild that he had not been able to consider them as anything but hysterical fantasies. But Wang's answer showed that Grettir's idea was also his. Instead of replying in terms of gravitational force, he had talked as if the ship were a subatomic particle.

But if the ship was not affected by the primary, why had Wellington's corpse been attracted by the primary?

"Our velocity in relation to the primary?" Grettir said.

"We cut off the acceleration as soon as the wires were reconnected," Wang said. "This was immediately after we came out into this . . . this space. We didn't apply any retrodrive. Our velocity, as indicated by power consumption, is ten megaparsecs per minute. That is," he added after a pause, "what the instruments show. But our radar, which should be totally ineffective at this velocity, indicates 50 kilometers per minute, relative to the big sphere."

Wang leaned back in his chair as if he expected Grettir to explode into incredulity. Grettir lit up another cigar. This time, his hands shook. He blew out a big puff of smoke and said, "Obviously, we're operating under different quote laws unquote *out here.*"

Wang sighed softly. "So you think so, too, Captain? Yes, different *laws.* Which means that every time we make a move through this space, we can't know what the result will be. May I ask what you plan to do, sir?"

By this question, which Wang would never have dared to voice before, though he had doubtless often thought it, Grettir knew that the navigator shared his anxiety. Beneath that apparently easy manner and soft voice was a pain just beneath the navel. The umbilical had been ripped out; Wang was hurting and bleeding inside. Was he, too, beginning to float away in a gray void? Bereft as no man had ever been bereft?

It takes a special type of man or woman to lose himself or herself from Earth or his native planet, to go out among the stars so far that the natal sun is not even a faint glimmer. It also takes special conditioning for the special type of man. He has to believe, in the deepest part of his unconscious, that his ship is a piece of Mother Earth. He has to believe; otherwise, he goes to pieces.

It can be done. Hundreds do it. But nothing had prepared even these farfarers for absolute divorce from the universe itself.

Grettir ached with the dread of the void. The void was coiling up inside him, a gray serpent, a slither of nothingness. Coiling. And what would happen when it uncoiled?

And what would happen to the crew when they were informed—as they must be—of the utter dissociation?

There was only one way to keep their minds from slipping their moorings. They must believe that they could get back into the world. Just as he must believe it.

"I'll play it by ear," Grettir said.

"What? Sir?"

"Play it by ear!" Grettir said more harshly than he had intended. "I was merely answering your question. Have you forgotten you asked me what I meant to do?"

"Oh, no, sir," Wang said. "I was just thinking . . ."

"Keep your mind on the job," Grettir said. He told Darl he would take over. He spoke the code to activate the ALL-STATIONS; a low rising-falling sound went into every room of the *Sleipnir*, and all screens flashed a black-and-green checked pattern. Then the warnings, visual and audible, died out, and the captain spoke.

He talked for two minutes. The bridgemen looked as if the lights had been turned off in their brains. It was almost impossible to grasp the concept of their being outside their universe. As difficult was thinking of their unimaginably vast native cosmos as only an "electron" orbiting around the nucleus of an "atom." If what the captain said was true (how could it be?), the ship was in the space between the superatoms of a supermolecule of a superuniverse.

Even though they knew that the *Sleipnir* had ballooned under the effect of nearly 300,000 times the speed of light, they could not wrap the fingers of their minds around the concept. It turned to smoke and drifted away.

It took ten minutes, ship's time, to turn and to complete the maneuvers which placed the *Sleipnir* in an orbit parallel to but outside the secondary, or, as Grettir thought of it, "our universe."

He gave his chair back to Darl and paced back and forth across the bridge while he watched the starscreen.

If they were experiencing the sundering, the cutting-off, they were keeping it under control. They had been told by their captain that they *were* going back in, not that they would make a *try* at re-entry. They had been through much with him, and he had never failed them. With this trust, they could endure the agony of dissolution.

As the *Sleipnir* established itself parallel to the secondary, Wellington's body curved around the primary again and began to pass the small sphere and ship. The arms of the mountainous body were extended stiffly to both sides, and her legs spread out. In the gray light, her skin was bluish-black from the ruptured veins and arteries below the skin. Her red hair, coiled in a Psyche knot, looked black. Her eyes, each of which was larger than the bridge of the *Sleipnir*, were open, bulging clots of black blood. Her lips were pulled back in a grimace, the teeth like a soot-streaked portcullis.

Cartwheeling, she passed the sphere and the ship.

Wang reported that there were three "shadows" on the surface of the primary. Those were keeping pace with the secondary, the corpse and the ship. Magnified on the bridge-bulkhead screen, each "shadow" was the silhouette of one of the three orbiting bodies. The shadows were only about one shade darker than the surface and were caused by a shifting pucker in the primary skin. The surface protruded along the edges of the shadows and formed a shallow depression within the edges.

If the shadow of the *Sleipnir* was a true indication of the shape of the vessel, the *Sleipnir* had lost its needle shape and was a spindle, fat at both ends and narrow-waisted.

When Wellington's corpse passed by the small sphere and the ship, her shadow or "print" reversed itself in shape. Where the head of the shadow should have been, the feet now were, and vice versa.

She disappeared around the curve of the primary and, on returning on the other side, her shadow had again become a "true" reflection. It remained so until she passed the secondary, after which the shadow once more reversed itself.

Grettir had been informed that there seemed to be absolutely no matter in the space outside the spheres. There was not one detectable atom or particle. Moreover, despite the lack of any radiation, the temperature of the hull, and ten meters beyond the hull, was a fluctuating 70° plus-or-minus 20° F.

4

Three orbits later, Grettir knew that the ship had diminished greatly in size. Or else the small sphere had expanded. Or both changes occurred. Moreover, on the visual screen, the secondary had lost its spherical shape and become a fat disk during the first circling of the ship to establish its orbit.

Grettir was puzzling over this and thinking of calling Van Voorden, the physicist chief, when Wellington's corpse came around the primary again. The body caught up with the other satellites, and for a moment the primary, secondary, and the *Sleipnir* were in a line, strung on an invisible cord.

Suddenly, the secondary and the corpse jumped toward each other. They ceased their motion when within a quarter kilometer of each other. The secondary regained its globular form as soon as it had attained its new orbit. Wellington's arms and legs, during this change in position, moved in as if she had come to life. Her arms folded themselves across her breasts, and her legs drew up so that her thighs were against her stomach.

Grettir called Van Voorden. The physicist said, "Out here, the cabin boy—if we had one—knows as much as I do about what's going on or what to expect. The data, such as they are, are too inadequate, too confusing. I can only suggest that there was an interchange of energy between Wellington and the secondary."

"A quantum jump?" Grettir said. "If that's so, why didn't the ship experience a loss or gain?"

Darl said, "Pardon, sir. But it did. There was a loss of 50 megakilowatts in 0.8 second."

Van Voorden said, "The *Sleipnir* may have decreased in relative size because of decrease in velocity. Or maybe velocity had nothing to do with it or only partially, anyway. Maybe the change in spatial interrelationships among bodies causes other changes. In shape, size, energy transfer and so forth. I don't know. Tell me, how big is the woman—corpse—relative to the ship now?"

"The radar measurements say she's eighty-three times as large. She increased. Or we've decreased."

Van Voorden's eyes grew even larger. Grettir thanked him and cut him off. He ordered the *Sleipnir* to be put in exactly the same orbit as the secondary but ten dekameters ahead of it.

Van Voorden called back. "The jump happened when we were in line with the other three bodies. Maybe the *Sleipnir* is some sort of *geometrical catalyst* under certain conditions. That's only an analogy, of course."

Wang verbally fed the order into the computer-interface, part of his wrist-console. The *Sleipnir* was soon racing ahead of the sphere. Radar reported that the ship and secondary were now approximately equal in size. The corpse, coming around the primary again, was still the same relative size as before.

Grettir ordered the vessel turned around so that the nose would be facing the sphere. This accomplished, he had the velocity reduced. The retrodrive braked them while the lateral thrusts readjusted forces to keep the ship in the same orbit. Since the primary had no attraction for the *Sleipnir*, the ship had to remain in orbit with a constant rebalancing of thrusts. The sphere, now ballooning, inched towards the ship.

"Radar indicates we're doing 26.6 dekameters per second relative to the primary," Wang said. "Power drain indicates we're making 25,000 times the speed of light. That, by the way, is not proportionate to what we were making when we left our world."

"More braking," Grettir said. "Cut it down to 15 dm."

The sphere swelled, filled the screen, and Grettir involuntarily braced himself for the impact, even though he was so far from expecting one that he had not strapped himself into a chair. There had been none when the ship had broken through the "skin" of the universe.

Grettir had been told of the distorting in the ship when it had left the universe and so was not entirely surprised. Nevertheless, he could not help being both frightened and bewildered when the front part of the bridge abruptly swelled and then rippled. Screen, bulkheads, deck and crew waved as if they were cloth in a strong wind. Grettir felt as if he were being folded into a thousand different angles at the same time.

Then Wang cried out, and the others repeated his cry. Wang rose from his seat and put his hands out before him. Grettir, standing behind and to one side of him, was frozen as he saw dozens of little objects, firefly-size, burning brightly, slip *through* the starscreen and bulkhead and drift towards him. He came out of his paralysis in time to dodge one tiny whitely glowing ball. But another struck his forehead, causing him to yelp.

A score of the bodies passed by him. Some were white; some blue; some green; one was topaz. They were at all levels, above his head, even with his waist, one almost touching the deck. He crouched down to let two pass over him, and as he did so, he saw Nagy, the communications officer, bent over and vomiting. The stuff sprayed out of his mouth and caught a little glow in it and snuffed it out in a burst of smoke.

Then the forepart of the bridge had reasserted its solidity and constancy of shape. There were no more burning objects coming through.

Grettir turned to see the aft bulkheads of the bridge quivering in the wake of the wave. And they, too, became normal. Grettir shouted the "override" code so that he could take control from Wang, who was screaming with pain. He directed the ship to change its course to an "upward vertical" direction. There was no "upward" sensation, because the artificial g-field within the ship readjusted. Suddenly, the forward part of the bridge became distorted again, and the waves reached through the fabric of the ship and the crew.

The starscreen, which had been showing nothing but the blackness of space, speckled by a few stars, now displayed the great gray sphere in one corner and the crepuscular light. Grettir, fighting the pain in his forehead and the nausea, gave another command. There was a delay of possibly thirty seconds, and then the *Sleipnir* began the turn that would take it back into a parallel orbit with the secondary.

Grettir, realizing what was happening shortly after being burned, had taken the *Sleipnir* back out of the universe. He put in a call for corpsmen and Doctor Wills and then helped Wang from his chair. There was an odor of burned flesh and hair in the bridge which the air-conditioning system had not as yet removed. Wang's face and hands were burned in five or six places, and part of the long coarse black hair on the right side of his head was burned.

Three corpsmen and Wills ran into the bridge. Wills started to apply a pseudoprotein jelly on Grettir's forehead, but Grettir told him to take care of Wang first. Wills worked swiftly and then, after spreading the jelly over Wang's burns and placing a false-skin bandage over the burns, treated the captain. As soon as the jelly was placed on his forehead, Grettir felt the pain dissolve.

"Third degree," Wills said. "It's lucky those things—whatever they are—weren't larger."

Grettir picked up his cigar, which he had dropped on the deck when he had first seen the objects racing towards him. The cigar was still burning. Near it lay a coal, swiftly blackening. He picked it up gingerly. It felt warm but could be held without too much discomfort.

Grettir extended his hand, palm up, so that the doctor could see the speck of black matter in it. It was even smaller than when it had floated into the bridge through the momentarily "opened" interstices of the molecules composing the hull and bulkheads.

"This is *a galaxy*," he whispered.

Doc Wills did not understand. "A galaxy of our universe," Grettir added.

Doc Wills paled, and he gulped loudly.

"You mean . . . ?"

Grettir nodded.

Wills said, "I hope . . . not our . . . Earth's . . . Galaxy!"

"I doubt it," Grettir said. "We were on the edge of the star fields farthest out, that is, the closest to the—skin?—of our universe. But if we had kept on going . . ."

Wills shook his head. Billions of stars, possibly millions of inhabitable, hence inhabited, planets, were in that little ball of fire, now cool and collapsed. Trillions of sentient beings and an unimaginable number of animals had died when their world collided with Grettir's forehead.

Wang, informed of the true cause of the burns, became ill again. Grettir ordered him to sick bay and replaced him with Gomez. Van Voorden entered the bridge. He said, "I suppose our main objective has to be our reentry. But why couldn't we make an attempt to penetrate the primary, the nucleus? Do you realize what an astounding . . . ?"

Grettir interrupted. "I realize. But our fuel supply is low, very low. If—I mean, *when* we get back through the 'skin,' we'll have a long way to go before we can return to Base. Maybe too long. I don't dare exceed a certain speed during reentry because of our size. It would be too dangerous. . . . I don't want to wipe out any more galaxies. God knows the psychological problems we are going to have when the guilt really hits. Right now, we're numbed. *No!* We're not going to do any exploring!"

"But there may be no future investigations permitted!" Van Voorden said. "There's too much danger to the universe itself to allow any more research by ships like ours!"

"Exactly," Grettir said. "I sympathize with your desire to do scientific research. But the safety of the ship and crew comes first. Besides, I think that if I were to order an exploration, I'd have mutiny on my hands. And I couldn't blame my men. Tell me, Van Voorden, don't you feel a sense of . . . dissociation?"

Van Voorden nodded and said, "But I'm willing to fight it. There is so much . . ."

"So much to find out," Grettir said. "Agreed. But the authorities will have to determine if that is to be done."

Grettir dismissed him. Van Voorden marched off. But he did not give the impression of a powerful anger. He was, Grettir thought, secretly relieved at the captain's decision. Van Voorden had made his protest for Science's sake. But as a human being, Van Voorden must want very much to get "home."

5

At the end of the ordered maneuver, the *Sleipnir* was in the same orbit as the universe but twenty kilometers ahead and again pointed toward it. Since there was no attraction between ship and primary, the *Sleipnir* had to use power to maintain the orbit; a delicate readjustment of lateral thrust was constantly required.

Grettir ordered braking applied. The sphere expanded on the starscreen, and then there was only a gray surface displayed. To the viewers the surface did not seem to spin, but radar had determined that the globe completed a revolution on its polar axis once every 33 seconds.

Grettir did not like to think of the implications of this. Van Voorden undoubtedly had received the report, but he had made no move to notify the captain. Perhaps, like Grettir, he believed that the fewer who thought about it, the better.

The mockup screen showed, in silhouette form, the relative sizes of the approaching spheres and the ship. The basketball was the universe; the toothpick, the *Sleipnir*. Grettir hoped that this reduction would be enough to avoid running into any more galaxies. Immediately after the vessel penetrated the "skin," the *Sleipnir* would be again braked, thus further diminishing it. There should be plenty of distance between the skin and the edge of the closest star fields.

"Here we go," Grettir said, watching the screen which indicated in meters the gap between ship and sphere. Again he involuntarily braced himself.

There was a rumble, a groan. The deck slanted upwards, then rolled to port. Grettir was hurled to the deck, spun over and over and brought up with stunning impact against a bulkhead. He was in a daze for a moment, and by the time he had recovered, the ship had reasserted its proper attitude. Gomez had placed the ship into "level" again. He had a habit of strapping himself into the navigator's chair although regulations did not require it unless the captain ordered it.

Grettir asked for a report on any damage and, while waiting

for it, called Van Voorden. The physicist was bleeding from a cut on his forehead.

"Obviously," he said, "it requires a certain force to penetrate the outer covering or energy shield or whatever it is that encloses the universe. We didn't have it. So—"

"Presents quite a problem," Grettir said. "If we go fast enough to rip through, we're too large and may destroy entire galaxies. If we go too slow, we can't get through."

He paused, then said, "I can think of only one method. But I'm ignorant of the consequences, which might be disastrous. Not for us but for the universe. I'm not sure I should even take such a chance."

He was silent so long that Van Voorden could not restrain himself. "Well?"

"Do you think that if we could make a hole in the skin, the rupture might result in some sort of collapse or cosmic disturbance?"

"You want to beam a hole in the skin?" Van Voorden said slowly. His skin was pale, but it had been that color before Grettir asked him the question. Grettir wondered if Van Voorden was beginning to crumble under the "dissociation."

"Never mind," Grettir said. "I shouldn't have asked you. You can't know what the effects would be any more than anyone else. I apologize. I must have been trying to make you share some of the blame if anything went wrong. Forget it."

Van Voorden stared, and he was still looking blank when Grettir cut off his image. He paced back and forth, once stepping over a tiny black object on the deck and then grimacing when he realized that it was too late for care. Millions of stars, billions of planets, trillions of creatures. All cold and dead. And if he experimented further in trying to get back into the native cosmos, then what? A collapsing universe?

But the *Sleipnir* had passed through the skin twice, and the rupture had not seemed to cause harm. The surface of the sphere was smooth and unbroken. It must be self-regulating and self-repairing.

Grettir stopped pacing and said aloud, "We came through

the skin twice without harm to it. So we're going to try the beam!"

Nobody answered him, but the look on their faces was evidence of their relief. Fifteen minutes later, the *Sleipnir* was just ahead of the sphere and facing it. After an unvarying speed and distance from the sphere had been maintained for several minutes, laser beams measured the exact length between the tip of the cannon and the surface of the globe.

The chief gunnery officer, Abdul White Eagle, set one of the fore cannons. Grettir delayed only a few seconds in giving the next order. He clenched his teeth so hard he almost bit the cigar in two, groaned slightly then said, "Fire!"

Darl transmitted the command. The beam shot out, touched the skin and vanished.

The starscreen showed a black hole in the gray surface at the equator of the sphere. The hole moved away and then was gone around the curve of the sphere. Exactly 33 seconds later, the hole was in its original position. It was shrinking. By the time four rotations were completed, the hole had closed in on itself.

Grettir sighed and wiped the sweat off his forehead. Darl reported that the hole would be big enough for the ship to get through by the second time it came around. After that, it would be too small.

"We'll go through during the second rotation," Grettir said. "Set up the compigator for an automatic entry; tie the cannon in with the compigator. There shouldn't be any problem. If the hole shrinks too fast, we'll enlarge it with the cannon."

He heard Darl say, "Operation begun, sir!" as Gomez spoke into his console. The white beam spurted out in a cone, flicked against the "shell" or "skin" and disappeared. A circle of blackness three times the diameter of the ship came into being and then moved to one side of the screen. Immediately, under the control of the compigator, the retrodrive of the *Sleipnir* went into action. The sphere loomed; a gray wall filled the starscreen. Then the edge of the hole came into view, and a blackness spread over the screen.

"We're going to make it," Grettir thought. "The compigator can't make a mistake."

He looked around him. The bridgemen were strapped to their chairs now. Most of the faces were set, they were well disciplined and brave. But if they felt as he did—they must—they were shoving back a scream far down in them. They could not endure this "homesickness" much longer. And after they got through, were back in the womb, he would have to permit them a most unmilitary behavior. They would laugh, weep, shout, whoop. And so would he.

The nose of the *Sleipnir* passed through the hole. Now, if anything went wrong, the fore cannon could not be used. But it was impossible that . . .

The klaxon whooped. Darl screamed, "Oh, my God! Something's wrong! The hole's shrinking too fast!"

Grettir roared, "Double the speed! No! Halve it!"

Increasing the forward speed meant a swelling in size of the *Sleipnir* but a contraction of the longitudinal axis and a lengthening of the lateral. The *Sleipnir* would get through the hole faster, but it would also narrow the gap between its hull and the edges of the hole.

Halving the speed, on the other hand, though it would make the ship smaller in relation to the hole, would also make the distance to be traversed greater. This might mean that the edges would still hit the ship.

Actually, Grettir did not know what order should be given or if any order would have an effect upon their chance to escape. He could only do what seemed best.

The grayness spread out from the perimeter of the starscreen. There was a screech of severed plastic running through the ship, quivering the bulkheads and decks, a sudden push forward of the crew as they felt the inertia, then a release as the almost instantaneous readjustment of the internal g-field canceled the external effects.

Everybody in the bridge yelled. Grettir forced himself to cut off his shout. He watched the starscreen. They were out in the gray again. The huge sphere shot across the screen. In the corner was the secondary and then a glimpse of a giant blue-black foot. More grayness. A whirl of other great spheres in the distance. The primary again. The secondary. Wellington's hand, like a malformed squid of the void.

When Grettir saw the corpse again, he knew that the ship had been deflected away from the sphere and was heading towards the corpse. He did not, however, expect a collision. The orbital velocity of the dead woman was greater than that of the secondary or of the *Sleipnir*.

Grettir, calling for a damage report, heard what he expected. The nose of the ship had been sheared off. Bearing 45 crewmen with it, it was now inside the "universe," heading toward a home it would never reach. The passageways leading to the cut-off part had been automatically sealed, of course, so that there was no danger of losing air.

But the retrodrives had also been sliced off. The *Sleipnir* could drive forward but could not brake itself unless it was first turned around to present its aft to the direction of motion.

6

Grettir gave the command to stabilize the ship first, then to reverse it. MacCool replied from the engine room that neither maneuver was, at the moment, possible. The collision and the shearing had caused malfunctions in the control circuits. He did not know what the trouble was, but the electronic trouble-scanner was searching through the circuits. A moment later, he called back to say that the device was itself not operating properly and that the troubleshooting would have to be done by his men until the device had been repaired.

MacCool was disturbed. He could not account for the breakdown because, theoretically, there should have been none. Even the impact and loss of the fore part should not have resulted in loss of circuit operation.

Grettir told him to do what he could. Meanwhile, the ship was tumbling and was obviously catching up with the vast corpse. There had been another unexplainable interchange of energy, position and momentum, and the *Sleipnir* and Mrs. Wellington were going to collide.

Grettir unstrapped himself and began walking back and forth across the bridge. Even though the ship was cartwheeling, the internal g-field neutralized the effect for the crew. The vessel seemed level and stable unless the starscreen was looked at. When Grettir watched the screen, he felt slightly queasy because he was, at times, standing upside down in relation to the corpse.

Grettir asked for a computation of when the collision would take place and of what part of the body the *Sleipnir* would strike. It might make a difference whether it struck a soft or hard part. The difference would not result in damage to the ship, but it would affect the angle and velocity of the rebound path. If the circuits were repaired before the convergence, or just after, Grettir would have to know what action to take.

Wang replied that he had already asked the compigator for an estimate of the area of collision if conditions remained as they were. Even as he spoke, a coded card issued from a slot in the bulkhead. Wang read it, handed it to Grettir.

Grettir said, "At any other time, I'd laugh. So we will return—literally—to the womb."

The card had also indicated that, the nearer the ship got to Wellington, the slower was its velocity. Moreover, the relative size of the ship, as reported by radar, was decreasing in direct proportion to its proximity to the body.

Gomez said, "I think we've come under the influence of that ... woman, as if she's become a planet and had captured a satellite. Us. She doesn't have any gravitational attraction or any charge in relation to us. But—"

"But there are other factors," Grettir said to her. "Maybe they are spatial relations, which, in this 'space,' may be the equivalent of gravity."

The *Sleipnir* was now so close that the body entirely filled the starscreen when the ship was pointed towards it. First, the enormous head came into view. The blood-clotted and bulging eyes stared at them. The nose slid by like a Brobdingnagian guillotine; the mouth grinned at them as if it were to enjoy gulping them down. Then the neck, a diorite column left exposed by the erosion of softer rock; the cleavage of the blackened

Himalayan breasts; the navel, the eye of a hurricane.

Then she went out of sight, and the secondary and primary and the gray-shrouded giants far off wheeled across the screen.

Grettir used the All-Stations to tell the nonbridge personnel what was happening. "As soon as MacCool locates the trouble, we will be on our way out. We have plenty of power left, enough to blast our way out of a hundred corpses. Sit tight. Don't worry. It's just a matter of time."

He spoke with a cheerfulness he did not feel, although he had not lied to them. Nor did he expect any reaction, positive or negative. They must be as numb as he. Their minds, their entire nervous systems, were boggling.

Another card shot out from the bulkhead-slot, a corrected impact prediction. Because of the continuing decrease in size of the vessel, it would strike the corpse almost dead-center in the navel. A minute later, another card predicted impact near the coccyx. A third card revised that to a collision with the top of the head. A fourth changed that to a strike on the lower part on the front of the right leg.

Grettir called Van Voorden again. The physicist's face shot up from the surface of Grettir's wrist-console but was stationary on the auxiliary bulkhead-screen. This gave a larger view and showed Van Voorden looking over his wrist-console at a screen on his cabin-bulkhead. It offered the latest impact report in large burning letters.

"Like the handwriting on the wall in the days of King Belshazzar," Van Voorden said. "And I am a Daniel come to judgment. So we're going to hit her leg, heh, *Many, many tickle up her shin*. Hee, hee!"

Grettir stared uncomprehendingly at him, then cut him off. A few seconds later, he understood Van Voorden's pun. He did not wonder at the man's levity at a moment so grave. It was a means of relieving his deep anxiety and bewilderment. It might also mean that he was already cracking up, since it was out of character for him. But Grettir could do nothing for him at that moment.

As the *Sleipnir* neared the corpse, it continued to shrink. However, the dwindling was not at a steady rate nor could the times of shrinkage be predicted. It operated in spurts of from two to thirty seconds duration at irregular intervals. And then, as the 300th card issued from the slot, it became evident that, unless some new factor entered, the *Sleipnir* would spin into the gaping mouth. While the head rotated "downward," the ship would pass through the great space between the lips.

And so it was. On the starscreen, the lower lip, a massive ridge, wrinkled with mountains and pitted with valleys, appeared. Flecks of lipstick floated by, black-red Hawaiis. A tooth like a jagged skyscraper dropped out of sight.

The *Sleipnir* settled slowly into the darkness. The walls shot away and upwards. The blackness outside knotted. Only a part of the gray "sky" was visible during that point of the cartwheel when the fore part of the starscreen was directed upwards. Then the opening became a thread of gray, a strand, and was gone.

Strangely—or was it so odd?—the officers and crew lost their feeling of dissociation. Grettir's stomach expanded with relief; the dreadful fragmenting was gone. He now felt as if something had been attached, or reattached, to his navel. Rubb, the psychology officer, reported that he had taken a survey of one out of fifty of the crew, and each described similar sensations.

Despite this, the personnel were free of only one anxiety and were far from being out of danger. The temperature had been slowly mounting ever since the ship had been spun off the secondary and had headed towards the corpse. The power system and air-conditioning had stabilized at 80° F for a while. But the temperature of the hull had gone upwards at a geometric progression, and the outer hull was now 2500 K. There was no danger of it melting as yet; it could resist up to 56,000 K. The airconditioning demanded more and more power, and after thirty minutes ship's time, Grettir had had to let the internal temperature rise to 98.2° F to ease the load.

Grettir ordered everybody into spacesuits, which could keep the wearers at a comfortable temperature. Just as the order was carried out, MacCool reported that he had located the source of malfunction.

"The Wellington woman did it!" he shouted. "She sure took

care of us! She inserted a monolith subparticle switch in the circuits; the switch had a timer which operated the switch after a certain time had elapsed. It was only coincidence that the circuits went blank right after we failed to get back into our world!"

7

"So she wanted to be certain that we'd be wrecked if she was frustrated in her attempts in the engine room," Grettir said. "You'd better continue the search for other microswitches or sabotage devices."

MacCool's face was long.

"We're ready to operate now . . . hell! We can't spare any power now because we need all we can get to keep the temperature down. I can spare enough to cancel the tumble. But that's all."

"Forget it for now," Grettir said. He had contacted Van Voorden, who seemed to have recovered. He confirmed the captain's theory about the rise in temperature. It was the rapid contraction of the ship that was causing the emission of heat.

"How is this contraction possible?" Grettir said. "Are the atoms of the ship, and of our bodies, coming closer together? If so, what happens when they come into contact with each other?"

"We've already passed that point of diminishment," Van Voorden said. "I'd say that our own atoms are shrinking also."

"But that's not possible," Grettir replied. Then, "Forget about that remark. What is possible? Whatever happens is possible."

Grettir cut him off and strode back and forth and wished that he could smoke a cigar. He had intended to talk about what the *Sleipnir* would find if it had managed to break back into its native universe. It seemed to Grettir that the universe would have changed so much that no one aboard the ship would recognize it. Every time the secondary—the universe—completed a revolution on its axis, trillions of Earth years, maybe quadrillions, might have passed. The Earth's sun might have become a lightless clot in space or even have disappeared altogether. Man, who might have survived on other planets, would no longer be homo sapiens.

Moreover, when the *Sleipnir* attained a supercosmic mass on its way out of the universe, it might have disastrously affected the other masses in the universe.

Yet none of these events would necessarily have occurred. It was possible that time inside that sphere was absolutely independent of time outside it. The notion was not so fantastic. God Almighty! Less than seventy minutes ago, Donna Wellington had been inside the ship. Now the ship was inside her.

And when the electrons and the nuclei of the atoms composing the ship and the crew came into contact, what then? Explosion?

Or were the elements made up of divisible subelements, and collapse would go on towards the inner infinity? He thought of the 20th-century stories of a man shrinking until the molecules became clusters of suns and the nuclei were the suns and the electrons were the planets. Eventually, the hero found himself on an electron-planet with atmosphere, seas, rivers, plains, mountains, trees, animals and aboriginal sentients.

These stories were only fantasies. Atomic matter was composed of wavicles, stuff describable in terms of both waves and particles. The parahomunculus hero would be in a cosmos as bewildering as that encountered by the crew of the *Sleipnir* on breaking into the extra-universe space.

That fantasy galloping across the sky of his mind, swift as the original *Sleipnir*, eight-legged horse of All-Father Odin of his ancestors' religion, would have to be dismissed. Donna Wellington was not a female Ymir, the primeval giant out of whose slain corpse was formed the world, the skull the sky, the blood the sea, the flesh the Earth, the bones the mountains.

No, the heat of contraction would increase until the men cooked in their suits. What happened after that would no longer be known to the crew and hence of no consequence.

"Captain!"

MacCool's face was on the auxiliary screen, kept open to the engine room. "We'll be ready to go in a minute."

Sweat mingled with tears to blur the image of the engineer's face. "We'll make it then," Grettir said.

Four minutes later, the tumble was stopped, the ship was pointed upwards and was on its way out. The temperature began dropping inside the ship at one degree F per 30 seconds. The blackness was relieved by a gray thread. The thread broadened into ribbon, and then the ribbon became the edges of two mountain ridges, one below and the one above hanging upside down.

"This time," Grettir said, "we'll make a hole more than large enough."

Van Voorden entered the bridge as the *Sleipnir* passed through the break. Grettir said, "The hole repairs itself even more quickly than it did the last time. That's why the nose was cut off. We didn't know that the bigger the hole, the swifter the rate of reclosure."

Van Voorden said, "Thirty-six hundred billion years old or even more! Why bother to go home when home no longer exists?"

"Maybe there won't be that much time gone," Grettir said. "Do you remember Minkowski's classical phrase? *From henceforth space in itself and time in itself sink to mere shadows, and only a kind of union of the two preserves an independent existence.*

"That phrase applied to the world inside the sphere, our world. Perhaps *out here* the union is somehow dissolved, the marriage of space and time is broken. Perhaps no time, or very little, has elapsed in our world."

"It's possible," Van Voorden said. "But you've overlooked one thing, Captain. If our world has not been marked by time while we've been gone, *we* have been marked. Scarred by unspace and untime. I'll never believe in cause and effect and order throughout the cosmos again. I'll always be suspicious and anxious. I'm a ruined man."

Grettir started to answer but could not make himself heard. The men and women on the bridge were weeping, sobbing, or laughing shrilly. Later, they would think of that *out there* as a nightmare and would try not to think of it at all. And if other nightmares faced them here, at least they would be nightmares they knew.

Riders of the Purple Wage
or The Great Gavage

1967

If Jules Verne could really have looked into the future, say 1966 A.D., he would have crapped in his pants. And 2166, oh, my!

—from Grandpa Winnegan's unpublished Ms. *How I Screwed Uncle Sam & Other Private Ejaculations*

THE COCK THAT CROWED BACKWARDS

Un and Sub, the giants, are grinding him for bread.

Broken pieces float up through the wine of sleep. Vast treadings crush abysmal grapes for the incubus sacrament.

He as Simple Simon fishes in his soul as pail for the leviathan.

He groans, half-wakes, turns over, sweating dark oceans, and groans again. Un and Sub, putting their backs to their work, turn the stone wheels of the sunken mill, muttering Fie, fye, fo, fum. Eyes glittering orange-red as a cat's in a cubbyhole, teeth dull white digits in the murky arithmetic.

Un and Sub, Simple Simons themselves, busily mix metaphors non-self-consciously.

Dunghill and cock's egg: up rises the cockatrice and gives first crow, two more to come, in the flushrush of blood of dawn of I-am-the-erection-and-the-strife.

It grows out and out until weight and length merge to curve it over, a not-yet weeping willow or broken reed. The one-eyed red head peeks over the edge of bed. It rests its chinless jaw, then, as body swells, slides over and down. Looking monocularly this way

30

and those, it sniffs archaically across the floor and heads for the door, left open by the lapsus linguae of malingering sentinels.

A loud braying from the center of the room makes it turn back. The three-legged ass, Baalim's easel, is heehawing. On the easel is the "canvas," an oval shallow pan of irradiated plastic, specially treated. The canvas is two meters high and forty-four centimeters deep. Within the painting is a scene that must be finished by tomorrow.

As much sculpture as painting, the figures are in alto-relief, rounded, some nearer the back of the pan than others. They glow with light from outside and also from the self-luminous plastic of the "canvas." The light seems to enter the figures, soak awhile, then break loose. The light is pale red, the red of dawn, of blood watered with tears, of anger, of ink on the debit side of the ledger.

This is one of his Dog Series: *Dogmas from a Dog, The Aerial Dogfight, Dog Days, the Sundog, Dog Reversed, The Dog of Flinders, Dog Berries, Dog Catcher, Lying Doggo, The Dog of the Right Angle*, and *Improvisations on a Dog*.

Socrates, Ben Jonson, Cellini, Swedenborg, Li Po, and Hiawatha are roistering in the Mermaid Tavern. Through a window, Daedalus is seen on top of the battlements of Cnossus, shoving a rocket up the ass of his son, Icarus, to give him a jet-assisted takeoff for his famous flight. In one corner crouches Og, Son of Fire. He gnaws on a sabertooth bone and paints bison and mammoths on the mildewed plaster. The barmaid, Athena, is bending over the table where she is serving nectar and pretzels to her distinguished customers. Aristotle, wearing goat's horns, is behind her. He has lifted her skirt and is tupping her from behind. The ashes from the cigarette dangling from his smirking lips have fallen onto her skirt, which is beginning to smoke. In the doorway of the men's room, a drunken Batman succumbs to a long-repressed desire and attempts to bugger the Boy Wonder. Through another window is a lake on the surface of which a man is walking, a green-tarnished halo hovering over his head. Behind him a periscope sticks out of the water.

Prehensile, the penisnake wraps itself around the brush and begins to paint. The brush is a small cylinder attached at one end to a hose which runs to a dome-shaped machine. From the other end of the cylinder extends a nozzle. The aperture of this can be decreased or increased by rotation of a thumb-dial on the cylinder. The paint which the nozzle deposits in a fine spray or in a thick stream or in whatever color or hue desired is controlled by several dials on the cylinder.

Furiously, proboscisean, it builds up another figure layer by layer. Then, it sniffs a musty odor of must and drops the brush and slides out the door and down the bend of wall of oval hall, describing the scrawl of legless creatures, a writing in the sand which all may read but few understand. Blood pumppumps in rhythm with the mills of Un and Sub to feed and swill the hot-blooded reptile. But the walls, detecting intrusive mass and extrusive desire, glow.

He groans, and the glandular cobra rises and sways to the fluting of his wish for cuntcealment. Let there not be light! The lights must be his cloaka. Speed past mother's room, nearest the exit. Ah! Sighs softly in relief but air whistles through the vertical and tight mouth, announcing the departure of the exsupress for Desideratum.

The door has become archaic; it has a keyhole. Quick! Up the ramp and out of the house through the keyhole and out onto the street. One person abroad a broad, a young woman with phosphorescent silver hair and snatch to match.

Out and down the street and coiling around her ankle. She looks down with surprise and then fear. He likes this; too willing were too many. He's found a diamond in the ruff.

Up around her kitten-ear-soft leg, around and around, and sliding across the dale of groin. Nuzzling the tender corkscrewed hairs and then, self-Tantalus, detouring up the slight convex of belly, saying hello to the bellybutton, pressing on it to ring upstairs, around and around the narrow waist and shyly and quickly snatching a kiss from each nipple. Then back down to form an expedition for climbing the mons veneris and planting the flag thereon.

Oh, delectation tabu and sickersacrosanct! There's a baby in there, ectoplasm beginning to form in eager preanticipation of actuality. Drop, egg, and shoot the chuty-chutes of flesh, hastening to gulp the lucky Micromoby Dick, outwriggling its million million brothers, survival of the fightingest.

A vast croaking fills the hall. The hot breath chills the skin. He sweats. Icicles coat the tumorous fuselage, and it sags under the weight of ice, and fog rolls around, whistling past the struts, and the ailerons and elevators are locked in ice, and he's losing altiattitude fast. Get up, get up! Venusberg somewhere ahead in the mists; Tannhäuser, blow your strumpets, send up your flares, I'm in a nose-dive.

Mother's door has opened. A toad squatfills the ovoid doorway. Its dewlap rises and falls bellows-like; its toothless mouth gawps. Ginungagap. Forked tongue shoots out and curls around the boar cuntstrictor. He cries out with both mouths and jerks this way and those. The waves of denial run through. Two webbed paws bend and tie the flopping body into a knot—a runny shapeshank, of course.

The woman strolls on. Wait for me! Out the flood roars, crashes into the knot, roars back, ebb clashing with flood. Too much and only one way to go. He jerkspurts, the firmament of waters falling, no Noah's ark or arc; he novas, a shatter of millions of glowing wriggling meteors, flashes in the pan of existence.

Thigh kingdom come. Groin and belly encased in musty armor, and he cold, wet, and trembling.

GOD'S PATENT ON DAWN EXPIRES

... the following spoken by Alfred Melophon Voxpopper, of the Aurora Pushups and Coffee Hour, Channel 69B. Lines taped during the 50th Folk Art Center Annual Demonstration and Competition, Beverly Hills, level 14. Spoken by Omar Bacchylides Runic, extemporaneously if you discount some forethought during the previous evening at the nonpublic tavern, The Private Universe, and you may because Runic did not remember a thing about that evening. Despite which he won First Laurel Wreath A, there being no Second, Third, etc., wreaths classified as A through Z, God bless our democracy.

A gray-pink salmon leaping up the falls of
    night
Into the spawning pool of another day.

Dawn—the red roar of the heliac bull
Charging over the horizon.

The photonic blood of bleeding night,
Stabbed by the assassin sun.

and so on for fifty lines punctuated and fractured by cheers,
handclaps, boos, hisses, and yelps.

Chib is half-awake. He peeps down into the narrowing dark as
the dream roars off into the subway tunnel. He peeps through
barely opened lids at the other reality: consciousness.

"Let my peeper go!" he groans with Moses and so, thinking
of long beards and horns (courtesy of Michelangelo), he thinks of
his great-great-grandfather.

The will, a crowbar, forces his eyelids open. He sees the fido
which spans the wall opposite him and curves up over half the
ceiling. Dawn, the paladin of the sun, is flinging its gray gauntlet
down.

Channel 69B, YOUR FAVORITE CHANNEL, LA's own, brings
you dawn. (Deception in depth. Nature's false dawn shadowed
forth with electrons shaped by devices shaped by man.)

Wake up with the sun in your heart and a song on your lips!
Thrill to the stirring lines of Omar Runic! See dawn as the birds
in the trees, as God, see it!

Voxpopper chants the lines softly while Grieg's *Anitra* wells
softly. The old Norwegian never dreamed of this audience and
just as well. A young man, Chibiabos Elgreco Winnegan, has a
sticky wick, courtesy of a late gusher in the oilfield of the unconscious.

"Off your ass and onto your steed," Chib says. "Pegasus runs
today."

He speaks, thinks, lives in the present tensely.

Chib climbs out of bed and shoves it into the wall. To leave
the bed sticking out, rumpled as an old drunkard's tongue, would

fracture the aesthetics of his room, destroy that curve that is the reflection of the basic universe, and hinder him in his work.

The room is a huge ovoid and in a corner is a small ovoid, the toilet and shower. He comes out of it looking like one of Homer's god-like Achaeans, massively thighed, great-armed, golden-brown-skinned, blue-eyed, auburn-haired—although beardless. The phone is simulating the tocsin of a South American tree frog he once heard over Channel 122.

"Open O sesame!"

INTER CAECOS REGNAT LUSCUS

The face of Rex Luscus spreads across the fido, the pores of skin like the cratered fields of a World War I battlefield. He wears a black monocle over the left eye, ripped out in a brawl among art critics during the *I Love Rembrandt Lecture Series*, Channel 109. Although he has enough pull to get a priority for eye-replacement, he has refused.

"*Inter caecos regnat luscus*," he says when asked about it and quite often when not. "Translation: among the blind, the one-eyed man is king. That's why I renamed myself Rex Luscus, that is, King One-eyed."

There is a rumor, fostered by Luscus, that he will permit the bioboys to put in an artificial protein eye when he sees the works of an artist great enough to justify focal vision. It is also rumored that he may do so soon, because of his discovery of Chibiabos El-greco Winnegan.

Luscus looks hungrily (he swears by adverbs) at Chib's to-mentum and outlying regions. Chib swells, not with tumescence but with anger.

Luscus says, smoothly, "Honey, I just want to reassure myself that you're up and about the tremendously important business of this day. You must be ready for the showing, must! But now I see you, I'm reminded I've not eaten yet. What about breakfast with me?"

"What're we eating?" Chib says. He does not wait for a reply. "No. I've too much to do today. Close O sesame!"

Rex Luscus' face fades away, goatlike, or, as he prefers to describe it, the face of Pan, a Faunus of the arts. He has even had his ears trimmed to a point. Real cute.

"Baa-aa-aa!" Chib bleats at the phantom. "Ba! Humbuggery! I'll never kiss your ass, Luscus, or let you kiss mine. Even if I lose the grant!"

The phone bells again. The dark face of Rousseau Red Hawk appears. His nose is as the eagle's, and his eyes are broken black glass. His broad forehead is bound with a strip of red cloth, which circles the straight black hair that glides down to his shoulders. His shirt is buckskin; a necklace of beads hangs from his neck. He looks like a Plains Indian, although Sitting Bull, Crazy Horse, or the noblest Roman Nose of them all would have kicked him out of the tribe. Not that they were anti-Semitic, they just could not have respected a brave who broke out into hives when near a horse.

Born Julius Applebaum, he legally became Rousseau Red Hawk on his Naming Day. Just returned from the forest reprimevalized, he is now reveling in the accursed fleshpots of a decadent civilization.

"How're you, Chib? The gang's wondering how soon you'll get here?"

"Join you? I haven't had breakfast yet, and I've a thousand things to do to get ready for the showing. I'll see you at noon!"

"You missed out on the fun last night. Some goddam Egyptians tried to feel the girls up, but we salaamed them against the walls."

Rousseau vanished like the last of the red men.

Chib thinks of breakfast just as the intercom whistles. Open O sesame! He sees the living room. Smoke, too thick and furious for the air-conditioning to whisk away, roils. At the far end of the ovoid, his little half-brother and half-sister sleep on a flato. Playing Mama-and-friend, they fell asleep, their mouths open in blessed innocence, beautiful as only sleeping children can be. Opposite the closed eyes of each is an unwinking eye like that of a Mongolian Cyclops.

"Ain't they cute?" Mama says. "The darlings were just too tired to toddle off."

The table is round. The aged knights and ladies are gathered around it for the latest quest of the ace, king, queen, and jack. They are armored only in layer upon layer of fat. Mama's jowls hang down like banners on a windless day. Her breasts creep and quiver on the table, bulge, and ripple.

"A gam of gamblers," he says aloud, looking at the fat faces, the tremendous tits, the rampant rumps. They raise their eyebrows. What the hell's the mad genius talking about now?

"Is your kid really retarded?" says one of Mama's friends, and they laugh and drink some more beer. Angela Ninon, not wanting to miss out on this deal and figuring Mama will soon turn on the sprayers anyway, pisses down her leg. They laugh at this, and William Conqueror says, "I open."

"I'm always open," Mama says, and they shriek with laughter.

Chib would like to cry. He does not cry, although he has been encouraged from childhood to cry any time he feels like it.

—It makes you feel better and look at the Vikings, what men they were and they cried like babies whenever they felt like it—Courtesy of Channel 202 on the popular program *What's A Mother Done?*

He does not cry because he feels like a man who thinks about the mother he loved and who is dead but who died a long time ago. His mother has been long buried under a landslide of flesh. When he was sixteen, he had a lovely mother.

Then she cut him off.

THE FAMILY THAT BLOWS IS THE FAMILY THAT GROWS
—from a poem by Edgar A. Grist, via Channel 88

"Son, I don't get much out of this. I just do it because I love you."

Then, fat, fat, fat! Where did she go? Down into the adipose abyss. Disappearing as she grew larger.

"Sonny, you could at least wrestle with me a little now and then."

"You cut me off, Mama. That was all right. I'm a big boy now. But you haven't any right to expect me to want to take it up again."

"You don't love me any more!"

"What's for breakfast, Mama?" Chib says.

"I'm holding a good hand, Chibby," Mama says. "As you've told me so many times, you're a big boy. Just this once, get your own breakfast."

"What'd you call me for?"

"I forgot when your exhibition starts. I wanted to get some sleep before I went."

"14:30, Mama, but you don't have to go."

Rouged green lips part like a gangrened wound. She scratches one rouged nipple. "Oh, I want to be there. I don't want to miss my own son's artistic triumphs. Do you think you'll get the grant?"

"If I don't, it's Egypt for us," he says.

"Those stinking Arabs!" says William Conqueror.

"It's the Bureau that's doing it, not the Arabs," Chib says. "The Arabs moved for the same reason we may have to move."

From Grandpa's unpublished Ms.: Whoever would have thought that Beverly Hills would become anti-Semitic?

"I don't want to go to Egypt!" Mama wails. "You got to get that grant, Chibby. I don't want to leave the clutch. I was born and raised here, well, on the tenth level, anyway, and when I moved all my friends went along. I won't go!"

"Don't cry, Mama," Chib says, feeling distress despite himself. "Don't cry. The government can't force you to go, you know. You got your rights."

"If you want to keep on having goodies, you'll go," says Conqueror. "Unless Chib wins the grant, that is. And I wouldn't blame him if he didn't even try to win it. It ain't his fault you can't say no to Uncle Sam. You got your purple and the yap Chib makes from selling his paintings. Yet it ain't enough. You spend faster than you get it."

Mama screams with fury at William, and they're off. Chib cuts off fido. Hell with breakfast; he'll eat later. His final painting for the Festival must be finished by noon. He presses a plate, and the bare egg-shaped room opens here and there, and painting equipment comes out like a gift from the electronic gods. Zeuxis would flip and Van Gogh would get the shakes if they could see the canvas and palette and brush Chib uses.

The process of painting involves the individual bending and twisting of thousands of wires into different shapes at various depths. The wires are so thin they can be seen only with magnifiers and manipulated with exceedingly delicate pliers. Hence, the goggles he wears and the long almost-gossamer instrument in his hand when he is in the first stages of creating a painting. After hundreds of hours of slow and patient labor (of love), the wires are arranged.

Chib removes his goggles to perceive the overall effect. He then uses the paint-sprayer to cover the wires with the colors and hues he desires. The paint dries hard within a few minutes. Chib attaches electrical leads to the pan and presses a button to deliver a tiny voltage through the wires. These glow beneath the paint and, Lilliputian fuses, disappear in blue smoke.

The result is a three-dimensional work composed of hard shells of paint on several levels below the exterior shell. The shells are of varying thicknesses and all are so thin that light slips through the upper to the inner shell when the painting is turned at angles. Parts of the shells are simply reflectors to intensify the light so that the inner images may be more visible.

When being shown, the painting is on a self-moving pedestal which turns the painting 12 degrees to the left from the center and then 12 degrees to the right from the center.

The fido tocsins. Chib, cursing, thinks of disconnecting it. At least, it's not the intercom with his mother calling hysterically. Not yet, anyway. She'll call soon enough if she loses heavily at poker.

Open O sesame!

SING, O MEWS, OF UNCLE SAM

Grandpa writes in his *Private Ejaculations:* Twenty-five years
after I fled with twenty billion dollars and then supposedly
died of a heart attack, Falco Accipiter is on my trail again.
The IRB detective who named himself Falcon Hawk when he
entered his profession. What an egotist! Yet, he is as sharp-
eyed and relentless as a bird of prey, and I would shiver if I
were not too old to be frightened by mere human beings.
Who loosed the jesses and hood? How did he pick up the old
and cold scent?

Accipiter's face is that of an overly suspicious peregrine that
tries to look everywhere while it soars, that peers up its own anus
to make sure that no duck has taken refuge there. The pale blue
eyes fling glances like knives shot out of a shirtsleeve and hurled
with a twist of the wrist. They scan all with sherlockian intake of
minute and significant detail. His head turns back and forth, ears
twitching, nostrils expanding and collapsing, all radar and sonar
and odar.

"Mr. Winnegan, I'm sorry to call so early. Did I get you out
of bed?"

"It's obvious you didn't!" Chib says. "Don't bother to intro-
duce yourself. I know you. You've been shadowing me for three
days."

Accipiter does not redden. Master of control, he does all his
blushing in the depths of his bowels, where no one can see. "If
you know me, perhaps you can tell me why I'm calling you?"

"Would I be dumbshit enough to tell you?"

"Mr. Winnegan, I'd like to talk to you about your great-
great-grandfather."

"He's been dead for twenty-five years!" Chib cries. "Forget
him. And don't bother me. Don't try for a search warrant. No
judge would give you one. A man's home is his hassle . . . I mean
castle."

He thinks of Mama and what the day is going to be like unless he gets out soon. But he has to finish the painting.

"Fade off, Accipiter," Chib says. "I think I'll report you to the BPHR. I'm sure you got a fido inside that silly-looking hat of yours."

Accipiter's face is as smooth and unmoving as an alabaster carving of the falcon-god Horus. He may have a little gas bulging his intestines. If so, he slips it out unnoticed.

"Very well, Mr. Winnegan. But you're not getting rid of me that easily. After all ..."

"Fade out!"

The intercom whistles thrice. What I tell you three times is Grandpa. "I was eavesdropping," says the 120-year-old voice, hollow and deep as an echo from a Pharaoh's tomb. "I want to see you before you leave. That is, if you can spare the Ancient of Daze a few minutes."

"Always, Grandpa," Chib says, thinking of how much he loves the old man. "You need any food?"

"Yes, and for the mind, too."

Der Tag. Dies Irae. Götterdämmerung. Armageddon. Things are closing in. Make-or-break day. Go-no-go time. All these calls and a feeling of more to come. What will the end of the day bring?

THE TROCHE SUN SLIPS INTO THE SORE THROAT
OF NIGHT
—from Omar Runic

Chib walks towards the convex door, which rolls into the interstices between the walls. The focus of the house is the oval family room. In the first quadrant, going clockwise, is the kitchen, separated from the family room by six-meter-high accordion screens, painted with scenes from Egyptian tombs by Chib, his too subtle comment on modern food. Seven slim pillars around the family room mark the borders of room and corridor. Between the pillars are more tall accordion screens, painted by Chib during his Amerind mythology phase.

The corridor is also oval-shaped; every room in the house opens onto it. There are seven rooms, six bedroom-workroom-study-toilet-shower combinations. The seventh is a storeroom.

Little eggs within bigger eggs within great eggs within a meg-amonolith on a planetary pear within an ovoid universe, the latest cosmogony indicating that infinity has the form of a hen's fruit. God broods over the abyss and cackles every trillion years or so.

Chib cuts across the hall, passes between two pillars, carved by him into nymphet caryatids, and enters the family room. His mother looks sidewise at her son, who she thinks is rapidly approaching insanity if he has not already overshot his mark. It's partly her fault; she shouldn't have gotten disgusted and in a moment of wackiness called It off. Now, she's fat and ugly, oh, God, so fat and ugly. She can't reasonably or even unreasonably hope to start up again.

It's only natural, she keeps telling herself, sighing, resentful, teary, that he's abandoned the love of his mother for the strange, firm, shapely delights of young women. But to give them up, too? He's not a bisex. He quit all that when he was thirteen. So what's the reason for his chastity? He isn't in love with the fornixator, either, which she would understand, even if she did not approve.

Oh, God, where did I go wrong? And then, There's nothing wrong with me. He's going crazy like his father—Raleigh Renaissance, I think his name was—and his aunt and his great-great-grandfather. It's all that painting and those radicals, the Young Radishes, he runs around with. He's too artistic, too sensitive. Oh, God, if something happens to my little boy, I'll have to go to Egypt.

Chib knows her thoughts since she's voiced them so many times and is not capable of having new ones. He passes the round table without a word. The knights and ladies of the canned Camelot see him through a beery veil.

In the kitchen, he opens an oval door in the wall. He removes a tray with food in covered dishes and cups, all wrapped in plastic.

"Aren't you going to eat with us?"

"Don't whine, Mama," he says and goes back to his room to pick up some cigars for his Grandpa. The door, detecting, amplifying, and transmitting the shifting but recognizable eidolon of epidermal electrical fields to the activating mechanism, balks. Chib is too upset. Magnetic maelstroms rage over his skin and distort the spectral configuration. The door half-rolls out, rolls in, changes its minds again, rolls out, rolls in.

Chib kicks the door and it becomes completely blocked. He decides he'll have a video or vocal sesame put in. Trouble is, he's short of units and coupons and can't buy the materials. He shrugs and walks along the curving, one-walled hall and stops in front of Grandpa's door, hidden from view of those in the living room by the kitchen screens.

"For he sang of peace and freedom,
Sang of beauty, love, and longing;
Sang of death, and life undying
In the Islands of the Blessed,
In the kingdom of Ponemah,
In the land of the Hereafter.
Very dear to Hiawatha
Was the gentle Chibiabos."

Chib chants the passwords; the door rolls back.

Light glares out, a yellowish red-tinged light that is Grandpa's own creation. Looking into the convex oval door is like looking into the lens of a madman's eyeball. Grandpa, in the middle of the room, has a white beard falling to midthigh and white hair cataracting to just below the back of his knees. Although beard and headhair conceal his nakedness, and he is not out in public, he wears a pair of shorts. Grandpa is somewhat old-fashioned, forgivable in a man of twelve decadencies.

Like Rex Luscus, he is one-eyed. He smiles with his own teeth, grown from buds transplanted thirty years ago. A big green cigar sticks out of one corner of his full red mouth. His nose is broad and smeared as if time had stepped upon it with a heavy foot. His forehead and cheeks are broad, perhaps due to a shot of Ojibway blood in his veins, though he was born Finnegan and even sweats celtically, giving off an aroma of whiskey. He holds his head high, and the blue-gray eye is like a pool at the bottom of a prediluvian pothole, remnant of a melted glacier.

All in all, Grandpa's face is Odin's as he returns from the Well of Mimir, wondering if he paid too great a price. Or it is the face of the windbeaten, sandblown Sphinx of Gizeh.

"Forty centuries of hysteria look down upon you, to paraphrase Napoleon," Grandpa says. "The rockhead of the ages. *What, then is Man?* sayeth the New Sphinx, Oedipus having resolved the question of the Old Sphinx and settling nothing because She had already delivered another of her kind, a smartass kid with a question nobody's been able to answer yet. And perhaps just as well it can't be."

"You talk funny," Chib says. "But I like it."

He grins at Grandpa, loving him.

"You sneak into here every day, not so much from love for me as to gain knowledge and insight. I have seen all, heard everything, and thought more than a little. I voyaged much before I took refuge in this room a quarter of a century ago. Yet confinement here has been the greatest Odyssey of all.

THE ANCIENT MARINATOR

I call myself. A marinade of wisdom steeped in the brine of oversalted cynicism and too long a life."

"You smile so, you must have just had a woman," Chib teases.

"No, my boy. I lost the tension in my ramrod thirty years ago. And I thank God for that, since it removes from me the temptation of fornication, not to mention masturbation. However, I have other energies left, hence, scope for other sins, and these are even more serious.

"Aside from the sin of sexual commission, which paradoxically involves the sin of sexual emission, I had other reasons for not asking that Old Black Magician Science for shots to starch me out again. I was too old for young girls to be attracted to me for anything but money. And I was too much a poet, a lover of beauty, to take on the wrinkled blisters of my generation or several just before mine.

"So now you see, my son. My clapper swings limberly in the bell of my sex. Ding, dong, ding, dong. A lot of dong, but not much ding."

Grandpa laughs deeply, a lion's roar with a spray of doves.

"I am but the mouthpiece of the ancients, a shyster pleading for long-dead clients. Come not to bury but to praise and forced by my sense of fairness to admit the faults of the past, too. I'm a queer crabbed old man, pent like Merlin in his tree trunk. Samolxis, the Thracian bear god, hibernating in his cave. The Last of the Seven Sleepers."

Grandpa goes to the slender plastic tube depending from the ceiling and pulls down the folding handles of the eyepiece.

"Accipiter is hovering outside our house. He smells something rotten in Beverly Hills, level 14. Could it be that Win-again Winnegan isn't dead? Uncle Sam is like a diplodocus kicked in the ass. It takes twenty-five years for the message to reach its brain."

Tears appear in Chib's eyes. He says, "Oh, God, Grandpa, I don't want anything to happen to you."

"What can happen to a 120-year-old man besides failure of brain or kidneys?"

"With all due respect, Grandpa," Chib says, "you do rattle on."

"Call me Id's mill," Grandpa says. "The flour it yields is baked in the strange oven of my ego—or half-baked, if you please."

Chib grins through his tears and says, "They taught me at school that puns are cheap and vulgar."

"What's good enough for Homer, Aristophanes, Rabelais, and Shakespeare is good enough for me. By the way, speaking of cheap and vulgar, I met your mother in the hall last night, before the poker party started. I was just leaving the kitchen with a bottle of booze. She almost fainted. But she recovered fast and pretended not to see me. Maybe she did think she'd seen a ghost. I doubt it. She'd have been blabbing all over town about it."

"She may have told her doctor," Chib says. "She saw you several weeks ago, remember? She may have mentioned it while she was bitching about her so-called dizzy spells and hallucinations."

"And the old sawbones, knowing the family history, called the IRB. Maybe."

Chib looks through the periscope's eyepiece. He rotates it and turns the knobs on the handle-ends to raise and lower the cyclops on the end of the tube outside. Accipiter is stalking around the aggregate of seven eggs, each on the end of a broad thin curved branchlike walk projecting from the central pedestal. Accipiter goes up the steps of a branch to the door of Mrs. Applebaum's. The door opens.

"He must have caught her away from the fornixator," Chib says. "And she must be lonely; she's not talking to him over fido. My God, she's fatter than Mama!"

"Why not?" Grandpa says. "Mr. and Mrs. Everyman sit on their asses all day, drink, eat, and watch fido, and their brains run to mud and their bodies to sludge. Caesar would have had no trouble surrounding himself with fat friends these days. You ate, too, Brutus?"

Grandpa's comment, however, should not apply to Mrs. Applebaum. She has a hole in her head, and people addicted to fornixation seldom get fat. They sit or lie all day and part of the night, the needle in the fornix area of the brain delivering a series of minute electrical jolts. Indescribable ecstasy floods through their bodies with every impulse, a delight far surpassing any of food, drink, or sex. It's illegal, but the government never bothers a user unless it wants to get him for something else, since a fornic rarely has children. Twenty per cent of LA have had holes drilled in their heads and tiny shafts inserted for access of the needle. Five per cent are addicted; they waste away, seldom eating, their distended bladders spilling poisons into the bloodstream.

Chib says, "My brother and sister must have seen you sometimes when you were sneaking out to mass. Could they . . . ?"

"They think I'm a ghost, too. In this day and age! Still, maybe it's a good sign that they can believe in something, even a spook."

"You better stop sneaking out to church."

"The Church, and you, are the only things that keep me going. It was a sad day, though, when you told me you couldn't believe. You would have made a good priest—with faults, of course—and I could have had private mass and confession in this room."

Chib says nothing. He's gone to instruction and observed services just to please Grandpa. The Church was an egg-shaped sea-shell which, held to the ear, gave only the distant roar of God receding like an ebb tide.

THERE ARE UNIVERSES BEGGING FOR GODS

yet He hangs around this one looking for work.
—from Grandpa's Ms.

Grandpa takes over the eyepiece. He laughs. "The Internal Revenue Bureau! I thought it'd been disbanded! Who the hell has an income big enough to report on any more? Do you suppose it's still active just because of me? Could be."

He calls Chib back to the scope, directed towards the center of Beverly Hills. Chib has a lane of vision between the seven-egged clutches on the branched pedestals. He can see part of the central plaza, the giant ovoids of the city hall, the federal bureaus, the Folk Center, part of the massive spiral on which set the houses of worship, and the dora (from pandora) where those on the purple wage get their goods and those with extra income get their goodies. One end of the big artificial lake is visible; boats and canoes sail on it and people fish.

The irradiated plastic dome that enfolds the clutches of Beverly Hills is sky-blue. The electronic sun climbs towards the zenith. There are a few white genuine-looking images of clouds and even a V of geese migrating south, their honks coming down faintly. Very nice for those who have never been outside the walls of LA. But Chib spent two years in the World Nature Rehabilitation and Conservation Corps—the WNRCC—and he knows the difference. Almost, he decided to desert with Rousseau Red Hawk and join the neo-Amerinds. Then, he was going to become a forest ranger. But this might mean he'd end up shooting or arresting Red Hawk. Besides, he didn't want to become a sammer. And he wanted more than anything to paint.

"There's Rex Luscus," Chib says. "He's being interviewed outside the Folk Center. Quite a crowd."

THE PELLUCIDAR BREAKTHROUGH

Luscus' middle name should have been Upmanship. A man of great erudition, with privileged access to the Library of Greater LA computer, and of Ulyssean sneakiness, he is always scoring over his colleagues.

He it was who founded the Go-Go School of Criticism.

Primalux Ruskinson, his great competitor, did some extensive research when Luscus announced the title of his new philosophy. Ruskinson triumphantly announced that Luscus had taken the phrase from obsolete slang, current in the mid-twentieth century.

Luscus, in the fido interview next day, said that Ruskinson was a rather shallow scholar, which was to be expected.

Go-go was taken from the Hottentot language. In Hottentot, *go-go* meant to examine, that is, to keep looking until something about the object—in this case, the artist and his works—has been observed.

The critics got in line to sign up at the new school. Ruskinson thought of committing suicide, but instead accused Luscus of having blown his way up the ladder of success.

Luscus replied on fido that his personal life was his own, and Ruskinson was in danger of being sued for violation of privacy. However, he deserved no more effort than a man striking at a mosquito.

"What the hell's a mosquito?" say millions of viewers. "Wish the bighead would talk language we could understand."

Luscus' voice fades off for a minute while the interpreters explain, having just been slipped a note from a monitor who's run off the word through the station's encyclopedia.

Luscus rode on the novelty of the Go-Go School for two years.

Then he re-established his prestige, which had been slipping somewhat, with his philosophy of the Totipotent Man.

This was so popular that the Bureau of Cultural Development and Recreation requisitioned a daily one-hour slot for a year-and-a-half in the initial program of totipotentializing.

Grandpa Winnegan's penned comment in his *Private Ejaculations:*

What about The Totipotent Man, that apotheosis of individuality and complete psychosomatic development, the democratic Übermensch, as recommended by Rex Luscus, the sexually one-sided? Poor old Uncle Sam! Trying to force the proteus of his citizens into a single stabilized shape so he can control them. And at the same time trying to encourage each and every to bring to flower his inherent capabilities—if any! The poor old long-legged, chin-whiskered, milk-hearted, flint-brained schizophrenic! Verily, the left hand knows not what the right hand is doing. As a matter of fact, the right hand doesn't know what the right hand is doing.

"What about the totipotent man?" Luscus replied to the chairman during the fourth session of the *Luscan Lecture Series.* "How does he conflict with the contemporary Zeitgeist? He doesn't. The totipotent man is the imperative of our times. He must come into being before the Golden World can be realized. How can you have a Utopia without utopians, a Golden World with humans of brass?"

It was during this Memorable Day that Luscus gave his talk on The Pellucidar Breakthrough and thereby made Chibiabos Winnegan famous. And more than incidentally gave Luscus his biggest score over his competitors.

"Pellucidar? Pellucidar?" Ruskinson mutters. "Oh, God, what's Tinker Bell doing now?"

"I'll take me some time to explain why I use this phrase to describe Winnegan's stroke of genius," Luscus continues. "First, let me seem to detour

FROM THE ARCTIC TO ILLINOIS

"Now, Confucius once said that a bear could not fart at the North Pole without causing a big wind in Chicago.

"By this he meant that all events, therefore, all men, are interconnected in an unbreakable web. What one man does, no matter how seemingly insignificant, vibrates through the strands and affects every man."

Ho Chung Ko, before his fido on the 30th level of Lhasa, Tibet, says to his wife, "That white prick has got it all wrong. Confucius didn't say that. Lenin preserve us! I'm going to call him up and give him hell."

His wife says, "Let's change the channel. Pai Ting Place is on now, and . . ."

Ngombe, 10th level, Nairobi: "The critics here are a bunch of black bastards. Now you take Luscus; he could see my genius in a second. I'm going to apply for emigration in the morning."

Wife: "You might at least ask me if I want to go! What about the kids . . . mother . . . friends . . . dog . . . ?" and so on into the lionless night of self-luminous Africa.

". . . ex-president Radinoff," Luscus continues, "once said that this is the 'Age of the Plugged-In Man.' Some rather vulgar remarks have been made about this, to me, insighted phrase. But Radinoff did not mean that human society is a daisy chain. He meant that the current of modern society flows through the circuit of which we are all part. This is the Age of Complete Interconnection. No wires can hang loose; otherwise we all short-circuit. Yet, it is undeniable that life without individuality is not worth living. Every man must be a *hapax legomenon* . . ."

Ruskinson jumps up from his chair and screams, "I know that phrase! I got you this time, Luscus!"

He is so excited he falls over in a faint, symptom of a widespread hereditary defect. When he recovers, the lecture is over. He springs to the recorder to run off what he missed. But Luscus has carefully avoided defining The Pellucidar Breakthrough. He will explain it at another lecture.

Grandpa, back at the scope, whistles, "I feel like an astronomer. The planets are in orbit around our house, the sun. There's

Accipiter, the closest, Mercury, although he's not the god of thieves but their nemesis. Next, Benedictine, your sad-sack Venus. Hard, hard, hard! The sperm would batter their heads flat against the stony ovum. You sure she's pregnant?

"Your Mama's out there, dressed fit to kill and I wish someone would. Mother Earth headed for the perigee of the gummint store to waste your substance."

Grandpa braces himself as if on a rolling deck, the blue-black veins on his legs thick as strangling vines on an ancient oak. "Brief departure from the role of Herr Doktor Sternscheissdreckschnuppe, the great astronomer, to that of der Unterseeboot Kapitan von Schooten die Fischen in der Barrel. Ach! I zee yet das tramp schteamer, Deine Mama, yawing, pitching, rolling in the seas of alcohol. Compass lost; rhumb dumb. Three sheets to the wind. Paddlewheels spinning in the air. The black gang sweating their balls off, stoking the furnaces of frustration. Propeller tangled in the nets of neurosis. And the Great White Whale a glimmer in the black depths but coming up fast, intent on broaching her bottom, too big to miss. Poor damned vessel, I weep for her. I also vomit with disgust.

"Fire one! Fire two! Baroom! Mama rolls over, a jagged hole in her hull but not the one you're thinking of. Down she goes, nose first, as befits a devoted fellationeer, her huge aft rising into the air. Blub, blub! Full fathom five!

"And so back from undersea to outer space. Your sylvan Mars, Red Hawk, has just stepped out of the tavern. And Luscus, Jupiter, the one-eyed All-Father of Art, if you'll pardon my mixing of Nordic and Latin mythologies, is surrounded by his swarm of satellites."

EXCRETION IS THE BITTER PART OF VALOR

Luscus says to the fido interviewers, "By this I mean that Winnegan, like every artist, great or not, produces art that is, first, secretion, unique to himself, then excretion. Excretion in the original sense of 'sifting out.' Creative excretion or discrete excretion. I know that my distinguished colleagues will make fun of this analogy, so I hereby challenge them to a fido debate whenever it can be arranged.

"The valor comes from the courage of the artist in showing his inner products to the public. The bitter part comes from the fact that the artist may be rejected or misunderstood in his time. Also from the terrible war that takes place in the artist with the disconnected or chaotic elements, often contradictory, which he must unite and then mold into a unique entity. Hence my 'discrete excretion' phrase."

Fido interviewer: "Are we to understand that everything is a big pile of shit but that art makes a strange seachange, forms it into something golden and illuminating?"

"Not exactly. But you're close. I'll elaborate and expound at a later date. At present, I want to talk about Winnegan. Now, the lesser artists give only the surface of things; they are photographers. But the great ones give the interiority of objects and beings. Winnegan, however, is the first to reveal more than one interiority in a single work of art. His invention of the alto-relief multilevel technique enables him to epiphanize—show forth—subterranean layer upon layer."

Primalux Ruskinson, loudly, "The Great Onion Peeler of Painting!"

Luscus, calmly after the laughter has died: "In one sense, that is well put. Great art, like an onion, brings tears to the eyes. However, the light on Winnegan's paintings is not just a reflection; it is sucked in, digested, and then fractured forth. Each of the broken beams makes visible, not various aspects of the figures beneath, but whole figures. Worlds, I might say.

"I call this The Pellucidar Breakthrough. Pellucidar is the hollow interior of our planet, as depicted in a now forgotten fantasy-romance of the twentieth-century writer, Edgar Rice Burroughs, creator of the immortal Tarzan."

Ruskinson moans and feels faint again. "Pellucid! Pellucidar! Luscus, you punning exhumist bastard!"

"Burroughs' hero penetrated the crust of Earth to discover another world inside. This was, in some ways, the reverse of the exterior, continents where the surface seas are, and vice versa. Just so, Winnegan has discovered an inner world, the obverse of the public image Everyman projects. And, like Burroughs' hero, he has returned with a stunning narrative of psychic dangers and exploration.

"And just as the fictional hero found his Pellucidar to be populated with stone-age men and dinosaurs, so Winnegan's world is, though absolutely modern in one sense, archaic in another. Abysmally pristine. Yet, in the illumination of Winnegan's world, there is an evil and inscrutable patch of blackness, and that is paralleled in Pellucidar by the tiny fixed moon which casts a chilling and unmoving shadow.

"Now, I did intend that the ordinary 'pellucid' should be part of Pellucidar. Yet 'pellucid' means 'reflecting light evenly from all surfaces' or 'admitting maximum passage of light without diffusion or distortion.' Winnegan's paintings do just the opposite. But—under the broken and twisted light, the acute observer can see a primeval luminosity, even and straight. This is the light that links all the fractures and multilevels, the light I was thinking of in my earlier discussion of the 'Age of the Plugged-In Man' and the polar bear.

"By intent scrutiny, a viewer may detect this, feel, as it were, the photonic fremitus of the heartbeat of Winnegan's world."

Ruskinson almost faints. Luscus' smile and black monocle make him look like a pirate who has just taken a Spanish galleon loaded with gold.

Grandpa, still at the scope, says, "And there's Maryam bint Yusuf, the Egyptian backwoodswoman you were telling me about. Your Saturn, aloof, regal, cold, and wearing one of those suspended whirling manycolored hats that're all the rage. Saturn's rings? Or a halo?"

"She's beautiful, and she'd make a wonderful mother for my children," Chib says.

"The chic of Araby. Your Saturn has two moons, mother and aunt. Chaperones! You say she'd make a good mother! How good a wife! Is she intelligent?"

"She's as smart as Benedictine."

"A dumbshit then. You sure can pick them. How do you

know you're in love with her? You've been in love with twenty women in the last six months."

"I love her. This is it."

"Until the next one. Can you really love anything but your painting? Benedictine's going to have an abortion, right?"

"Not if I can talk her out of it," Chib says. "To tell the truth, I don't even like her any more. But she's carrying my child."

"Let me look at your pelvis. No, you're male. For a moment, I wasn't sure, you're so crazy to have a baby."

"A baby is a miracle to stagger sextillions of infidels."

"It beats a mouse. But don't you know that Uncle Sam has been propagandizing his heart out to cut down on propagation? Where've you been all your life?"

"I got to go, Grandpa."

Chib kisses the old man and returns to his room to finish his latest painting. The door still refuses to recognize him, and he calls the gummint repair shop, only to be told that all technicians are at the Folk Festival. He leaves the house in a red rage. The bunting and balloons are waving and bobbing in the artificial wind, increased for this occasion, and an orchestra is playing by the lake.

Through the scope, Grandpa watches him walk away.

"Poor devil! I ache for his ache. He wants a baby, and he is ripped up inside because that poor devil Benedictine is aborting their child. Part of his agony, though he doesn't know it, is identification with the doomed infant. His own mother has had innumerable—well, quite a few—abortions. But for the grace of God, he would have been one of them, another nothingness. He wants this baby to have a chance, too. But there is nothing he can do about it, nothing.

"And there is another feeling, one which he shares with most of humankind. He knows he's screwed up his life, or something has twisted it. Every thinking man and woman knows this. Even the smug and dimwitted realize this unconsciously. But a baby, that beautiful being, that unsmirched blank tablet, unformed angel, represents a new hope. Perhaps it won't screw up. Perhaps it'll grow up to be a healthy confident reasonable good-humored unselfish loving man or woman. 'It won't be like me or my next-door neighbor,' the proud, but apprehensive, parent swears.

"Chib thinks this and swears that his baby will be different. But, like everybody else, he's fooling himself. A child has one father and mother, but it has trillions of aunts and uncles. Not only those that are its contemporaries; the dead, too. Even if Chib fled into the wilderness and raised the infant himself, he'd be giving it his own unconscious assumptions. The baby would grow up with beliefs and attitudes that the father was not even aware of. Moreover, being raised in isolation, the baby would be a very peculiar human being indeed.

"And if Chib raises the child in this society, it's inevitable that it will accept at least part of the attitudes of its playmates, teachers, and so on ad nauseam.

"So, forget about making a new Adam out of your wonderful potential-teeming child, Chib. If it grows up to become at least half-sane, it's because you gave it love and discipline and it was lucky in its social contacts and it was also blessed at birth with the right combination of genes. That is, your son or daughter is now both a fighter and a lover.

ONE MAN'S NIGHTMARE IS ANOTHER MAN'S WET DREAM

Grandpa says.

"I was talking to Dante Alighieri just the other day, and he was telling me what an inferno of stupidity, cruelty, perversity, atheism, and outright peril the sixteenth century was. The nineteenth left him gibbering, hopelessly searching for adequate enough invectives.

"As for this age, it gave him such high-blood pressure, I had to slip him a tranquilizer and ship him out via time machine with an attendant nurse. She looked much like Beatrice and so should have been just the medicine he needed—maybe."

Grandpa chuckles, remembering that Chib, as a child, took

him seriously when he described his time-machine visitors, such notables as Nebuchadnezzar, King of the Grass-Eaters; Samson, Bronze Age Riddler and Scourge of the Philistines; Moses, who stole a god from his Kenite father-in-law and who fought against circumcision all his life; Buddha, the Original Beatnik; No-Moss Sisyphus, taking a vacation from his stone-rolling; Androcles and his buddy, the Cowardly Lion of Oz; Baron von Richthofen, the Red Knight of Germany; Beowulf; Al Capone; Hiawatha; Ivan the Terrible; and hundreds of others.

The time came when Grandpa became alarmed and decided that Chib was confusing fantasy with reality. He hated to tell the little boy that he had been making up all those wonderful stories, mostly to teach him history. It was like telling a kid there wasn't any Santa Claus.

And then, while he was reluctantly breaking the news to his grandson, he became aware of Chib's barely suppressed grin and knew that it was his turn to have his leg pulled. Chib had never been fooled or else had caught on without any shock. So, both had a big laugh and Grandpa continued to tell of his visitors.

"There are no time machines," Grandpa says. "Like it or not, Miniver Cheevy, you have to live in this your time.

"The machines work in the utility-factory levels in a silence broken only by the chatter of a few mahouts. The great pipes at the bottom of the seas suck up water and bottom sludge. The stuff is automatically carried through pipes to the ten production levels of LA. There the inorganic chemicals are converted into energy and then into the matter of food, drink, medicines, and artifacts. There is very little agriculture or animal husbandry outside the city walls, but there is superabundance for all. Artificial but exact duplication of organic stuff, so who knows the difference?

"There is no more starvation or want anywhere, except among the self-exiles wandering in the woods. And the food and goods are shipped to the pandoras and dispensed to the receivers of the purple wage. *The purple wage.* A Madison-Avenue euphemism with connotations of royalty and divine right. Earned by just being born.

"Other ages would regard ours as a delirium, yet ours has benefits others lacked. To combat transiency and rootlessness, the megalopolis is compartmented into small communities. A man can live all his life in one place without having to go elsewhere to get anything he needs. With this has come a provincialism, a small-town patriotism and hostility towards outsiders. Hence, the bloody juvenile gang-fights between towns. The intense and vicious gossip. The insistence on conformity to local mores.

"At the same time, the small-town citizen has fido, which enables him to see events anywhere in the world. Intermingled with the trash and the propaganda, which the government thinks is good for the people, is any amount of superb programs. A man may get the equivalent of a Ph.D. without stirring out of his house.

"Another Renaissance has come, a fruition of the arts comparable to that of Pericles' Athens and the city-states of Michelangelo's Italy or Shakespeare's England. Paradox. More illiterates than ever before in the world's history. But also more literates. Speakers of classical Latin outnumber those of Caesar's day. The world of aesthetics bears a fabulous fruit. And, of course, fruits.

"To dilute the provincialism and also to make international war even more unlikely, we have the world policy of *homogenization*. The voluntary exchange of a part of one nation's population with another's. Hostages to peace and brotherly love. Those citizens who can't get along on just the purple wage or who think they'll be happier elsewhere are induced to emigrate with bribes.

"A Golden World in some respects; a nightmare in others. So what's new with the world? It was always thus in every age. Ours has had to deal with overpopulation and automation. How else could the problem be solved? It's Buridan's ass (actually, the ass was a dog) all over again, as in every time. Buridan's ass, dying of hunger because it can't make up its mind which of two equal amounts of food to eat.

"History: *a pons asinorum* with men the asses on the bridge of time.

"No, those two comparisons are not fair or right. It's Hobson's horse, the only choice being the beast in the nearest stall. Zeitgeist rides tonight, and the devil take the hindmost!

"The mid-twentieth-century writers of the Triple Revolution document forecast accurately in some respects. But they deemphasized what lack of work would do to Mr. Everyman. They believed that all men have equal potentialities in developing artistic tendencies, that all could busy themselves with arts, crafts, and hobbies or education for education's sake. They wouldn't face the 'undemocratic' reality that only about ten per cent of the population—if that—are inherently capable of producing anything worth while, or even mildly interesting, in the arts. Crafts, hobbies, and a lifelong academic education pale after a while, so back to the booze, fido, and adultery.

"Lacking self-respect, the fathers become free-floaters, nomads on the steppes of sex. Mother, with a capital M, becomes the dominant figure in the family. She may be playing around, too, but she's taking care of the kids; she's around most of the time. Thus, with father a lower-case figure, absent, weak, or indifferent, the children often become homosexual or ambisexual. The wonderland is also a fairyland.

"Some features of this time could have been predicted. Sexual permissiveness was one, although no one could have seen how far it would go. But then no one could have foreknown of the Panamorite sect, even if America has spawned lunatic-fringe cults as a frog spawns tadpoles. Yesterday's monomaniac is tomorrow's messiah, and so Sheltey and his disciples survived through years of persecution and today their precepts are embedded in our culture."

Grandpa again fixes the cross-reticules of the scope on Chib.

"There he goes, my beautiful grandson, bearing gifts to the Greeks. So far, that Hercules has failed to clean up his psychic Augean stable. Yet, he may succeed, that stumblebum Apollo, that Edipus Wrecked. He's luckier than most of his contemporaries. He's had a permanent father, even if a secret one, a zany old man hiding from so-called justice. He has gotten love, discipline, and a superb education in this starred chamber. He's also fortunate in having a profession.

"But Mama spends far too much and also is addicted to gambling, a vice which deprives her of her full gauranteed income. I'm supposed to be dead, so I don't get the purple wage. Chib has to make up for all this by selling or trading his paintings. Luscus has helped him by publicizing him, but at any moment

Luscus may turn against him. The money from the paintings is still not enough. After all, money is not the basic of our economy; it's a scarce auxiliary. Chib needs the grant but won't get it unless he lets Luscus make love to him.

"It's not that Chib rejects homosexual relations. Like most of his contemporaries, he's sexually ambivalent. I think that he and Omar Runic still blow each other occasionally. And why not? They love each other. But Chib rejects Luscus as a matter of principle. He won't be a whore to advance his career. Moreover, Chib makes a distinction which is deeply embedded in this society. He thinks that uncompulsive homosexuality is natural (whatever that means?) but that compulsive homosexuality is, to use an old term, queer. Valid or not, the distinction is made.

"So, Chib may go to Egypt. But what happens to me then?

"Never mind me or your mother, Chib. No matter what. Don't give in to Luscus. Remember the dying words of Singleton, Bureau of Relocation and Rehabilitation Director, who shot himself because he couldn't adjust to the new times.

" 'What if a man gain the world and lose his ass?' "

At this moment, Grandpa sees his grandson, who has been walking along with somewhat drooping shoulders, suddenly straighten them. And he sees Chib break into a dance, a little improvised shuffle followed by a series of whirls. It is evident that Chib is whooping. The pedestrians around him are grinning.

Grandpa groans and then laughs. "Oh, God, the goatish energy of youth, the unpredictable shift of spectrum from black sorrow to bright orange joy! Dance, Chib, dance your crazy head off! Be happy, if only for a moment! You're young yet, you've got the bubbling of unconquerable hope deep in your springs! Dance, Chib, dance!"

He laughs and wipes a tear away.

SEXUAL IMPLICATIONS OF THE CHARGE OF THE LIGHT BRIGADE

is so fascinating a book that Doctor Jespersen Joyce Bathymens, psycholinguist for the federal Bureau of Group Reconfiguration and Intercommunicability, hates to stop reading. But duty beckons.

"A radish is not necessarily reddish," he says into the recorder. "The Young Radishes so named their group because a radish is a radicle, hence, radical. Also, there's a play on roots and on red-ass, a slang term for anger, and possibly on ruttish and rattish. And undoubtedly on rude-ickle, Beverly Hills dialectical term for a repulsive, unruly, and socially ungraceful person.

"Yet the Young Radishes are not what I would call Left Wing; they represent the current resentment against Life-In-General and advocate no radical policy of reconstruction. They howl against Things As They Are, like monkeys in a tree, but never give constructive criticism. They want to destroy without any thought of what to do after the destruction.

"In short, they represent the average citizen's grousing and bitching, being different in that they are more articulate. There are thousands of groups like them in LA and possibly millions all over the world. They had normal life as children. In fact, they were born and raised in the same clutch, which is one reason why they were chosen for this study. What phenomenon produced ten such creative persons, all mothered in the seven houses of Area 69-14, all about the same time, all practically raised together, since they were put together in the playpen on top of the pedestal while one mother took her turn baby-sitting and the others did whatever they had to do, which . . . where was I?

"Oh, yes, they had a normal life, went to the same school, palled around, enjoyed the usual sexual play among themselves, joined the juvenile gangs and engaged in some rather bloody warfare with the Westwood and other gangs. All were distinguished however, by an intense intellectual curiosity and all became active in the creative arts.

"It has been suggested—that might be true—that that mysterious stranger, Raleigh Renaissance, was the father of all ten. This is possible but can't be proved. Raleigh Renaissance was living in the house of Mrs. Winnegan at the time, but he seems to have been unusually active in the clutch, and, indeed, all over Beverly Hills. Where this man came from, who he was, and where he went are still unknown despite intensive search by various agencies. He had no ID or other cards of any kind yet he went unchallenged for a long time. He seems to have had something on the Chief of Police of Beverly Hills and possibly on some of the federal agents stationed in Beverly Hills.

"He lived for two years with Mrs. Winnegan, then dropped out of sight. It is rumored that he left LA to join a tribe of white neo-Amerinds, sometimes called the Seminal Indians.

"Anyway, back to the Young (pun on Jung?) Radishes. They are revolting against the Father Image of Uncle Sam, whom they both love and hate. Uncle is, of course, linked by their subconsciouses with *unco*, a Scottish word meaning strange, uncanny, weird, this indicating that their own fathers were strangers to them. All come from homes where the father was missing or weak, a phenomenon regrettably common in our culture.

"I never knew my own father . . . Tooney, wipe that out as irrelevant. *Unco* also means news or tidings, indicating that the unfortunate young men are eagerly awaiting news of the return of their fathers and perhaps secretly hoping for reconciliation with Uncle Sam, that is, their fathers.

"Uncle Sam. Sam is short for Samuel, from the Hebrew *Shemu'el*, meaning Name of God. All the Radishes are atheists, although some, notably Omar Runic and Chibiabos Winnegan, were given religious instruction as children (Panamorite and Roman Catholic, respectively).

"Young Winnegan's revolt against God, and against the Catholic Church, was undoubtedly reinforced by the fact that his mother forced strong *cath*artics upon him when he had a chronic constipation. He probably also resented having to learn his *cate*chism when he preferred to play. And there is the deeply significant and traumatic incident in which a *cath*eter was used on him. (This refusal to excrete when young will be analyzed in a later report.)

"Uncle Sam, the Father Figure. *Figure* is so obvious a play that I won't bother to point it out. Also perhaps on *figger*, in the sense of 'a fig on thee!'—look this up in Dante's *Inferno*, some Italian or other in Hell said, 'A fig on thee, God!' biting his thumb in the ancient gesture of defiance and disrespect. Hmm? Biting the thumb—an infantile characteristic?

"Sam is also a multileveled pun on phonetically, orthographically, and semisemantically linked words. It is significant that young Winnegan can't stand to be called *dear*; he claims that his mother called him that so many times it nauseates him. Yet the word has a deeper meaning to him. For instance, *sambar* is an Asiatic *deer* with *three*-pointed antlers. (Note the *sam*, also.) Obviously, the three points symbolize, to him, the Triple Revolution document, the historic dating point of the beginning of our era, which Chib claims to hate so. The three points are also archetypes of the Holy Trinity, which the Young Radishes frequently blaspheme against.

"I might point out that in this the group differs from others I've studied. The others expressed an infrequent and mild blasphemy in keeping with the mild, indeed pale, religious spirit prevalent nowadays. Strong blasphemers thrive only when strong believers thrive.

"Sam also stands for *same*, indicating the Radishes' subconscious desire to conform.

"Possibly, although this particular analysis may be invalid, Sam corresponds to Samekh, the fifteenth letter of the Hebrew alphabet. (Sam! Ech!?) In the old style of English spelling, which the Radishes learned in their childhood, the fifteenth letter of the Roman alphabet is O. In the Alphabet Table of my dictionary, Webster's 128th New Collegiate, the Roman O is in the same horizontal column as the Arabic Dad. Also with the Hebrew Mem. So we get a double connection with the missing and longed for Father (or Dad) and with the overdominating Mother (or Mem).

"I can make nothing out of the Greek Omicron, also in the same horizontal column. But give me time; this takes study.

"Omicron. The little O! The lower-case omicron has an egg shape. The little egg is their father's sperm fertilized? The womb? The basic shape of modern architecture?

"Sam Hill, an archaic euphemism for Hell. Uncle Sam is a Sam Hill of a father? Better strike that out, Tooney. It's possible that these highly educated youths have read about this obsolete phrase, but it's not confirmable. I don't want to suggest any connections that might make me look ridiculous.

"Let's see. Samisen. A Japanese musical instrument with *three* strings. The Triple Revolution document and the Trinity again. Trinity? Father, Son, and Holy Ghost. Mother the thoroughly despised figure, hence, the Wholly Goose? Well, maybe not. Wipe that out, Tooney.

"Samisen. Son of Sam? Which leads naturally to Samson, who pulled down the temple of the Philistines on them and on himself. These boys talk of doing the same thing. Chuckle. Reminds me of myself when I was their age, before I matured. Strike out that last remark, Tooney.

"Samovar. The Russian word means, literally, self-boiler. There's no doubt the Radishes are boiling with revolutionary fervor. Yet their disturbed psyches know, deep down, that Uncle Sam is their everloving Father-Mother, that he has only their best interests at heart. But they force themselves to hate him, hence, they self-boil.

"A samlet is a young salmon. Cooked salmon is a yellowish pink or pale red, near to a radish in color, in their unconsciouses, anyway. Samlet equals Young Radish; they feel they're being cooked in the great pressure cooker of modern society.

"How's that for a trinely furned phase—I mean, finely turned phrase, Tooney? Run this off, edit as indicated, smooth it out, you know how, and send it off to the boss. I got to go. I'm late for lunch with Mother; she gets very upset if I'm not there on the dot.

"Oh, postscript! I recommend that the agents watch Winnegan more closely. His friends are blowing off psychic steam through talk and drink, but he has suddenly altered his behavior pattern. He has long periods of silence, he's given up smoking, drinking, and sex."

A PROFIT IS NOT WITHOUT HONOR

even in this day. The gummint has no overt objection to privately owned taverns, run by citizens who have paid all license fees, passed all examinations, posted all bonds, and bribed the local politicians and police chief. Since there is no provision made for them, no large buildings available for rent, the taverns are in the homes of the owners themselves.

The Private Universe is Chib's favorite, partly because the proprietor is operating illegally. Dionysus Gobrinus, unable to hew his way through the roadblocks, prise-de-chevaux, barbed wire, and booby-traps of official procedure, has quit his efforts to get a license.

Openly, he paints the name of his establishment over the mathematical equations that once distinguished the exterior of the house. (Math prof at Beverly Hills U. 14, named Al-Khwarizmi Descartes Lobachevsky, he has resigned and changed his name again.) The atrium and several bedrooms have been converted for drinking and carousing. There are no Egyptian customers, probably because of their supersensitivity about the flowery sentiments painted by patrons on the inside walls.

A BAS, ABU
MOHAMMED WAS THE SON OF A VIRGIN DOG
THE SPHINX STINKS
REMEMBER THE RED SEA!
THE PROPHET HAS A CAMEL FETISH

Some of those who wrote the taunts have fathers, grandfathers, and great-grandfathers who were themselves the objects of similar insults. But their descendants are thoroughly assimilated, Beverly Hillsians to the core. Of such is the kingdom of men.

Gobrinus, a squat cube of a man, stands behind the bar, which is square as a protest against the ovoid. Above him is a big sign:

ONE MAN'S MEAD IS ANOTHER MAN'S POISSON

Gobrinus has explained this pun many times, not always to his listener's satisfaction. Suffice it that Poisson was a mathematician and that Poisson's frequency distribution is a good approximation to the binomial distribution as the number of trials increases and probability of success in a single trial is small.

When a customer gets too drunk to be permitted one more

drink, he is hurled headlong from the tavern with furious combustion and utter ruin by Gobrinus, who cries, "Poisson! Poisson!"

Chib's friends, the Young Radishes, sitting at a hexagonal table, greet him, and their words unconsciously echo those of the federal psycholinguist's estimate of his recent behavior.

"Chib, monk! Chibber as ever! Looking for a chibbie, no doubt! Take your pick!"

Madame Trismegista, sitting at a little table with a Seal-of-Solomon-shape top, greets him. She has been Gobrinus' wife for two years, a record, because she will knife him if he leaves her. Also, he believes that she can somehow juggle his destiny with the cards she deals. In this age of enlightenment, the soothsayer and astrologer flourish. As science pushes forward, ignorance and superstition gallop around the flanks and bite science in the rear with big dark teeth.

Gobrinus himself, a Ph.D., holder of the torch of knowledge (until lately, anyway), does not believe in God. But he is sure the stars are marching towards a baleful conjunction for him. With a strange logic, he thinks that his wife's cards control the stars; he is unaware that card-divination and astrology are entirely separate fields.

What can you expect of a man who claims that the universe is asymmetric?

Chib waves his hand at Madame Trismegista and walks to another table. Here sits

A TYPICAL TEEMAGER

Benedictine Serinus Melba. She is tall and slim and has narrow lemurlike hips and slender legs but big breasts. Her hair, black as the pupils of her eyes, is parted in the middle, plastered with perfumed spray to the skull, and braided into two long pigtails. These are brought over her bare shoulders and held together with a golden brooch just below her throat. From the brooch, which is in the form of a musical note, the braids part again, one looping under each breast. Another brooch secures them, and they separate to circle behind her back, are brooched again, and come back to meet on her belly. Another brooch holds them, and the twin waterfalls flow blackly over the front of her bell-shaped skirt.

Her face is thickly farded with green, aquamarine, a shamrock beauty mark, and topaz. She wears a yellow bra with artificial pink nipples; frilly lace ribbons hang from the bra. A demicorselet of bright green with black rosettes circles her waist. Over the corselet, half-concealing it, is a wire structure covered with a shimmering pink quilty material. It extends out in back to form a semifuselage or a bird's long tail, to which are attached long yellow and crimson artificial feathers.

An ankle-length diaphanous skirt billows out. It does not hide the yellow and dark-green striped lace-fringed garter-panties, white thighs, and black net stockings with green clocks in the shape of musical notes. Her shoes are bright blue with topaz high heels.

Benedictine is costumed to sing at the Folk Festival; the only thing missing is her singer's hat. Yet, she came to complain, among other things, that Chib has forced her to cancel her appearance and so lose her chance at a great career.

She is with five girls, all between sixteen and twenty-one, all drinking P (for popskull).

"Can't we talk in private, Benny?" Chib says.

"What for?" Her voice is a lovely contralto ugly with inflection.

"You got me down here to make a public scene," Chib says.

"For God's sake, what other kind of scene is there?" she shrills. "Look at him! He wants to talk to me alone!"

It is then that he realizes she is afraid to be alone with him. More than that, she is incapable of being alone. Now he knows why she insisted on leaving the bedroom door open with her girl-friend, Bela, within calling distance. And listening distance.

"You said you was just going to use your finger!" she shouts. She points at the slightly rounded belly. "I'm going to have a baby! You rotten smooth-talking sick bastard!"

"That isn't true at all," Chib says. "You told me it was all right, you loved me."

" 'Love! Love!' he says! What the hell do I know what I said, you got me so excited! Anyway, I didn't say you could stick it in! I'd never say that, never! And then what you *did! What* you did! My God, I could hardly walk for a week, you bastard, you!"

Chib sweats. Except for Beethoven's Pastoral welling from the fido, the room is silent. His friends grin. Gobrinus, his back turned, is drinking scotch. Madame Trismegista shuffles her cards, and she farts with a fiery conjunction of beer and onions. Benedictine's friends look at their Mandarin-long fluorescent fingernails or glare at him. Her hurt and indignity is theirs and vice versa.

"I can't take those pills. They make me break out and give me eye trouble and screw up my monthlies! You know that! And I can't stand those mechanical uteruses! And you lied to me anyway! You said you took a pill!"

Chib realizes she's contradicting herself, but there's no use trying to be logical. She's furious because she's pregnant; she doesn't want to be inconvenienced with an abortion at this time, and she's out for revenge.

Now how, Chib wonders, how could she get pregnant *that* night? No woman, no matter how fertile, could have managed that. She must have been knocked up before or after. Yet she swears that it was that night, the night he was

THE KNIGHT OF THE BURNING PESTLE OR FOAM, FOAM ON THE RANGE

"No, no!" Benedictine cries.

"Why not? I love you," Chib says. "I want to marry you."

Benedictine screams, and her friend Bela, out in the hall, yells, "What's the matter? What happened?"

Benedictine does not reply. Raging, shaking as if in the grip of a fever, she scrambles out of bed, pushing Chib to one side. She runs to the small egg of the bathroom in the corner, and he follows her.

"I hope you're not going to do what I think . . . ?" he says.

Benedictine moans, "You sneaky no-good son of a bitch!"

In the bathroom, she pulls down a section of wall, which becomes a shelf. On its top, attached by magnetic bottoms to the shelf, are many containers. She seizes a long thin can of spermatocide, squats, and inserts it. She presses the button on its bottom, and it foams with a hissing sound even its cover of flesh cannot silence.

Chib is paralyzed for a moment. Then he roars.

Benedictine shouts, "Stay away from me, you rude-ickle!"

From the door to the bedroom comes Bela's timid, "Are you all right, Benny?"

"I'll all-right her!" Chib bellows.

He jumps forward and takes a can of tempoxy glue from the shelf. The glue is used by Benedictine to attach her wigs to her head and will hold anything forever unless softened by a specific defixative.

Benedictine and Bela both cry out as Chib lifts Benedictine up and then lowers her to the floor. She fights, but he manages to spray the glue over the can and the skin and hairs around it.

"What're you doing?" she screams.

He pushes the button on the bottom of the can to full-on position and then sprays the bottom with glue. While she struggles, he holds her arms tight against her body and keeps her from rolling over and so moving the can in or out. Silently, Chib counts to thirty, then to thirty more to make sure the glue is thoroughly dried. He releases her.

The foam is billowing out around her groin and down her legs and spreading out across the floor. The fluid in the can is under enormous pressure in the indestructible unpunchable can, and the foam expands vastly if exposed to open air.

Chib takes the can of defixative from the shelf and clutches it in his hand, determined that she will not have it. Benedictine jumps up and swings at him. Laughing like a hyena in a tentful of nitrous oxide, Chib blocks her fist and shoves her away. Slipping on the foam, which is ankle-deep by now. Benedictine falls and then slides backward out of the bedroom on her buttocks, the can clunking.

She gets to her feet and only then realizes fully what Chib has done. Her scream goes up, and she follows it. She dances around, yanking at the can, her screams intensifying with every tug and resultant pain. Then she turns and runs out of the room or tries to. She skids; Bela is in her way; they cling together and both ski out of the room, doing a half-turn while going through the door. The foam swirls out so that the two look like Venus and friend rising from the bubble-capped waves of the Cyprian Sea.

Benedictine shoves Bela away but not without losing some flesh to Bela's long sharp fingernails. Bela shoots backwards through the door toward Chib. She is like a novice ice skater trying to maintain her balance. She does not succeed and shoots by Chib, wailing, on her back, her feet up in the air.

Chib slides his bare feet across the floor gingerly, stops at the bed to pick up his clothes, but decides he'd be wiser to wait until he's outside before he puts them on. He gets to the circular hall just in time to see Benedictine crawling past one of the columns that divides the corridor from the atrium. Her parents, two middle-aged behemoths, are still sitting on a flato, beer cans in hand, eyes wide, mouths open, quivering.

Chib does not even say goodnight to them as he passes along the hall. But then he sees the fido and realizes that her parents had switched it from EXT. to INT. and then to Benedictine's room. Father and mother have been watching Chib and daughter and it is evident from father's not-quite dwindled condition that father was very excited by this show, superior to anything seen on exterior fido.

"You peeping bastards!" Chib roars.

Benedictine has gotten to them and on her feet and she is stammering, weeping, indicating the can and then stabbing her finger at Chib. At Chib's roar, the parents heave up from the flato as two leviathans from the deep. Benedictine turns and starts to run towards him, her arms outstretched, her longnailed fingers curved, her face a medusa's. Behind her streams the wake of the livid witch and father and mother on the foam.

Chib shoves up against a pillar and rebounds and skitters off, helpless to keep himself from turning sidewise during the maneuver. But he keeps his balance. Mama and Papa have gone down together with a crash that shakes even the solid house. They are up, eyes rolling and bellowing like hippos surfacing. They charge him but separate, Mama shrieking now, her face, despite the fat, Benedictine's. Papa goes around one side of the pillar; Mama, the other. Benedictine has rounded another pillar, holding to it with one hand to keep her from slipping. She is between Chib and the door to the outside.

Chib slams against the wall of the corridor, in an area free of foam. Benedictine runs towards him. He dives across the floor, hits it, and rolls between two pillars and out into the atrium.

Mama and Papa converge in a collision course. The Titanic meets the iceberg, and both plunge swiftly. They skid on their faces and bellies towards Benedictine. She leaps into the air, trailing foam on them as they pass beneath her.

By now it is evident that the government's claim that the can is good for 40,000 shots of death-to-sperm, or for 40,000 copulations, is justified. Foam is all over the place ankle-deep—knee-high in some places—and still pouring out.

Bela is on her back now and on the atrium floor, her head driven into the soft folds of the flato.

Chib gets up slowly and stands for a moment, glaring around him, his knees bent, ready to jump from danger but hoping he won't have to since his feet will undoubtedly fly away from under him.

"Hold it, you rotten son of a bitch!" Papa roars. "I'm going to kill you! You can't do this to my daughter!"

Chib watches him turn over like a whale in a heavy sea and try to get to his feet. Down he goes again, grunting as if hit by a harpoon. Mama is no more successful than he.

Seeing that his way is unbarred—Benedictine having disappeared somewhere—Chib skis across the atrium until he reaches an unfoamed area near the exit. Clothes over his arm, still holding the defixative, he struts towards the door.

At this moment Benedictine calls his name. He turns to see her sliding from the kitchen at him. In her hand is a tall glass. He wonders what she intends to do with it. Certainly, she is not offering him the hospitality of a drink.

Then she scoots into the dry region of the floor and topples forward with a scream. Nevertheless, she throws the contents of the glass accurately.

Chib screams when he feels the boiling hot water, painful as if he had been circumcised unanesthetized.

Benedictine, on the floor, laughs. Chib, after jumping around and shrieking, the can and clothes dropped, his hands holding the scalded parts, manages to control himself. He stops his antics, seizes Benedictine's right hand, and drags her out into the streets of Beverly Hills. There are quite a few people out this night, and they follow the two. Not until Chib reaches the lake does he stop and there he goes into the water to cool off the burn, Benedictine with him.

The crowd has much to talk about later, after Benedictine and Chib have crawled out of the lake and then run home. The crowd talks and laughs quite a while as they watch the sanitation department people clean the foam off the lake surface and the streets.

"I was so sore I couldn't walk for a month!" Benedictine screams.

"You had it coming," Chib says. "You've got no complaints. You said you wanted my baby, and you talked as if you meant it."

"I must've been out of my mind!" Benedictine says. "No, I wasn't! I never said no such thing! You lied to me! You forced me!"

"I would never force anybody," Chib said. "You know that. Quit your bitching. You're a free agent, and you consented freely. You have free will."

Omar Runic, the poet, stands up from his chair. He is a tall thin red-bronze youth with an aquiline nose and very thick red lips. His kinky hair grows long and is cut into the shape of the *Pequod*, that fabled vessel which bore mad Captain Ahab and his mad crew and the sole survivor Ishmael after the white whale. The coiffure is formed with a bowsprit and hull and three masts and yardarms and even a boat hanging on davits.

Omar Runic claps his hands and shouts, "Bravo! A philosopher! Free will it is; free will to seek the Eternal Verities—if any—or Death and Damnation! I'll drink to free will! A toast, gentlemen! Stand up, Young Radishes, a toast to our leader!"

And so begins

THE MAD P PARTY

Madame Trismegista calls, "Tell your fortune, Chib! See what the stars tell through the cards!"

He sits down at her table while his friends crowd around.

"O.K., Madame. How do I get out of this mess?"

She shuffles and turns over the top card.

"Jesus! The ace of spades!"

"You're going on a long journey!"

"Egypt!" Rousseau Red Hawk cries. "Oh, no, you don't want to go there, Chib! Come with me to where the buffalo roam and . . ."

Up comes another card.

"You will soon meet a beautiful dark lady."

"A goddam Arab! Oh, no, Chib, tell me it's not true!"

"You will win great honors soon."

"Chib's going to get the grant!"

"If I get the grant, I don't have to go to Egypt," Chib says. "Madame Trismegista, with all due respect, you're full of crap."

"Don't mock, young man. I'm not a computer. I'm tuned to the spectrum of psychic vibrations."

Flip. "You will be in great danger, physically and morally."

Chib says, "That happens at least once a day."

Flip. "A man very close to you will die twice."

Chib pales, rallies, and says, "A coward dies a thousand deaths."

"You will travel in time, return to the past."

"Zow!" Red Hawk says. "You're outdoing yourself, Madame. Careful! You'll get a psychic hernia, have to wear an ectoplasmic truss!"

"Scoff if you want to, you dumbshits," Madame says. "There are more worlds than one. The cards don't lie, not when I deal them."

"Gobrinus!" Chib calls. "Another pitcher of beer for the Madame."

The young Radishes return to their table, a legless disc held up in the air by a graviton field. Benedictine glares at them and goes into a huddle with the other teemagers. At a table nearby sits Pinkerton Legrand, a gummint agent, facing them so that the fido under his one-way window of a jacket beams in on them. They know he's doing this. He knows they know and has reported so to his superior. He frowns when he sees Falco Accipiter enter. Legrand does not like an agent from another department messing around on his case. Accipiter does not even look at Legrand. He orders a pot of tea and then pretends to drop into the teapot a pill that combines with tannic acid to become P.

Rousseau Red Hawk winks at Chib and says, "Do you really think it's possible to paralyze all of LA with a single bomb?"

"Three bombs!" Chib says loudly so that Legrand's fido will pick up the words. "One for the control console of the desalinization plant, a second for the backup console, the third for the nexus of the big pipe that carries the water to the reservoir on the 20th level."

Pinkerton Legrand turns pale. He downs all the whiskey in his glass and orders another, although he has already had too many. He presses the plate on his fido to transmit a triple top-priority. Lights blink redly in HQ; a gong clangs repeatedly; the chief wakes up so suddenly he falls off his chair.

Accipiter also hears, but he sits stiff, dark, and brooding as the diorite image of a Pharaoh's falcon. Monomaniac, he is not to be diverted by talk of inundating all LA, even if it will lead to action. On Grandpa's trail, he is now here because he hopes to use Chib as the key to the house. One "mouse"—as he thinks of his criminals—one "mouse" will run to the hole of another.

"When do you think we can go into action?" Huga Wells-Erb Heinsturbury, the science-fiction authoress, says.

"In about three weeks," Chib says.

At HQ, the chief curses Legrand for disturbing him. There are thousands of young men and women blowing off steam with these plots of destruction, assassination, and revolt. He does not understand why the young punks talk like this, since they have everything handed them free. If he had his way, he'd throw them into jail and kick them around a little or more than.

"After we do it, we'll have to take off for the big outdoors," Red Hawk says. His eyes glisten. "I'm telling you, boys, being a free man in the forest is the greatest. You're a genuine individual, not just one of the faceless breed."

Red Hawk believes in this plot to destroy LA. He is happy because, though he hasn't said so, he has grieved while in Mother Nature's lap for intellectual companionship. The other savages can hear a deer at a hundred yards, detect a rattlesnake in the bushes, but they're deaf to the footfalls of philosophy, the neigh of Nietzsche, the rattle of Russell, the honkings of Hegel.

"The illiterate swine!" he says aloud. The others say, "What?"

"Nothing. Listen, you guys must know how wonderful it is. You were in the WNRCC."

"I was 4-F," Omar Runic says. "I got hay fever."

"I was working on my second M.A.," Gibbon Tacitus says.

"I was in the WNRCC band," Sibelius Amadeus Yehudi says. "We only got outside when we played the camps, and that wasn't often."

"Chib, you were in the Corps. You loved it, didn't you?"

Chib nods but says, "Being a neo-Amerind takes all your time just to survive. When could I paint? And who would see the paintings if I did get time? Anyway, that's no life for a woman or a baby."

Red Hawk looks hurt and orders a whiskey mixed with P.

Pinkerton Legrand doesn't want to interrupt his monitoring, yet he can't stand the pressure in his bladder. He walks towards the room used as the customers' catch-all. Red Hawk, in a nasty mood caused by rejection, sticks his leg out. Legrand trips, catches himself, and stumbles forward. Benedictine puts out her leg. Legrand falls on his face. He no longer has any reason to go to the urinal except to wash himself off.

Everybody except Legrand and Accipiter laughs. Legrand jumps up, his fists doubled. Benedictine ignores him and walks over to Chib, her friends following. Chib stiffens. She says, "You perverted bastard! You told me you were just going to use your finger!"

"You're repeating yourself," Chib says. "The important thing is, what's going to happen to the baby?"

"What do you care?" Benedictine says. "For all you know, it might not even be yours!"

"That'd be a relief," Chib says, "if it weren't. Even so, the baby should have a say in this. He might want to live—even with you as his mother."

"In this miserable life!" she cries. "I'm going to do it a favor. I'm going to the hospital and get rid of it. Because of you, I have to miss out on my big chance at the Folk Festival! There'll be agents from all over there, and I won't get a chance to sing for them!"

"You're a liar," Chib says. "You're all dressed up to sing."

Benedictine's face is red; her eyes, wide; her nostrils, flaring. "You spoiled my fun!"

She shouts, "Hey, everybody, want to hear a howler! This great artist, this big hunk of manhood, Chib the divine, he can't get a hard-on unless he's gone down on!"

Chib's friends look at each other. What's the bitch screaming about? So what's new?

From Grandpa's *Private Ejaculations:* Some of the features of the Panamorite religion, so reviled and loathed in the 21st century, have become everyday facts in modern times. Love, love, love, physical and spiritual! It's not enough to just kiss your children and hug them. But oral stimulation of the genitals of infants by the parents and relatives has resulted in some curious conditioned reflexes. I could write a book about this aspect of mid-22nd century life and probably will.

Legrand comes out of the washroom. Benedictine slaps Chib's face. Chib slaps her back. Gobrinus lifts up a section of the bar and hurtles through the opening, crying, "Poisson! Poisson!"

He collides with Legrand, who lurches into Bela, who screams, whirls, and slaps Legrand, who slaps back. Benedictine empties a glass of P in Chib's face. Howling, he jumps up and swings his fist. Benedictine ducks, and the fist goes over her shoulder into a girl-friend's chest.

Red Hawk leaps up on the table and shouts, "I'm a regular bearcat, half-alligator and half . . ."

The table, held up in a graviton field, can't bear much weight. It tilts and catapults him into the girls, and all go down. They bite and scratch Red Hawk, and Benedictine squeezes his testicles. He screams, writhes, and hurls Benedictine with his feet onto the top of the table. It has regained its normal height and altitude, but now it flips over again, tossing her to the other side. Legrand, tippytoeing through the crowd on his way to the exit, is knocked down. He loses some front teeth against somebody's knee cap. Spitting blood and teeth, he jumps up and slugs a bystander.

Gobrinus fires off a gun that shoots a tiny Very light. It's supposed to blind the brawlers and so bring them to their senses while they're regaining their sight. It hangs in the air and shines like

A STAR OVER BEDLAM

The Police Chief is talking via fido to a man in a public booth. The man has turned off the video and is disguising his voice.

"They're beating the shit out of each other in The Private Universe."

The Chief groans. The Festival has just begun, and They are at it already.

"Thanks. The boys'll be on the way. What's your name? I'd like to recommend you for a Citizen's Medal."

"What! And get the shit knocked out of me, too! I ain't no stoolie; just doing my duty. Besides, I don't like Gobrinus or his customers. They're a bunch of snobs."

The Chief issues orders to the riot squad, leans back, and drinks a beer while he watches the operation on fido. What's the matter with these people, anyway? They're always mad about something.

The sirens scream. Although the bolgani ride electrically driven noiseless tricycles, they're still clinging to the centuries-old tradition of warning the criminals that they're coming. Five trikes pull up before the open door of The Private Universe. The police dismount and confer. Their two-storied cylindrical helmets are black and have scarlet roaches. They wear goggles for some reason although their vehicles can't go over 15 m.p.h. Their jackets are black and fuzzy, like a teddy bear's fur, and huge golden epaulets decorate their shoulders. The shorts are electric-blue and fuzzy; the jackboots, glossy black. They carry electric shock sticks and guns that fire chokegas pellets.

Gobrinus blocks the entrance. Sergeant O'Hara says, "Come on, let us in. No, I don't have a warrant of entry. But I'll get one."

"If you do, I'll sue," Gobrinus says. He smiles. While it is true that government red tape was so tangled he quit trying to acquire a tavern legally, it is also true that the government will protect him in this issue. Invasion of privacy is a tough rap for the police to break.

O'Hara looks inside the doorway at the two bodies on the floor, at those holding their heads and sides and wiping off blood, and at Accipiter, sitting like a vulture dreaming of carrion. One of the bodies gets up on all fours and crawls through between Gobrinus' legs out into the street.

"Sergeant, arrest that man!" Gobrinus says. "He's wearing an illegal fido. I accuse him of invasion of privacy."

O'Hara's face lights up. At least he'll get one arrest to his credit. Legrand is placed in the paddywagon, which arrives just after the ambulance. Red Hawk is carried out as far as the doorway by his friends. He opens his eyes just as he's being carried on a stretcher to the ambulance and he mutters.

O'Hara leans over him. "What?"

"I fought a bear once with only my knife, and I came out better than with those cunts. I charge them with assault and battery, murder and mayhem."

O'Hara's attempt to get Red Hawk to sign a warrant fails because Red Hawk is now unconscious. He curses. By the time Red Hawk begins feeling better, he'll refuse to sign the warrant. He won't want the girls and their boy-friends laying for him, not if he has any sense at all.

Through the barred window of the paddy-wagon, Legrand screams, "I'm a gummint agent! You can't arrest me!"

The police get a hurry-up call to go to the front of the Folk Center, where a fight between local youths and Westwood invaders is threatening to become a riot. Benedictine leaves the tavern. Despite several blows in the shoulders and stomach, a kick in the buttocks, and a bang on the head, she shows no sign of losing the fetus.

Chib, half-sad, half-glad, watches her go. He feels a dull grief that the baby is to be denied life. By now he realizes that part of his objection to the abortion is identification with the fetus; he knows what Grandpa thinks he does not know. He realizes that his birth was an accident—lucky or unlucky. If things had gone otherwise, he would not have been born. The thought of his non-existence—no painting, no friends, no laughter, no hope, no love—horrifies him. His mother, drunkenly negligent about contraception, has had any number of abortions, and he could have been one of them.

Watching Benedictine swagger away (despite her torn clothes), he wonders what he could ever have seen in her. Life with her, even with a child, would have been gritty.

In the hope-lined nest of the mouth
Love flies once more, nestles down,
Coos, flashes feathered glory, dazzles,
And then flies away, crapping,
As is the wont of birds,
To jet-assist the take off.
—Omar Runic

Chib returns to his home, but he still can't get back into his room. He goes to the storeroom. The painting is seven-eighths finished but was not completed because he was dissatisfied with it. Now he takes it from the house and carries it to Runic's house, which is in the same clutch as his. Runic is at the Center, but he always leaves his doors open when he's gone. He has equipment which Chib uses to finish the painting, working with a sureness and intensity he lacked the first time he was creating it. He then leaves Runic's house with the huge oval canvas held above his head.

He strides past the pedestals and under their curving branches with the ovoids at their ends. He skirts several small grassy parks with trees, walks beneath more houses, and in ten minutes is nearing the heart of Beverly Hills. Here mercurial Chib sees

ALL IN THE GOLDEN AFTERNOON, THREE LEADEN LADIES

drifting in a canoe on Lake Issus. Maryam bint Yusuf, her mother, and aunt listlessly hold fishing poles and look towards the gay colors, music, and the chattering crowd before the Folk Center. By now the police have broken up the juvenile fight and are standing around to make sure nobody else makes trouble.

The three women are dressed in the somber clothes, completely body-concealing, of the Mohammedan Wahhabi fundamentalist sect. They do not wear veils; not even the Wahhabi now insist on this. Their Egyptian brethren ashore are clad in modern garments, shameful and sinful. Despite which, the ladies stare at them.

Their menfolk are at the edge of the crowd. Bearded and costumed like sheiks in a Foreign Legion fido show, they mutter gargling oaths and hiss at the iniquitous display of female flesh. But they stare.

This small group has come from the zoological preserves of Abyssinia, where they were caught poaching. Their gummint gave them three choices. Imprisonment in a rehabilitation center, where they would be treated until they became good citizens if it took the rest of their lives. Emigration to the megalopolis of Haifa, Israel. Or emigration to Beverly Hills, LA.

What, dwell among the accursed Jews of Israel? They spat and chose Beverly Hills. Alas, Allah had mocked them! They were now surrounded by Finkelsteins, Applebaums, Siegels, Weintraubs, and others of the infidel tribes of Isaac. Even worse, Beverly Hills had no mosque. They either traveled forty kilometers every day to the 16th level, where a mosque was available, or used a private home.

Chib hastens to the edge of the plastic-edged lake and puts down his painting and bows low, whipping off his somewhat battered hat. Maryam smiles at him but loses the smile when the two chaperones reprimand her.

"*Ya kelb! Ya ibn kelb!*" the two shout at him.

Chib grins at them, waves his hat, and says, "Charmed, I'm sure, mesdames! Oh, you lovely ladies remind me of the Three Graces."

He then cries out, "I love you, Maryam! I love you! Thou art like the Rose of Sharon to me! Beautiful, doe-eyed, virginal! A fortress of innocence and strength, filled with a fierce motherhood and utter faithfulness to the one true love! I love thee, thou art the only light in a black sky of dead stars! I cry to you across the void!"

Maryam understands World English, but the wind carries his words away from her. She simpers, and Chib cannot help feeling a momentary repulsion, a flash of anger as if she has somehow betrayed him. Nevertheless, he rallies and shouts, "I invite you to come with me to the showing! You and your mother and aunt will be my guests. You can see my paintings, my soul, and know what kind of man is going to carry you off on his Pegasus, my dove!"

> There is nothing as ridiculous as the verbal outpourings of a young poet in love. Outrageously exaggerated. I laugh. But I am also touched. Old as I am, I remember my first loves, the fires, the torrents of words, lightning-sheathed, ache-winged. Dear lasses, most of you are dead; the rest, withered. I blow you a kiss.
>
> —Grandpa

Maryam's mother stands up in the canoe. For a second, her profile is to Chib, and he sees intimations of the hawk that Maryam will be when she is her mother's age. Maryam now has a gently aquiline face—"the sweep of the sword of love"—Chib has called that nose. Bold but beautiful. However, her mother does look like a dirty old eagle. And her aunt—uneaglish but something of the camel in those features.

Chib suppresses the unfavorable, even treacherous, comparisons. But he cannot suppress the three bearded, robed, and unwashed men who gather around him.

Chib smiles but says, "I don't remember inviting you."

They look blank since rapidly spoken LA English is a huftymagufty to them. Abu—generic name for any Egyptian in Beverly Hills—rasps an oath so ancient even the pre-Mohammed Meccans knew it. He forms a fist. Another Arab steps towards the painting and draws back a foot as if to kick it.

At this moment, Maryam's mother discovers that it is as dangerous to stand in a canoe as on a camel. It is worse, because the three women cannot swim.

Neither can the middle-aged Arab who attacks Chib, only to find his victim sidestepping and then urging him on into the lake with a foot in the rear. One of the young men rushes Chib; the other starts to kick at the painting. Both halt on hearing the three women scream and on seeing them go over into the water.

Then the two run to the edge of the lake, where they also go into the water, propelled by one of Chib's hands in each of their backs. A bolgan hears the six of them screaming and thrashing around and runs over to Chib. Chib is becoming concerned because Maryam is having trouble staying above the water. Her terror is not faked.

What Chib does not understand is why they are all carrying on so. Their feet must be on the bottom; the surface is below their chins. Despite which, Maryam looks as if she is going to drown. So do the others, but he is not interested in them. He should go in after Maryam. However, if he does, he will have to get a change of clothes before going to the showing.

At this thought, he laughs loudly and then even more loudly as the bolgan goes in after the women. He picks up the painting and walks off laughing. Before he reaches the Center, he sobers.

"Now, how come Grandpa was so right? How does he read me so well? Am I fickle, too shallow? No, I have been too deeply in love too many times. Can I help it if I love Beauty, and the beauties I love do not have enough Beauty? My eye is too demanding; it cancels the urgings of my heart."

THE MASSACRE OF THE INNER SENSE

The entrance hall (one of twelve) which Chib enters was designed by Grandpa Winnegan. The visitor comes into a long curving tube lined with mirrors at various angles. He sees a triangular door at the end of the corridor. The door seems to be too tiny for anybody over nine years old to enter. The illusion makes the visitor feel as if he's walking up the wall as he progresses towards the door. At the end of the tube, the visitor is convinced he's standing on the ceiling.

But the door gets larger as he approaches until it becomes huge. Commentators have guessed that this entrance is the architect's symbolic representation of the gateway to the world of art. One should stand on his head before entering the wonderland of aesthetics.

On going in, the visitor thinks at first that the tremendous room is inside out or reversed. He gets even dizzier. The far wall actually seems the near wall until the visitor gets reorientated. Some people can't adjust and have to get out before they faint or vomit.

On the right hand is a hatrack with a sign: HANG YOUR HEAD HERE. A double pun by Grandpa, who always carries a joke too far for most people. If Grandpa goes beyond the bounds of verbal good taste, his great-great-grandson has overshot the moon in his paintings. Thirty of his latest have been revealed, including the last three of his Dog Series: *Dog Star, Dog Would* and *Dog Tiered.* Ruskinson and his disciples are threatening to throw up. Luscus and his flock praise, but they're restrained. Luscus has told them to wait until he talks to young Winnegan before they go all-out. The fido men are busy shooting and interviewing both and trying to provoke a quarrel.

The main room of the building is a huge hemisphere with a bright ceiling which runs through the complete spectrum every nine minutes. The floor is a giant chessboard, and in the center of each square is a face, each of a great in the various arts. Michel-angelo, Mozart, Balzac, Zeuxis, Beethoven, Li Po, Twain, Dos-toyevsky, Farmisto, Mbuzi, Cupel, Krishnagurti, etc. Ten squares are left faceless so that future generations may add their own nom-inees for immortality.

The lower part of the wall is painted with murals depicting significant events in the lives of the artists. Against the curving wall are nine stages, one for each of the Muses. On a console above each stage is a giant statue of the presiding goddess. They are naked and have overripe figures: huge-breasted, broad-hipped, sturdy-legged, as if the sculptor thought of them as Earth god-desses, not refined intellectual types.

The faces are basically structured like the smooth placid faces of classical Greek statues, but they have an unsettling expression around the mouths and eyes. The lips are smiling but seem ready to break into a snarl. The eyes are deep and menacing. DON'T SELL ME OUT, they say. IF YOU DO . . .

A transparent plastic hemisphere extends over each stage and has acoustic properties which keep people who are not beneath the shell from hearing the sounds emanating from the stage and vice versa.

Chib makes his way through the noisy crowd towards the stage of Polyhymnia, the Muse who includes painting in her prov-ince. He passes the stage on which Benedictine is standing and pouring her lead heart out in an alchemy of golden notes. She sees Chib and manages somehow to glare at him and at the same time to keep smiling at her audience. Chib ignores her but observes that she has replaced the dress ripped in the tavern. He sees also the many policemen stationed around the building. The crowd does not seem in an explosive mood. Indeed, it seems happy, if boisterous. But the police know how deceptive this can be. One spark . . .

Chib goes by the stage of Calliope, where Omar Runic is ex-temporizing. He comes to Polyhymnia's, nods at Rex Luscus, who waves at him, and sets his painting on the stage. It is titled *The Massacre of the Innocents* (subtitle: *Dog in the Manger*).

The painting depicts a stable.

The stable is a grotto with curiously shaped stalactites. The light that breaks—or fractures—through the cave is Chib's red. It penetrates every object, doubles its strength, and then rays out jaggedly. The viewer, moving from side to side to get a complete look, can actually see the many levels of light as he moves, and thus he catches glimpses of the figures under the exterior figures.

The cows, sheep, and horses are in stalls at the end of the cave. Some are looking with horror at Mary and the infant. Others have their mouths open, evidently trying to warn Mary. Chib has used the legend that the animals in the manger were able to talk to each other the night Christ was born.

Joseph, a tired old man, so slumped he seems back-boneless, is in a corner. He wears two horns, but each has a halo, so it's all right.

Mary's back is to the bed of straw on which the infant is supposed to be. From a trapdoor in the floor of the cave, a man is reaching to place a huge egg on the straw bed. He is in a cave beneath the cave and is dressed in modern clothes, has a boozy expression, and, like Joseph, slumps as if invertebrate. Behind him a grossly fat woman, looking remarkably like Chib's mother, has the baby, which the man passed on to her before putting the foundling egg on the straw bed.

The baby has an exquisitely beautiful face and is suffused with a white glow from his halo. The woman has removed the halo from his head and is using the sharp edge to butcher the baby.

Chib has a deep knowledge of anatomy, since he has dissected many corpses while getting his Ph.D. in art at Beverly Hills U. The body of the infant is not unnaturally elongated, as so many of Chib's figures are. It is more than photographic; it seems to be an actual baby. Its viscera is unraveled through a large bloody hole.

The onlookers are struck in their viscera as if this were not a painting but a real infant, slashed and disemboweled, found on their doorsteps as they left home.

The egg has a semitransparent shell. In its murky yolk floats a hideous little devil, horns, hooves, tail. Its blurred features resemble a combination of Henry Ford's and Uncle Sam's. When the viewers shift to one side or the other, the faces of others appear: prominents in the development of modern society.

The window is crowded with wild animals that have come to adore but have stayed to scream soundlessly in horror. The beasts in the foreground are those that have been exterminated by man or survive only in zoos and natural preserves. The dodo, the blue whale, the passenger pigeon, the quagga, the gorilla, orangutan, polar bear, cougar, lion, tiger, grizzly bear, California condor, kangaroo, wombat, rhinoceros, bald eagle.

Behind them are other animals and, on a hill, the dark crouching shapes of the Tasmanian aborigine and Haitian Indian.

"What is your considered opinion of this rather remarkable painting, Doctor Luscus?" a fido interviewer asks.

Luscus smiles and says, "I'll have a considered judgment in a few minutes. Perhaps you'd better talk to Doctor Ruskinson first. He seems to have made up his mind at once. Fools and angels, you know."

Ruskinson's red face and scream of fury are transmitted over the fido.

"The shit heard around the world!" Chib says loudly.

"INSULT! SPITTLE! PLASTIC DUNG! A BLOW IN THE FACE OF ART AND A KICK IN THE BUTT FOR HUMANITY! INSULT! INSULT!"

"Why is it such an insult, Doctor Ruskinson?" the fido man says. "Because it mocks the Christian faith, and also the Panamorite faith? It doesn't seem to me it does that. It seems to me that Winnegan is trying to say that men have perverted Christianity, maybe all religions, all ideals, for their own greedy self-destructive purposes, that man is basically a killer and a perverter. At least, that's what I get out of it, although of course I'm only a simple layman, and ..."

"Let the critics make the analysis, young man!" Ruskinson snaps. "Do you have a double Ph.D., one in psychiatry and one in art? Have you been certified as a critic by the government?

"Winnegan, who has no talent whatsoever, let alone this genius that various self-deluded blowhards prate about, this abomination from Beverly Hills, presents his junk—actually a mishmash which has attracted attention solely because of a new technique that any electronic technician could invent—I am enraged that a mere gimmick, a trifling novelty, can not only fool certain sectors of the public but highly educated and federally certified critics such as Doctor Luscus here—although there will always be scholarly asses who bray so loudly, pompously, and obscurely that . . ."

"Isn't it true," the fido man says, "that many painters we now call great, Van Gogh for one, were condemned or ignored by their contemporary critics? And . . ."

The fido man, skilled in provoking anger for the benefit of his viewers, pauses. Ruskinson swells, his head a bloodvessel just before aneurysm.

"I'm no ignorant layman!" he screams. "I can't help it that there have been Luscuses in the past! I know what I'm talking about! Winnegan is only a micrometeorite in the heaven of Art, not fit to shine the shoes of the great luminaries of painting. His reputation has been pumped up by a certain clique so it can shine in the reflected glory, the hyenas, biting the hand that feeds them, like mad dogs . . ."

"Aren't you mixing your metaphors a little bit?" the fido man says.

Luscus takes Chib's hand tenderly and draws him to one side where they're out of fido range.

"Darling Chib," he coos, "now is the time to declare yourself. You know how vastly I love you, not only as an artist but for yourself. It must be impossible for you to resist any longer the deeply sympathetic vibrations that leap unhindered between us. God, if you only knew how I dreamed of you, my glorious godlike Chib, with . . ."

"If you think I'm going to say yes because you have the power to make or break my reputation, to deny me the grant, you're wrong," Chib says. He jerks his hand away.

Luscus' good eye glares. He says, "Do you find me repulsive? Surely it can't be on moral grounds . . ."

"It's the principle of the thing," Chib says. "Even if I were in love with you, which I'm not, I wouldn't let you make love to me. I want to be judged on my merit alone, that only. Come to think of it, I don't give a damn about anybody's judgment. I don't want to hear praise or blame from you or anybody. Look at my paintings and talk to each other, you jackals. But don't try to make me agree with your little images of me."

THE ONLY GOOD CRITIC IS A DEAD CRITIC

Omar Runic has left his dais and now stands before Chib's paintings. He places one hand on his naked left chest, on which is tattooed the face of Herman Melville, Homer occupying the other place of honor on his right breast. He shouts loudly, his black eyes like furnace doors blown out by explosion. As has happened before, he is seized with inspiration derived from Chib's paintings.

"Call me Ahab, not Ishmael.
For I have hooked the Leviathan.
I am the wild ass's colt born to a man.
Lo, my eye has seen it all!
My bosom is like wine that has no vent.
I am a sea with doors, but the doors are stuck.
Watch out! The skin will burst; the doors will break.

"You are Nimrod, I say to my friend, Chib.
And now is the hour when God says to his angels,
If this is what he can do as a beginning, then
Nothing is impossible for him.
He will be blowing his horn before
The ramparts of Heaven and shouting for
The Moon as hostage, the Virgin as wife,
And demanding a cut on the profits
From the Great Whore of Babylon."

"Stop that son of a bitch!" the Festival Director shouts. "He'll cause a riot like he did last year!"

The bolgani begin to move in. Chib watches Luscus, who is talking to the fido man. Chib can't hear Luscus, but he's sure Luscus is not saying complimentary things about him.

"Melville wrote of me long before I was born.
I'm the man who wants to comprehend
The Universe but comprehend on my terms.
I am Ahab whose hate must pierce, shatter,
All impediment of Time, Space, or Subject
Mortality and hurl my fierce
Incandescence into the Womb of Creation,
Disturbing in its Lair whatever Force or
Unknown Thing-in-Itself crouches there,
Remote, removed, unrevealed."

The Director gestures at the police to remove Runic. Ruskinson is still shouting, although the cameras are pointing at Runic or Luscus. One of the Young Radishes, Huga Wells-Erb Heinsturbury, the science-fiction authoress, is shaking with hysteria generated by Runic's voice and with a lust for revenge. She is sneaking up on a *Time* fido man. *Time* has long ago ceased to be a magazine, since there are no magazines, but became a government-supported communications bureau. *Time* is an example of Uncle Sam's left-hand, right-hand, hands-off policy of providing communications bureaus with all they need and at the same time permitting the bureau executives to determine the bureau policies. Thus, government provision and free speech are united. This is fine, in theory, anyway.

Time has revived several of its original policies, that is, truth and objectivity must be sacrificed for the sake of a witticism and science-fiction must be put down. *Time* has sneered at every one of Heinsturbury's works, and so she is out to get some personal satisfaction for the hurt caused by the unfair reviews.

"*Quid nunc? Cui bono?*
Time? Space? Substance? Accident?
When you die—Hell? Nirvana?
Nothing is nothing to think about.
The canons of philosophy boom.
Their projectiles are duds.
The ammo heaps of theology blow up,
Set off by the saboteur Reason.
Call me Ephraim, for I was halted

At the Ford of God and could not tongue
The sibilance to let me pass.
Well, I can't pronounce shibboleth,
But I can say shit!"

Huga Wells-Erb Heinsturbury kicks the *Time* fido man in the balls. He throws up his hands, and the football-shaped, football-sized camera sails from his hands and strikes a youth on the head. The youth is a Young Radish, Ludwig Euterpe Mahlzart. He is smoldering with rage because of the damnation of his tone poem, *Jetting The Stuff Of Future Hells,* and the camera is the extra fuel needed to make him blaze up uncontrollably. He punches the chief musical critic in his fat belly.

Huga, not the *Time* man, is screaming with pain. Her bare toes have struck the hard plastic armor with which the *Time* man, recipient of many such a kick, protects his genitals. Huga hops around on one foot while holding the injured foot in her hands. She twirls into a girl, and there is a chain effect. A man falls against the *Time* man, who is stooping over to pick up his camera.

"Ahaaa!" Huga screams and tears off the *Time* man's helmet and straddles him and beats him over the head with the optical end of the camera. Since the solid-state camera is still working, it is sending to billions of viewers some very intriguing, if dizzying, pictures. Blood obscures one side of the picture, but not so much that the viewers are wholly cheated. And then they get another novel shot as the camera flies into the air again, turning over and over.

A bolgan has shoved his shock-stick against her back, causing her to stiffen and propel the camera in a high arc behind her. Huga's current lover grapples with the bolgan; they roll on the floor; a Westwood juvenile picks up the shock-stick and has a fine time goosing the adults around him until a local youth jumps him.

"Riots are the opium of the people," the Police Chief groans. He calls in all units and puts in a call to the Chief of Police of Westwood, who is, however, having his own troubles.

Runic beats his breast, and howls.

"Sir, I exist! And don't tell me,
As you did Crane, that that creates
No obligation in you towards me.
I am a man; I am unique.
I've thrown the Bread out the window,
Pissed in the Wine, pulled the plug
From the bottom of the Ark, cut the Tree
For firewood, and if there were a Holy
Ghost, I'd goose him.
But I know that it all does not mean
A God damned thing.
That nothing means nothing,
That is is is and not-is not is is-not
That a rose is a rose is a
That we are here and will not be
And that is all we can know!"

Ruskinson sees Chib coming towards him, squawks, and tries
to escape. Chib seizes the canvas of *Dogmas from a Dog* and batters Ruskinson over the head with it. Luscus protests in horror,
not because of the damage done to Ruskinson but because the
painting might be damaged. Chib turns around and batters
Luscus in the stomach with the oval's edge.

"The earth lurches like a ship going down,
Its back almost broken by the flood of
Excrement from the heavens and the deeps,
What God in His terrible munificence
Has granted on hearing Ahab cry,
Bullshit! Bullshit!

"I weep to think that this is Man
And this his end. But wait!
On the crest of the flood, a three-master
Of antique shape. The Flying Dutchman!
And Ahab is astride a ship's deck once more.
Laugh, you Fates, and mock, you Norns!
For I am Ahab and I am Man,

And though I cannot break a hole
through the wall of What Seems
To grab a handful of What Is,
Yet, I will keep on punching.
And I and my crew will not give up,
Though the timbers split beneath our feet
And we sink to become indistinguishable
From the general excrement.

"For a moment that will burn on the
Eye of God forever, Ahab stands
Outlined against the blaze of Orion,
Fist clenched, a bloody phallus,
Like Zeus exhibiting the trophy of
The unmanning of his father Cronus.
And then he and his crew and ship
Dip and hurtle headlong over
The edge of the world.
And from what I hear, they are still

F
a
l
l
i
n
g"

Chib is shocked into a quivering mass by a jolt from a bolgan's electrical riot stick. While he is recovering, he hears his Grandpa's voice issuing from the transceiver in his hat.

"Chib, come quick! Accipiter has broken in and is trying to get through the door of my room!"

Chib gets up and fights and shoves his way to the exit. When he arrives, panting, at his home he finds that the door to Grandpa's room has been opened. The IRB men and electronic technicians are standing in the hallway. Chib bursts into Grandpa's room. Accipiter is standing in its middle and is quivering and pale. Nervous stone. He sees Chib and shrinks back, saying, "It wasn't my fault. I had to break in. It was the only way I could find out for sure. It wasn't my fault; I didn't touch him."

Chib's throat is closing in on itself. He cannot speak. He kneels down and takes Grandpa's hand. Grandpa has a slight smile on his blue lips. Once and for all, he has eluded Accipiter. In his hand is the latest sheet of his Ms.:

THROUGH BALAKLAVAS OF HATE, THEY CHARGE TOWARDS GOD

For most of my life, I have seen only a truly devout few and a great majority of truly indifferent. But there is a new spirit abroad. So many young men and women have revived, not a love for God, but a violent antipathy towards Him. This excites and restores me. Youths like my grandson and Runic shout blasphemies and so worship Him. If they did not believe, they would never think about Him. I now have some confidence in the future.

TO THE STICKS VIA THE STYX

Dressed in black, Chib and his mother go down the tube entrance to level 13B. It's luminous-walled, spacious, and the fare is free. Chib tells the ticket-fido his destination. Behind the wall, the protein computer, no larger than a human brain, calculates. A coded ticket slides out of a slot. Chib takes the ticket, and they go to the bay, a great incurve, where he sticks the ticket into a slot. Another ticket protrudes, and a mechanical voice repeats the information on the ticket in World and LA English, in case they can't read.

Gondolas shoot into the bay and decelerate to a stop. Wheelless, they float in a continually rebalancing graviton field. Sections of the bay slide back to make ports for the gondolas. Passengers step into the cages designated for them. The cages move forward; their doors open automatically. The passengers step into the gondolas. They sit down and wait while the safety meshmold closes over them. From the recess of the chassis, transparent plastic curves rise and meet to form a dome.

Automatically timed, monitored by redundant protein computers for safety, the gondolas wait until the coast is clear. On receiving the go-ahead, they move slowly out of the bay to the tube. They pause while getting another affirmation, trebly checked in microseconds. Then they move swiftly into the tube.

Whoosh! Whoosh! Other gondolas pass them. The tube glows yellowly as if filled with electrified gas. The gondola accelerates rapidly. A few are still passing it, but Chib's speeds up and soon none can catch up with it. The round posterior of a gondola ahead is a glimmering quarry that will not be caught until it slows before mooring at its destined bay. There are not many gondolas in the tube. Despite a 100-million population, there is little traffic on the north-south route. Most LAers stay in the self-sufficient walls of their clutches. There is more traffic on the east-west tubes, since a small percentage prefer the public ocean beaches to the municipality swimming pools.

The vehicle screams southward. After a few minutes, the tube begins to slope down, and suddenly it is at a 45-degree angle to the horizontal. They flash by level after level.

Through the transparent walls, Chib glimpses the people and architecture of other cities. Level 8, Long Beach, is interesting. Its homes look like two cut-quartz pie plates, one on top of another, open end on open end, and the unit mounted on a column of carved figures, the exit-entrance ramp a flying buttress.

At level 3A, the tube straightens out. Now the gondola races past establishments the sight of which causes Mama to shut her eyes. Chib squeezes his mother's hand and thinks of the half-brother and cousin who are behind the yellowish plastic. This level contains fifteen percent of the population, the retarded, the incurable insane, the too-ugly, the monstrous, the senile aged. They swarm here, the vacant or twisted faces pressed against the tube wall to watch the pretty cars float by.

"Humanitarian" medical science keeps alive the babies that *should*—by Nature's imperative—have died. Ever since the 20th century, humans with defective genes have been saved from death. Hence, the continual spreading of these genes. The tragic thing is that science can now detect and correct defective genes in the ovum and sperm. Theoretically, all human beings could be blessed with totally healthy bodies and physically perfect brains. But the rub is that we don't have near enough doctors and facilities to keep up with the births. This despite the ever decreasing birth rate.

Medical science keeps people living so long that senility strikes. So, more and more slobbering mindless decrepits. And also an accelerating addition of the mentally addled. There are therapies and drugs to restore most of them to "normalcy," but not enough doctors and facilities. Some day there may be, but that doesn't help the contemporary unfortunate.

What to do now? The ancient Greeks placed defective babies in the fields to die. The Eskimos shipped out their old people on ice floes. Should we gas our abnormal infants and seniles? Sometimes, I think it's the merciful thing to do. But I can't ask somebody else to pull the switch when I won't.

I would shoot the first man to reach for it.
—from Grandpa's *Private Ejaculations*

The gondola approaches one of the rare intersections. Its passengers see down the broad-mouthed tube to their right. An express flies towards them; it looms. Collision course. They know better, but they can't keep from gripping the mesh, gritting their teeth, and bracing their legs. Mama gives a small shriek. The flier hurtles over them and disappears, the flapping scream of air a soul on its way to underworld judgment.

The tube dips again until it levels out on 1. They see the round below and the massive self-adjusting pillars supporting the megalopolis. They whiz by over a little town, quaint, early 21st century LA preserved as a museum, one of many beneath the cube.

Fifteen minutes after embarking, the Winnegans reach the end of the line. An elevator takes them to the ground, where they enter a big black limousine. This is furnished by a private-enterprise mortuary, since Uncle Sam or the LA government will pay for cremation but not for burial. The Church no longer insists on interment, .eaving it to the religionists to choose between being wind-blown ashes or underground corpses.

The sun is halfway towards the zenith. Mama begins to have trouble breathing and her arms and neck redden and swell. The three times she's been outside the walls, she's been attacked with this allergy despite the air conditioning of the limousine. Chib pats her hand while they're riding over a roughly patched road. The archaic eighty-year-old, fuel-cell-powered, electric-motor-driven vehicle is, however, rough-riding only by comparison with the gondola. It covers the ten kilometers to the cemetery speedily, stopping once to let deer cross the road.

Father Fellini greets them. He is distressed because he is forced to tell them that the Church feels that Grandpa has committed sacrilege. To substitute another man's body for his corpse, to have mass said over it, to have it buried in sacred ground is to blaspheme. Moreover, Grandpa died an unrepentant criminal. At least, to the knowledge of the Church, he made no contrition just before he died.

Chib expects this refusal. St. Mary's of BH-14 has declined to perform services for Grandpa within its walls. But Grandpa has often told Chib that he wants to be buried beside his ancestors, and Chib is determined that Grandpa will get his wish.

Chib says, "I'll bury him myself! Right on the edge of the graveyard!"

"You can't do that!" the priest, mortuary officials, and a federal agent say simultaneously.

"The Hell I can't! Where's the shovel?"

It is then that he sees the thin dark face and falciform nose of Accipiter. The agent is supervising the digging up of Grandpa's (first) coffin. Nearby are at least fifty fido men shooting with their minicameras, the transceivers floating a few decameters near them. Grandpa is getting full coverage, as befits the Last Of The Billionaires and The Greatest Criminal Of The Century.

Fido interviewer: "Mr. Accipiter, could we have a few words from you? I'm not exaggerating when I say that there are probably at least ten billion people watching this historic event. After all, even the grade-school kids know of Win-again Winnegan.

"How do you feel about this? You've been on the case for 26

years. The successful conclusion must give you great satisfaction."

Accipiter, unsmiling as the essence of diorite: "Well, actually, I've not devoted full time to this case. Only about three years of accumulative time. But since I've spent at least several days each month on it, you might say I've been on Winnegan's trail for 26 years."

Interviewer: "It's been said that the ending of this case also means the end of the IRB. If we've not been misinformed, the IRB was only kept functioning because of Winnegan. You had other business, or course, during this time, but the tracking down of counterfeiters and gamblers who don't report their income has been turned over to other bureaus. Is this true? If so, what do you plan to do?"

Accipiter, voice flashing a crystal of emotion: "Yes, the IRB is being disbanded. But not until after the case against Winnegan's grand-daughter and her son is finished. They harbored him and are, therefore, accessories after the fact.

"In fact, almost the entire population of Beverly Hills, level 14, should be on trial. I know, but can't prove it as yet, that everybody, including the municipal Chief of Police, was well aware that Winnegan was hiding in that house. Even Winnegan's priest knew it, since Winnegan frequently went to mass and to confession. His priest claims that he urged Winnegan to turn himself in and also refused to give him absolution unless he did so.

"But Winnegan, a hardened 'mouse'—I mean, criminal, if ever I saw one, refused to follow the priest's urgings. He claimed that he had not committed a crime, that, believe it or not, Uncle Sam was the criminal. Imagine the effrontery, the depravity, of the man!"

Interviewer: "Surely you don't plan to arrest the entire population of Beverly Hills 14?"

Accipiter: "I have been advised not to."

Interviewer: "Do you plan on retiring after this case is wound up?"

Accipiter: "No. I intend to transfer to the Greater LA Homicide Bureau. Murder for profit hardly exists any more, but there are still crimes of passion, thank God!"

Interviewer: "Of course, if young Winnegan should win his case against you—he has charged you with invasion of domestic privacy, illegal housebreaking, and directly causing his great-great-grandfather's death—then you won't be able to work for the Homicide Bureau or any police department."

Accipiter, flashing several crystals of emotion: "It's no wonder we law enforcers have such a hard time operating effectively! Sometimes, not only the majority of citizens seem to be on the law-breaker's side but my own employers . . ."

Interviewer: "Would you care to complete that statement? I'm sure your employers are watching this channel. No? I understand that Winnegan's trial and yours are, for some reason, scheduled to take place *at the same time.* How do you plan to be present at both trials? Heh, heh! Some fido-casters are calling you The Simultaneous Man!"

Accipiter, face darkening: "Some idiot clerk did that! He incorrectly fed the data into the legal computer. And he, or somebody, turned off the error-override circuit, and the computer burned up. The clerk is suspected of deliberately making the error—by me anyway, and let the idiot sue me if he wishes—anyway, there have been too many cases like this, and . . ."

Interviewer: "Would you mind summing up the course of this case for our viewers' benefit? Just the highlights, please."

Accipiter: "Well, ah, as you know, fifty years ago all large private-enterprise businesses had become government bureaus. All except the building construction firm, the Finnegan Fifty-three States Company, of which the president was Finn Finnegan. He was the father of the man who is to be buried—somewhere—today.

"Also, all unions except the largest, the construction union, were dissolved or were government unions. Actually, the company and its union were one, because all employees got ninety-five per cent of the money, distributed more or less equally among them. Old Finnegan was both the company president and union business agent-secretary.

"By hook or crook, mainly by crook, I believe, the firm-union had resisted the inevitable absorption. There were investigations into Finnegan's methods: coercion and blackmail of U.S. Senators and even U.S. Supreme Court Justices. Nothing was, however, proved."

Interviewer: "For the benefit of our viewers who may be a little hazy on their history, even fifty years ago money was used only for the purchase of nonguaranteed items. Its other use, as today, was as an index of prestige and social esteem. At one time, the government was thinking of getting rid of currency entirely, but a study revealed that it had great psychological value. The income tax was also kept, although the government had no use for money, because the size of a man's tax determined prestige and also because it enabled the government to remove a large amount of currency from circulation."

Accipiter: "Anyway, when old Finnegan died, the federal government renewed its pressure to incorporate the construction workers and the company officials as civil servants. But young Finnegan proved to be as foxy and vicious as his old man. I don't suggest, of course, that the fact that his uncle was President of the U.S. at that time had anything to do with young Finnegan's success."

Interviewer: "Young Finnegan was seventy years old when his father died."

Accipiter: "During this struggle, which went on for many years, Finnegan decided to rename himself Winnegan. It's a pun on Win Again. He seems to have had a childish, even imbecilic, delight in puns, which, frankly, I don't understand. Puns, I mean."

Interviewer: "For the benefit of our non-American viewers, who may not know of our national custom of Naming Day ... this was originated by the Panamorites. When a citizen comes of age, he may at any time thereafter take a new name, one which he believes to be appropriate to his temperament or goal in life. I might point out that Uncle Sam, who's been unfairly accused of trying to impose conformity upon his citizens, encourages this individualistic approach to life. This despite the increased record-keeping required on the government's part.

"I might also point out something else of interest. The government claimed that Grandpa Winnegan was mentally incompetent. My listeners will pardon me, I hope, if I take up a moment of your time to explain the basis of Uncle Sam's assertion. Now, for the benefit of those among you who are unacquainted with an early 20th-century classic, *Finnegan's Wake,* despite your government's wish for you to have a free lifelong education, the author, James Joyce, derived the title from an old vaudeville song."

(Half-fadeout while a monitor briefly explains "vaudeville.")

"The song was about Tim Finnegan, an Irish hod carrier who fell off a ladder while drunk and was supposedly killed. During the Irish wake held for Finnegan, the corpse is accidentally splashed with whiskey. Finnegan, feeling the touch of the whiskey, the 'water of life,' sits up in his coffin and then climbs out to drink and dance with the mourners.

"Grandpa Winnegan always claimed that the vaudeville song was based on reality, you can't keep a good man down, and that the original Tim Finnegan was his ancestor. This preposterous statement was used by the government in its suit against Winnegan.

"However, Winnegan produced documents to substantiate his assertion. Later—too late—the documents were proved to be forgeries."

Accipiter: "The government's case against Winnegan was strengthened by the rank and file's sympathy with the government. Citizens were complaining that the business-union was undemocratic and discriminatory. The officials and workers were getting relatively high wages, but many citizens had to be contented with their guaranteed income. So, Winnegan was brought to trial and accused, justly, of course, of various crimes, among which were subversion of democracy.

"Seeing the inevitable, Winnegan capped his criminal career. He somehow managed to steal 20 billion dollars from the federal deposit vault. This sum, by the way, was equal to half the currency than existing in Greater LA. Winnegan disappeared with the money, which he had not only stolen but had not paid income tax on. Unforgivable. I don't know why so many people have glamorized this villain's feat. Why, I've even seen fido shows with him as the hero, thinly disguised under another name, of course."

Interviewer: "Yes, folks, Winnegan committed the Crime Of The Age. And, although he has finally been located, and is to be buried today—somewhere—the case is not completely closed. The federal government says it is. But where is the money, the 20 billion dollars?"

Accipiter: "Actually, the money has no value now except as collector's items. Shortly after the theft, the government called in all currency and then issued new bills that could not be mistaken for the old. The government had been wanting to do something like this for a long time, anyway, because it believed that there was too much currency, and it only reissued half the amount taken in.

"I'd like very much to know where the money is. I won't rest until I do. I'll hunt it down if I have to do it on my own time."

Interviewer: "You may have plenty of time to do that if young Winnegan wins his case. Well, folks, as most of you may know, Winnegan was found dead in a lower level of San Francisco about a year after he disappeared. His grand-daughter identified the body, and the fingerprints, earprints, retinaprints, teethprints, blood-type, hair-type, and a dozen other identity prints matched out."

Chib, who has been listening, thinks that Grandpa must have spent several millions of the stolen money arranging this. He does not know, but he suspects that a research lab somewhere in the world grew the duplicate in a biotank.

This happened two years after Chib was born. When Chib was five, his grandpa showed up. Without letting Mama know he was back, he moved in. Only Chib was his confidant. It was, of course, impossible for Grandpa to go completely unnoticed by Mama, yet she now insisted that she had never seen him. Chib thought that this was to avoid prosecution for being an accessory after the crime. He was not sure. Perhaps she had blocked off his "visitations" from the rest of her mind. For her it would be easy, since she never knew whether today was Tuesday or Thursday and could not tell you what year it was.

Chib ignores the mortuarians, who want to know what to do with the body. He walks over to the grave. The top of the ovoid coffin is visible now, with the long elephantlike snout of the digging machine sonically crumbling the dirt and then sucking it up. Accipiter, breaking through his lifelong control, is smiling at the fidomen and rubbing his hands.

"Dance a little, you son of a bitch," Chib says, his anger the only block to the tears and the wail building up in him.

The area around the coffin is cleared to make room for the grappling arms of the machine. These descend, hook under, and lift the black, irradiated-plastic, mocksilver-arabesqued coffin up and out and onto the grass. Chib, seeing the IRB men begin to open the coffin, starts to say something but closes his mouth. He watches intently, his knees bent as if getting ready to jump. The fidomen close in, their eyeball-shaped cameras pointing at the group around the coffin.

Groaning, the lid rises. There is a big bang. Dense dark smoke billows. Accipiter and his men, blackened, eyes wide and white, coughing, stagger out of the cloud. The fidomen are running every which way or stooping to pick up their cameras. Those who were standing far enough back can see that the explosion took place at the bottom of the grave. Only Chib knows that the raising of the coffin lid has activated the detonating device in the grave.

He is also the first to look up into the sky at the projectile soaring from the grave because only he expected it. The rocket climbs up to five hundred feet while the fidomen train their cameras on it. It bursts apart and from it a ribbon unfolds between two round objects. The objects expand to become balloons while the ribbon becomes a huge banner.

On it, in big black letters, are the words

WINNEGAN'S FAKE!

Twenty billions of dollars buried beneath the supposed bottom of the grave burn furiously. Some bills, blown up in the geyser of fireworks, are carried by the wind while IRB men, fidomen, mortuary officials, and municipality officials chase them.

Mama is stunned.

Accipiter looks as if he is having a stroke.

Chib cries and then laughs and rolls on the ground.

Grandpa has again screwed Uncle Sam and has also pulled his greatest pun where all the world can see it.

"Oh, you old man!" Chib sobs between laughing fits. "Oh, you old man! How I love you!"

While he is rolling on the ground again, roaring so hard his ribs hurt, he feels a paper in his hand. He stops laughing and gets on his knees and calls after the man who gave it to him. The man says, "I was paid by your grandfather to hand it to you when he was buried."

Chib reads.

I hope nobody was hurt, not even the IRB men.

Final advice from the Wise Old Man In The Cave. Tear loose. Leave LA. Leave the country. Go to Egypt. Let your mother ride the purple wage on her own. She can do it if she practices thrift and self-denial. If she can't, that's not your fault.

You are fortunate indeed to have been born with talent, if not genius, and to be strong enough to want to rip out the umbilical cord. So do it. Go to Egypt. Steep yourself in the ancient culture. Stand before the Sphinx. Ask her (actually, it's a he) the Question.

Then visit one of the zoological preserves south of the Nile. Live for a while in a reasonable facsimile of Nature as she was before mankind dishonored and disfigured her. There, where Homo Sapiens(?) evolved from the killer ape, absorb the spirit of that ancient place and time.

You've been painting with your penis, which I'm afraid was more stiffened with bile than with passion for life. Learn to paint with your heart. Only thus will you become great and true.

Paint.

Then, go wherever you want to go. I'll be with you as long as you're alive to remember me. To quote Runic, "I'll be the Northern Lights of your soul."

Hold fast to the belief that there will be others to love you just as much as I did or even more. What is more important, you must love them as much as they love you.

Can you do this?

Don't Wash the Carats
A Polytropical Paramyth

1968

T HE KNIFE SLICES the skin. The saw rips into bone. Gray dust flies. The plumber's helper (the surgeon is economical) clamps its vacuum onto the plug of bone. Ploop! Out comes the section of skull. The masked doctor, Van Mesgeluk, directs a beam of light into the cavern of cranium.

He swears a large oath by Hippocrates, Aesculapius, and the Mayo Brothers. The patient doesn't have a brain tumor. He's got a diamond.

The assistant surgeon, Beinschneider, peers into the well and, after him, the nurses.

"Amazing!" Van Mesgeluk says. "The diamond's not in the rough. It's cut!"

"Looks like a 58-facet brilliant, 127.1 carats," says Beinschneider, who has a brother-in-law in the jewelry trade. He sways the light at the end of the drop cord back and forth. Stars shine; shadows run.

"Of course, it's half buried. Maybe the lower part isn't diamond. Even so . . ."

"Is he married?" a nurse says.

Van Mesgeluk rolls his eyes. "Miss Lustig, don't you ever think of anything but marriage?"

"Everything reminds me of wedding bells," she replies, thrusting out her hips.

"Shall we remove the growth?" Beinschneider says.

"It's malignant," Van Mesgeluk says. "Of course, we remove it."

He thrusts and parries with a fire and skill that bring cries of admiration and a clapping of hands from the nurses and even cause Beinschneider to groan a bravo, not unmingled with jealousy. Van Mesgeluk then starts to insert the tongs but pulls them back when the first lightning bolt flashes beneath and across the opening in the skull. There is a small but sharp crack and, very faint, the roll of thunder.

"Looks like rain," Beinschneider says. "One of my brothers-in-law is a meteorologist."

"No. It's heat lightning," Van Mesgeluk says.

"With thunder?" says Beinschneider. He eyes the diamond with a lust his wife would give diamonds for. His mouth waters; his scalp turns cold. Who owns the jewel? The patient? He has no rights under this roof. Finders keepers? Eminent domain? Internal Revenue Service?

"It's mathematically improbable, this phenomenon," he says. "What's California law say about mineral rights in a case like this?"

"You can't stake out a claim!" Van Mesgeluk roars. "My God, this is a human being, not a piece of land!"

More lightning cracks whitely across the opening, and there is a rumble as of a bowling ball on its way to a strike.

"I said it wasn't heat lightning," Van Mesgeluk growls.

Beinschneider is speechless.

"No wonder the e.e.g. machine burned up when we were diagnosing him," Van Mesgeluk says. "There must be several thousand volts, maybe a hundred thousand, playing around down there. But I don't detect much warmth. Is the brain a heat sink?"

"You shouldn't have fired that technician because the machine burned up," Beinschneider says. "It wasn't her fault, after all."

"She jumped out of her apartment window the next day," Nurse Lustig says reproachfully. "I wept like a broken faucet at her funeral. And almost got engaged to the undertaker." Lustig rolls her hips.

"Broke every bone in her body, yet there wasn't a single break in her skin," Van Mesgeluk says. "Remarkable phenomenon."

"She was a human being, not a phenomenon!" Beinschneider says.

"But psychotic," Van Mesgeluk replies. "Besides, that's my

line. She was thirty-three years old but hadn't had a period in ten years."

"It was that plastic intrauterine device," Beinschneider says. "It was clogged with dust. Which was bad enough, but the dust was radioactive. All those tests . . ."

"Yes," the chief surgeon says. "Proof enough of her psychosis. I did the autopsy, you know. It broke my heart to cut into that skin. Beautiful. Like Carrara marble. In fact, I snapped the knife at the first pass. Had to call in an expert from Italy. He had a diamond-tipped chisel. The hospital raised hell about the expense, and Blue Cross refused to pay."

"Maybe she was making a diamond," says Nurse Lustig. "All that tension and nervous energy had to go somewhere."

"I always wondered where the radioactivity came from," Van Mesgeluk says. "Please confine your remarks to the business at hand, Miss Lustig. Leave the medical opinions to your superiors."

He peers into the hole. Somewhere between heaven of skull and earth of brain, on the horizon, lightning flickers.

"Maybe we ought to call in a geologist. Beinschneider, you know anything about electronics?"

"I got a brother-in-law who runs a radio and TV store."

"Good. Hook up a step-down transformer to the probe, please. Wouldn't want to burn up another machine."

"An e.e.g. now?" Beinschneider says. "It'd take too long to get a transformer. My brother-in-law lives clear across town. Besides, he'd charge double if he had to reopen the store at this time of the evening."

"Discharge him, anyway," the chief surgeon says. "Ground the voltage. Very well. We'll get that growth out before it kills him and worry about scientific research later."

He puts on two extra pairs of gloves.

"Do you think he'll grow another?" Nurse Lustig says. "He's not a bad-looking guy. I can tell he'd be simpatico."

"How the hell would I know?" says Van Mesgeluk. "I may be a doctor, but I'm not quite God."

"God who?" says Beinschneider, the orthodox atheist. He drops the ground wire into the hole; blue sparks spurt out. Van

Mesgeluk lifts out the diamond with the tongs. Nurse Lustig takes it from him and begins to wash it off with tap water.

"Let's call in your brother-in-law," Van Mesgeluk says. "The jewel merchant, I mean."

"He's in Amsterdam. But I could phone him. However, he'd insist on splitting the fee, you know."

"He doesn't even have a degree!" Van Mesgeluk cries. "But call him. How is he on legal aspects of mineralogy?"

"Not bad. But I don't think he'll come. Actually, the jewel business is just a front. He gets his big bread by smuggling in chocolate-covered LSD drops."

"Is that ethical?"

"It's top-quality Dutch chocolate," Beinschneider says stiffly.

"Sorry. I think I'll put in a plastic window over the hole. We can observe any regrowth."

"Do you think it's psychosomatic in origin?"

"Everything is, even the sex urge. Ask Miss Lustig."

The patient opens his eyes. "I had a dream," he says. "This dirty old man with a long white beard . . ."

"A typical archetype," Van Mesgeluk says. "Symbol of the wisdom of the unconscious. A warning . . ."

". . . his name was Plato," the patient says. "He was the illegitimate son of Socrates. Plato, the old man, staggers out of a dark cave at one end of which is a bright klieg light. He's holding a huge diamond in his hand; his fingernails are broken and dirty. The old man cries, 'The Ideal is Physical! The Universal is the Specific Concrete! Carbon, actually. Eureka! I'm rich! I'll buy all of Athens, invest in apartment buildings, Great Basin, COMSAT!

" 'Screw the mind!' the old man screams. 'It's all mine!' "

"Would you care to dream about King Midas?" Van Mesgeluk says.

Nurse Lustig shrieks. A lump of sloppy grayish matter is in her hands.

"The water changed it back into a tumor!"

"Beinschneider, cancel that call to Amsterdam!"

"Maybe he'll have a relapse," Beinschneider says.

Nurse Lustig turns savagely upon the patient. "The engagement's off!"

"I don't think you loved the real me," the patient says, "whoever you are. Anyway, I'm glad you changed your mind. My last wife left me, but we haven't been divorced yet. I got enough trouble without a bigamy charge.

"She took off with my surgeon for parts unknown just after my hemorrhoid operation. I never found out why."

The Jungle Rot Kid on the Nod

1968

I F WILLIAM BURROUGHS instead of Edgar Rice Burroughs had written the Tarzan novels . .

Foreward
Tapes cut and respliced at random by Brachiate Bruce, the old mainliner chimp, the Kid's asshole buddy, cool blue in the orgone box

from the speech in Parliament of Lord Greystoke alias The Jungle Rot Kid, a full house, SRO, the Kid really packing them in.

—Capitalistic pricks! Don't send me no more foreign aid! You corrupting my simple black folks, they driving around the old plantation way down on the Zambezi River in air-conditioned Cadillacs, shooting horse, flapping ubangi at me . . . Bwana him not in the cole cole ground but him sure as shit gonna be soon. Them M-16s, tanks, mortars, flamethrowers coming up the jungle trail, ole Mao Charley promised us!

Lords, Ladies, Third Sex! I tole you about apeomorphine but you dont lissen! You got too much invested in the Mafia and General Motors, I say you gotta kick the money habit too. Get them green things offen your back . . . nothing to lose but your chains that is stocks, bonds, castles, Rollses, whores, soft toilet paper, connection with The Man . . . it a long long way to the jungle but it worth it, build up your muscle and character cut/

. . . you call me here at my own expense to degrade humiliate me strip me of loincloth and ancient honored title! You hate me cause you hung up on civilization and I never been hooked. You over a barrel with smog freeways TV oily beaches taxes inflation frozen dinners time-clocks carcinogens neckties all that shit. Call me noble savage . . . me tell you how it is where its at with my personal tarzanic *purusharta* . . . involves kissing off *dharma* and *artha* and getting a fix on *moksha* through *kama* . . .

Old Lord Bromley-Rimmer who wear a merkin on his bald head and got pecker and balls look like dried-up grapes on top a huge hairy cut-in fold-out thing it disgust you to see it, he grip young Lord Materfutter's crotch and say—Dearie what kinda gibberish that, Swahili, what?

Young Lord Materfutter say—Bajove, some kinda African cricket doncha know what?

. . . them fuckin Ayrabs run off with my Jane again . . . intersolar communist venusian bankers plot . . . so it back to the jungle again, hit the arboreal trail, through the middle tearass, dig Numa the lion, the lost civilizations kick, tell my troubles to Sam Tantor alias The Long Dong Kid. Old Sam always writing amendments to the protocols of the elders of mars, dipping his trunk in the blood of innocent bystanders, writing amendments in the sand with blood and no one could read what he had written there selah

Me, I'm only fuckin free man in the world . . . live in state of anarchy, up trees . . . every kid and lotsa grownups (so-called) dream of the Big Tree Fix, of swinging on vines, freedom, live by the knife and unwritten code of the jungle . . .

Ole Morphodite Lord Bromley-Rimmer say—Dearie, that Anarchy, that one a them new African nations what?

The Jungle Rot Kid bellowing in the House of Lords like he calling ole Sam Tantor to come running help him outta his mess, he really laying it on them blueblood pricks.

. . . I got *satyagraha* in the ole original Sanskrit sense of course up the ass, you fat fruits. I quit. So long. Back to the Dark Continent . . . them sheiks of the desert run off with Jane again . . . blood will flow . . .

Fadeout. Lord Materfutter's face phantom of erection wheezing paregoric breath. —Dig that leopardskin jockstrap what price glory what? cut/

This here extracted from John Clayton's diary which he write in French God only know why . . . *Sacre bleu! Nom d'un con!* Alice she dead, who gonna blow me now? The kid screaming his head off, he sure don't look like black-haired gray-eyed fine-chis-

eled featured scion of noble British family which come over with
Willie the Bastard and his squarehead-frog goons on the Anglo-
Saxon Lark. No more milk for him no more ass for me, carry me
back to old Norfolk / / double cut

The Gorilla Thing fumbling at the lock on the door of old log
cabin which John Clayton built hisself. Eyes stabbing through the
window. Red as two diamonds in a catamite's ass. John Clayton,
he rush out with a big axe, gonna chop me some anthropoid
wood.

Big hairy paws strong as hold of pusher on old junkie whirl
Clayton around. Stinking breath. Must smoke banana peels.
Whoo! Whoo! Gorilla Express dingdonging up black tunnel of
my rectum. Piles burst like rotten tomatoes, sighing softly. Death
come. And come. And come. Blazing bloody orgasms. Not a bad
way to go . . . but you cant touch my inviolate white soul . . . too
late to make a deal with the Gorilla Thing? Give him my title,
Jaguar, moated castle, ole faithful family retainer he go down on
you, opera box . . . *ma tante de pisse* . . . who take care of the
baby, carry on family name? *Vive la bourgerie!* cut/

Twenty years later give take a couple, the Jungle Rot Kid trail
the killer of Big Ape Mama what snatch him from cradle and raise
him as her own with discipline security warm memory of hairy
teats hot unpasteurized milk . . . the Kid swinging big on vines
from tree to tree, fastern hot baboonshit through a tin horn. Ant
hordes blitzkrieg him like agenbite of intwat, red insect-things
which is exteriorized thoughts of the Monster Ant-Mother of the
Crab Nebula in secret war to take over this small planet, this Peoria Earth.

Monkey on his back, Nkima, eat the red insect-things, wipe
out trillions with flanking bowel movement, Ant-Mother close up
galactic shop for the day . . .

The Kid drop his noose around the black-assed motherkiller
and haul him up by the neck into the tree in front of God and
local citizens which is called gomangani in ape vernacular.

—You gone too far this time the Kid say as he core out the
motherkillers asshole with fathers old hunting knife and bugger
him old Turkish custom while the motherkiller rockin and rollin
in death agony.

Heavy metal Congo jissom ejaculate catherinewheeling all over local gomangani, they say—Looka that!

Old junkie witch doctor coughing his lungs out in sick gray African morning, shuffling through silver dust of old kraal.

—You say my son's dead, kilt by the Kid?

Jungle drums beat like aged wino's temples morning after. Get Whitey!

The Kid sometime known as Genocide John really liquidate them dumbshit gomangani. Sure is a shame to waste all that black gash the Kid say but it the code of the jungle. Noblesse obleege.

The locals say—We dont haffa put up with this shit and they split. The Kid dont have no fun nomore and this chimp ass mighty hairy not to mention chimp habit of crapping when having orgasm. Then along come Jane alias Baltimore Blondie, she on the lam from Rudolph Rassendale type snarling—You marry me Jane else I foreclose on your father's ass.

The Kid rescue Jane and they make the domestic scene big, go to Europe on The Civilized Caper but the Kid find out fast that the code of the jungle conflict with local ordinances. The fuzz say you cant go around putting a full-nelson on them criminals and breakin their necks even if they did assault you they got civil rights too. The Kid's picture hang on post office and police station walls everywhere, he known as Archetype Archie and by the Paris fuzz as *La Magnifique Merde*—50,000 francs dead or alive. With the heat moving in, the Kid and Baltimore Blondie cut out for the tree house.

Along come La sometime known as Sacrifice Sal elsewhere as Disembowelment Daisy. She queen of Opar, ruler of hairy little men-things of the hidden colony of ancient Atlantis, the Kid always dig the lost cities kick. So the Kid split with Jane for awhile to ball La.

—Along come them fuckin Ayrabs again and abduct Jane, gangbang her . . . she aint been worth a shit since . . . cost me all the jewels and golden ingots I heisted offa Opar to get rid of her clap, syph, yaws, crabs, pyorrhea, double-barreled dysentery, busted rectum, split urethra, torn nostrils, pierced eardrums, bruised kidneys, nymphomania, old hashish habit, and things too disgusting to mention . . .

Along come The Rumble To End All Rumbles 1914 style, and them fuckin Huns abduct Jane ... they got preying-mantis eyes with insect lust. Black anti-orgone Horbigerian Weltanschauung, they take orders from green venusians who telepath through von Hindenburg.

—*Ja Wohl!* bark Leutnant Herrlipp von Dreckfinger at his Kolonel, Bombastus von Arschangst. —Ve use die Baltimore snatch to trap der gottverdammerungt Jungle Rot Kid, dot pseudo-Aryan *Oberaffenmensch*, unt ve kill him unt den all Afrika iss ours! Drei cheers for Der Kaiser unt die Krupp Familie!

The Kid balling La again but he drop her like old junkie drop pants for a shot of horse, he track down the Hun, it the code of the jungle.

Cool blue orgone bubbles sift down from evening sky, the sinking sun a bloody kotex which spread stinking scarlet gashworms over the big dungball of Earth. Night move in like fuzz with Black Maria. Mysterious sounds of tropical wilds ... Numa roar, wild boars grunt like they constipated, parrots with sick pukegreen feathers and yellow eyes like old goofball bum Panama 1910 cry *Rache!*

Hun blood flow, kraut necks crack like cinnamon sticks, the Kid put his foot on dead ass of slain Teuton and give the victory cry of the bull ape, it even scare the shit outta Numa King of the Beasts fadeout

The Kid and his mate live in the old tree house now ... surohc lakcaj fo mhtyhr ot ffo kcaj* chimps, Numa roar, Sheeta the panther cough like an old junkie. Jane alias The Baltimore Bitch nag, squawk, whine about them mosquitoes tsetse flies antthings hyenas and them uppity gomangani moved into the neighborhood, they'll turn a decent jungle into slums in three days, I aint prejudiced ya unnerstand some a my best friends are Waziris, whynt ya ever take me out to dinner, Nairobi only a thousand miles away, they really swingin there for chrissakes and cut/

... trees chopped down for the saw mills, animals kilt off, rivers stiff stinking with dugout-sized tapewormy turds, broken gin

---

* Old Brachiate Bruce splice in tape backward here.

bottles, contraceptive jelly and all them disgusting things snatches use, detergents, cigarette filters . . . and the great apes shipped off to USA zoos, they send telegram: SOUTHERN CALIFORNIA CLIMATE AND WELFARE PROGRAM SIMPLY FABULOUS STOP NO TROUBLE GETTING A FIX STOP CLOSE TO TIAJUANA STOP WHAT PRICE FREEDOM INDIVIDUALITY EXISTENTIAL PHILOSOPHY CRAP STOP . . . Opar a tourist trap, La running the native-art made-in-Japan concession and you cant turn around without rubbing sparks off black asses.

The African drag really got the Kid down now . . . Jane's voice and the jungle noises glimmering off like a comet leaving Earth forever for the cold interstellar abysms . . .

The Kid never move a muscle staring at his big toe, thinking of nothing—wouldn't you?—not even La's diamond-studded snatch, he off the woman kick, off the everything kick, fulla horse, on the nod, lower spine ten degrees below absolute zero like he got a direct connection with The Liquid Hydrogen Man at Cape Kennedy . . .

The Kid ride with a one-way ticket on the Hegelian Express thesis antithesis synthesis, sucking in them cool blue orgone bubbles and sucking off the Eternal Absolute . . .

The Oogenesis of Bird City

1970

THE PRESIDENT OF the U.S.A. sat at the desk of the mayor of Upper Metropolitan Los Angeles, Level 1. There was no question of where the mayor was to sit. Before the office of mayor could be filled, the electorate had to move into the city.

The huge room was filled with U.S. cabinet heads and bureau chiefs, senators, state governors, industrial and educational magnates, union presidents, and several state GIP presidents. Most of them were watching the TV screens covering one part of the curving wall.

Nobody looked through the big window behind the President, even though this gave a view of half of the city. Outside the municipal building, the sky was blue with a few fleecy clouds. The midsummer sun was just past the zenith, yet the breeze was cool; it was 73°F everywhere in the city. Of the 200,000 visitors, at least one-third were collected around tourguides. Most of the hand-carried football-sized TV cameras of the reporters were focused at that moment on one man.

Government spieler: "Ladies 'n gentlemen, you've been personally conducted through most of this city and you now know almost as much as if you'd stayed home and watched it on TV. You've seen everything but the interior of the houses, the inside of your future homes. You've been amazed at what Uncle Sam, and the state of California, built here, a Utopia, an Emerald City of Oz, with you as the Wizard . . ."

Heckler (a large black woman with an M.A. in Elementary School Electronic Transference): "The houses look more like the eggs that Dorothy used to frighten the Nome King with!"

Spieler (managing to glare and smile at the same time):

"Lady, you've been shooting your mouth off so much, you must be an agent for the Anti-Bodies! You didn't take the pauper's oath; you took the peeper's oath!"

Heckler (bridling): "I'll sue you for defamation of character and public ridicule!"

Spieler (running his gaze up and down her whale-like figure): "Sue, sue, sooie! No wonder you're so sensitive about eggs, lady. There's something ovoid about you!"

The crowd laughed. The President snorted disgustedly and spoke into a disc strapped to his wrist. A man in the crowd, the message relayed through his ear plug, spoke into his wrist transmitter, but the spieler gestured as if to say, "This is my show! Jump in the lake if you don't like it!"

Spieler: "You've seen the artificial lake in the center of the city with the municipal and other buildings around it. The Folk Art Center, the Folk Recreation Center, the hospital, university, research center, and the PANDORA, the people's all-necessities depot of regulated abundance. You've been delighted and amazed with the fairyland of goodies that Uncle Sam, and the State of California, offers you free. Necessities and luxuries, too, since *Luxury Is A Necessity*, to quote the FBC. You want anything—anything!—you go to the PANDORA, press some buttons, and presto! you're rich beyond your dreams!"

Heckler: "When the lid to Pandora's box was opened, all the evils in the world flew out, and . . ."

Spieler: "No interruptions, lady! We're on a strict time schedule . . ."

Heckler: "Why? We're not going anyplace!"

Spieler: "I'll tell you where you can go, lady."

Heckler: "But . . ."

Spieler: "But me no buts, lady! You know, you ought to go on a diet!"

Heckler: (struggling to control her temper): "Don't get personal, big mouth! I'm big, all right, and I got a wallop, too, remember that. Now, Pandora's box . . ."

The spieler made a vulgar remark, at which the crowd laughed. The heckler shouted but could not be heard above the noise.

The President shifted uneasily. Kingbrook, the 82-year-old senator from New York, harumphed and said, "The things they permit nowadays in public media. Really, it's disgusting . . ."

Some of the screens on the wall of the mayor's office showed various parts of the interior of the city. One screen displayed a view from a helicopter flying on the oceanside exterior of Upper Metropolitan LA. It was far enough away to get the entire structure in its camera, including the hundred self-adjusting cylinders that supported the Brobdingnagian plastic cube and the telescoping elevator shafts dangling from the central underbase. Beneath the shadow of box and legs was the central section of the old city and the jagged sprawl of the rest of Los Angeles and surrounding cities.

The President stabbed towards the screen with a cigarette and said, "Screen 24, gentlemen. The dark past below. The misery of a disrupted ant colony. Above it, the bright complex of the future. The chance for everyone to realize the full potentiality as a human being."

Spieler: "Before I conduct you into this house, which is internally just like every other private residence . . ."

Heckler: "Infernally, you mean. They all look just alike on the outside, too."

Spieler: "Lady, you're arousing my righteous wrath. Now, folks, you noticed that all the buildings, municipal and private, are constructed like eggs. This futuristic design was adopted because the egg shape, according to the latest theory, is that of the universe. No corners, all curving, infinity within a confined space, if you follow me."

Heckler: "I don't!"

Spieler: "Take off a little weight, lady, and you'll be in shape to keep up with the rest of us. The ovoid form gives you a feeling of unbounded space yet of security-closeness. When you get inside . . ."

Every house was a great smooth white plastic egg lifted 18.28 meters above the floor of the city by a thick truncated-cone support. (Offscreen commentators explained that 18.18 meters was 60 feet, for the benefit of older viewers who could not adjust to the new system of measurement.) On two sides of the cone were stairs ending at a horizontal door on the lower side of the ovoid. These opened automatically to permit entrance. Also, a door opened in the cone base, and an elevator inside lifted the sick or crippled or, as the spieler put it, "the just plain lazy, everybody's got a guaranteed right to be lazy." The hollow base also housed several electrical carts for transportation around the city.

The President saw Kierson, the Detroit automobile magnate, frown at the carts. The auto industry had shifted entirely from internal combustion motors to electrical and nuclear power ten years ago, and now Kierson saw the doom of these. The President made a mental note to pacify and reassure him on this point later.

Spieler: ". . . *Variety Within Unity*, folks. You've heard a lot about that on FBC, and these houses are an example. In reply to the lady's anxiety about the houses all looking alike, every home owner can paint the outside of his house to express his individuality. Anything goes. From reproductions of Rembrandt to psychedelic dreams to dirty words, if you got the guts. Everything's free, including speech . . ."

Heckler: "They'll look like a bunch of Easter eggs!"

Spieler: "Lady, Uncle Sam *is* The Big Easter Bunny!"

The spieler took the group into the house, and the cameramen went into the atrium, kitchen, and the ten rooms to show the viewers just what the citizens-to-be were getting for nothing.

"For nothing!" Senator Kingbrook growled. "The taxpayers are paying through the nose, through every orifice, with their sweat and blood for this!"

The President said, mildly, "They won't have to in the future, as I'll explain."

"You don't have to explain anything to any of us," Kingbrook said. "We all know all about the economy of abundance versus the economy of scarcity. And about your plans for the transitional stage, which you call ORE, *obverse-reverse* economy, but which I call *schizophrenic horrors in tremens!*"

The President smiled and said, "You'll have your say, Senator."

The men and women in the room were silent for a while as they watched the spieler extol the splendors and virtues of the house with its soundproof walls, the atrium with its pool, the workshop with machinery for crafts, the storeroom, the bedroom-studios, TV in every room, *retractable* and inflatable furniture, air-conditioning, microfilm library, and so on.

Government shill: "This is fabulous! A hell of a lot better than any noisy rat-ridden dump on the ground!"

Spieler (quoting an FBC slogan): *"Happy and free as the birds in the air!* That's why everybody calls this Bird City and why the citizens are known as freebirds! Everything first class! Everything free!"

Heckler: "Except freedom to live where you want to in the type of house you want!"

Spieler: "Lady, unless you're a millionaire, you won't be able to get a house on the ground that isn't just like every other house. And then you'd have to worry about it being burned down. Lady, you'd gripe if you was hung with a new rope!"

The group went outside where the spieler pointed out that, though they were three hectometers above ground, they had trees and grass in small parks. If they wanted to fish or boat, they could use the lake in the municipal-building area.

Shill: "Man, this is living!"

Spieler: "The dome above the city looks just like the sky outside. The sun is an electronic reproduction; its progress exactly coincides with that of the real sun. Only, you don't have to worry about it getting too cold or too hot in here or about it raining. We even got birds in here."

Heckler: "What about the robins? Come springtime, how're they going to get inside without a pass?"

Spieler: "Lady, you got a big mouth! Whyn't you . . ."

The President rose from his chair. Kingbrook's face was wrinkled, fissured, and folded with old age. The red of his anger made his features look like hot lava on a volcano slope just after an eruption. His rich rumble pushed against the eardrums of those in the room as if they were in a pressure chamber.

"A brave new concentration camp, gentlemen! Fifty billion dollars worth to house 50,000 people! The great bankruptopolis of the future! I estimate it'll cost one trillion dollars just to enclose this state's population in these glorified chicken runs!"

"Not if ORE is put into effect," the President said. He held up his hand to indicate silence and said, "I'd like to hear Guild-man, gentlemen. Then we can have our conferences."

Senator Beaucamp of Mississippi muttered, "One trillion dollars! That would house, feed, and educate the entire population of my state for twenty years!"

The President signalled to cut off all screens except the FBC channel. The private network commentators were also speaking, but the federal commentator was the important one. His pitch was being imitated—if reluctantly—by the private networks. Enough pressure and threats had been applied to make them wary of going all-out against the President. Although the mass media had been restrained, the speech of private persons had not been repressed. For one thing, the public needed a safety valve. Occasionally, a private speaker was given a chance to express himself on TV and radio. And so, a cavalry charge of invective had been and was being hurled at the President. He had been denounced as an ultra-reactionary, a degenerate liberal, a Communist, a Fascist, a vulture, a pig, a Puritan, a pervert, a Hitler, etc., and had been hung *in absentia* so many times that an enterprising manufacturer of effigies had made a small fortune—though taxes made it even smaller.

From cavalry to Calvary, he thought. All charges admitted. All charges denied. I am human, and that takes in everything. Even the accusation of fanaticism. I know that what I'm doing is right, or, at least, the only known way. When the Four Horsemen ride, the countercharge cannot be led by a self-doubter.

The voice of the Great Guildman, as he was pleased to be called, throbbed through the room. Chief FBC commentator, bureau executive, Ph.D. in Mass Communications, G-90 rating, one who spoke with authority, whose personal voltage was turned full-on, who could, some said, have talked God into keeping Adam and Eve in the garden.

"... cries out! The people, the suffering earth itself, cry out! The air is poisoned! The water is poisoned! The soil is poisoned! Mankind is poisoned with the excess of his genius for survival! The wide walls of the Earth have become narrowed! Man, swelling like a tumor with uncontrolled growth, kills the body that gave him birth! He is squeezing himself into an insane mold which crushes his life out, crushes all hope for an abundant life, security, peace, quiet, fulfillment, dignity . . ."

The audience, tuning in on forty channels, was well aware of this; he was painting a picture the oils of which had been squeezed from their own pain. And so Guildman did not tarry overlong at these points. He spoke briefly of the dying economy of scarcity, obsolete in the middle 1900's but seeming vigorous, like a sick man with a fatal disease who keeps going on larger and larger shots of drugs and on placebos. Then he splashed bright colors over the canvas of the future.

Guildman went on about the population expansion, automation, the ever-growing permanently depressed class and its riots and insurrections, the ever-decreasing and ever-overburdened taxpayers with their strikes and riots, the Beverly Hills Massacre, the misery, crime, anger, etc.

The President repressed an impulse to squirm. There would be plenty of blacks and grays in The Golden World (the President's own catch-phrase). Utopia could never exist. The structure of human society, in every respect, had a built-in instability, which meant that there would always be a certain amount of suffering and maladjustment. There were always victims of change.

But that could not be helped. And it was a good thing that change was the unchanging characteristic of society. Otherwise, stagnation, rigidity, and loss of hope for improvement would result.

Beaucamp leaned close to the President and said softly, "Plenty of people have pointed out that the economy of abundance eventually means the death of capitalism. You've never commented on this, but you can't keep silent much longer."

"When I do speak," the President said, "I'll point out that EOA also means the death of socialism and communism. Besides, there's nothing sacred in an economic system, except to those who confuse money with religion. Systems are made for man, not vice versa."

Kingbrook rose from his sofa, his bones cracking, and walked stiffly towards the President.

"You've rammed through this project despite the opposition of the majority of taxpayers! You used methods that were not only unconstitutional, sir! I know for a fact that criminal tactics were used, blackmail and intimidation, sir! But you will go no more on your Caesar's road! This project has beggared our once wealthy nation, and we are not going to build any more of your follies! Your grandiose—and wicked—Golden World will be as tarnished as brass, as green as fool's gold, by the time that I am through with you! Don't underestimate me and my colleagues, sir!"

"I know of your plans to impeach me," the President said with a slight smile. "Now, Senators Beaucamp and Kingbrook, and you, Governor Corrigan, would you step into the mayor's apartment? I'd like to have a few words—I hope they're few—with you."

Kingbrook, breathing heavily, said, "My mind is made up, Mr. President. I know what's wrong and what's right for our country. If you have any veiled threats or insidious proposals, make them in public, sir! In this room, before these gentlemen!"

The President looked at the embarrassed faces, the stony, the hostile, the gleeful, and then glanced at his wristwatch. He said, "I only ask five minutes."

He continued, "I'm not slighting any of you. I intend to talk to all of you in groups selected because of relevant subjects. Three to five minutes apiece will let us complete our business before the post-dedication speeches. Gentlemen!" And he turned and strode through the door.

A few seconds passed, and then the three, stiff-faced, stiff-backed, walked in.

"Sit down or stand as you please," the President said.

There was a silence. Kingbrook lit a cigar and took a chair. Corrigan hesitated and then sat near Kingbrook. Beaucamp remained standing. The President stood before them.

He said, "You've seen the people who toured this city. They're the prospective citizens. What is their outstanding common characteristic?"

Kingbrook snorted and said something under his breath. Beaucamp glared at him and said, "I didn't hear your words, but I know what you said! Mr. President, I intend to speak loudly and clearly about this arrogant discrimination! I had one of my men run the list of accepted citizens through a computer, and he reports that the citizens will be 100 percent Negro! And ⅞ths are welfares!"

"The other eighth are doctors, technicians, teachers, and other professionals," the President said. "All volunteers. There, by the way, goes the argument that no one will work if he doesn't have to. These people will be living in this city and getting no money for their labor. We had to turn down many volunteers because there was no need for them."

"Especially since the government has been using public funds to brainwash us with the Great-Love-and-Service-for-Humanity campaign for twenty years," Kingbrook said.

"I never heard you making any speeches knocking love or service," the President said. "However, there is another motive which caused so many to offer their services. Money may die out, but the desire for prestige won't. The wish for prestige is at least as old as mankind itself and maybe older."

"I can't believe that no whites asked to live here," Beaucamp said.

"The rule was, first apply, first accepted," the President said. "The whole procedure was computer-run, and the application blanks contained no reference to race."

Corrigan said, "You know that computers have been gimmicked or their operators bribed."

The President said, "I am sure that an investigation would uncover nothing crooked."

"The gyps," Corrigan said, then stopped at Beaucamp's glare. "I mean, the guaranteed income people, or welfares as we called them when I was a kid, well, the GIP whites will be screaming discrimination."

"The whites could have volunteered," the President said.

Beaucamp's lip was curled. "Somebody spread the word. Of course, that would have nothing to do with lack of Caucasian applications."

Kingbrook rumbled like a volcano preparing to erupt. He said, "What're we arguing about this for? This . . . Bird City . . . was built over an all-colored section. So why shouldn't its citizens be colored? Let's stick to the point. You want to build more cities just like this, Mr. President, extend them outwards from this until you have one solid megalopolis on stilts extending from Santa Barbara to Long Beach. But you can't build here or in other states without absolutely bankrupting the country. So you want to get us to back your legislative proposals for your so-called ORE. That is, split the economy of the nation in half. One half will continue operating just as before; that half will be made up of private-enterprise industries and of the taxpayers who own or work for these industries. This half will continue to buy and sell and use money as it has always done.

"But the other half will be composed of GIP's, living in cities like this, and the government will take care of their every need. The government will do this by automating the mines, farms, and industries it now owns or plans on obtaining. It will not use money anywhere in its operations, and the entire process of input-output will be a closed circuit. Everybody in ORE will be GIP personnel, even the federal and state government service, except, of course, that the federal, legislative, and executive branches will maintain their proper jurisdiction."

"That *sounds* great," Corrigan said. "The ultimate result, or so you've *said*, Mr. President, is to relieve the taxpayer of his crushing burden and to give the GIP a position in society in which he will no longer be considered by others as a parasite. It sounds appealing. But there are many of us who aren't fooled by your fine talk."

"I'm not trying to fool anybody," the President said.

Corrigan said, angrily, "It's obvious what the end result will be! When the taxpayer sees the GIP living like a king without turning a hand while he has to work his tail off, he's going to want the same deal. And those who refuse to give up won't have enough money to back their stand because the GIP won't be spending any money. The small businessmen who live off their sales to the GIP will go under. And the larger businesses will, too. Eventually, the businessman and his employees will fold their fiscal and pecuniary tents and go to live in your everything-free cornucopias!

"So, if we're seduced by your beautiful scheme for a half-and-half economy, we'll take the first step into the quicksand. After that, it'll be too late to back out. Down we go!"

"I'd say, *Up we go*," the President said. "So! It's All-or-None, as far as you're concerned? And you vote for None! Well, gentlemen, over one-half of the nation is saying All because that's the only way to go and they've nothing to lose and everything to gain. If you kill the switchover legislation in Congress, I'll see that the issues are submitted to the people for their yea or nay. But that would take too much time, and time is vital. Time is what I'm buying. Or I should say, trading."

Beaucamp said, "Mister President, you didn't point out the racial composition of the city just to pass the time."

The President began pacing back and forth before them. He said, "The civil rights revolution was born about the same time that you and I, Mr. Beaucamp, were born. Yet, it's still far from achieving its goals. In some aspects, it's regressed. It was tragic that the Negroes began to get the education and political power they needed for advancement just as automation began to bloom. The Negro found that there were only jobs for the professionals and the skilled. The unskilled were shut out. This happened to the untrained white, too, and competition for work between the unskilled white and black became bitter. Bloodily bitter, as the past few years have shown us."

"We know what's been going on, Mr. President," Beaucamp said.

"Yes. Well, it's true isn't it, that the black as a rule, doesn't particularly care to associate or live with the whites? He just wants the same things whites have. But at the present rate of progress, it'll take a hundred years or more before he gets them. In fact, he may never do so if the present economy continues."

Kingbrook rumbled, "The point, Mr. President!"

The President stopped pacing. He looked hard at them and said, "But in an economy of abundance, in this type of city, he— the Negro—will have everything the whites have. He will have a high standard of living, a true democracy, color-free justice. He'll have his own judges, police, legislators. If he doesn't care to, he doesn't ever have to have any personal contact with whites."

Kingbrook's cigar sagged. Beaucamp sucked in his breath. Corrigan jumped up from his chair.

Beaucamp said, "That's ghettoism!"

"Not in the original sense," the President said. "The truth now, Mr. Beaucamp. Don't your people prefer to live with their own kind? Where they'll be free of that shadow, that wall, always between white and colored in this country?"

Beaucamp said, "Not to have to put up with honkeys! Excuse the expression, sir. It slipped out. You know we would! But . . ."

"No one will be forbidden to live in any community he chooses. There won't be any discrimination on the federal level. Those in the government, military, or Nature rehabilitation service will have equal opportunity. But, given the choice . . ."

The President turned to Kingbrook and Corrigan. "Publicly, you two have always stood for integration. You would have committed political suicide, otherwise. But I know your private opinions. You have also been strong states-righters. No secret about that. So, when the economy of abundance is in full swing, the states will become self-sufficient. They won't depend on federal funds."

"Because there'll be no dependence on money?" Corrigan said. "Because there'll be no money? Because money will be as extinct as the dodo?"

The ridges on Kingbrook's face shifted as if they were the gray backs of an elephant herd milling around to catch a strange scent. He said, "I'm not blasphemous. But now I think I know how Christ felt when tempted by Satan."

He stopped, realizing that he had made a Freudian slip.

"And you're not Christ and I'm not Satan," he said hurriedly. "We're just human beings trying to find a mutually agreeable way out of this mess."

Beaucamp said, "We're horse traders. And the horse is the future. A dream. Or a nightmare."

The President looked at his watch and said, "What about it, Mr. Beaucamp?"

"What can I trade? A dream of an end to contempt, dislike, hatred, treachery, oppression. A dream of the shadow gone, the wall down. Now you offer me abundance, dignity, and joy—if my people stay within the plastic walls."

"I don't know what will develop after the walls of the cities have been built," the President said. "But there is nothing evil about self-segregation, if it's not compulsive. It's done all the time by human beings of every type. If it weren't, you wouldn't have social classes, clubs, etc. And if, after our citizens are given the best in housing and food, luxuries, a free lifelong education, a wide spectrum of recreations, everything within reason, if they still go to Hell, then we might as well give up on the species."

"A man needs incentive; he needs work. By the sweat of his brow . . ." Kingbrook said.

Kingbrook was too old, the President thought. He was half stone, and the stone thought stone thoughts and spoke stone words. The President looked out the big window. Perhaps it had been a mistake to build such a "futuristic" city. It would be difficult enough for the new citizens to adjust. Perhaps the dome of Bird City should have contained buildings resembling those they now lived in. Later, more radical structures could have been introduced.

As it was, the ovoid shape was supposed to give a sense of security, a feeling of return-to-the-womb and also to suggest a rebirth. Just now, they looked like so many space capsules ready to take off into the blue the moment the button was pressed.

But this city, and those that would be added to it, meant a sharp break with the past, and any break always caused some pain.

He turned when someone coughed behind him. Senator Kingbrook was standing, his hand on his chest. The senator was going to make a speech.

The President looked at his watch and shook his head. Kingbrook smiled as if the smile hurt him, and he dropped his hand.

"It's yes, Mr. President. I'll back you all the way. And the impeachment proceedings will be dropped, of course. But . . ."

"I don't want to be rude," the President said. "But you can save your justifications for your constituents."

Beaucamp said, "I say yes. Only . . ."

"No ifs, ands, or buts."

"No. Only . . ."

"And you, Governor Corrigan?" the President said.

Corrigan said, "All of us are going along with you for reasons that shouldn't be considered—from the viewpoint of ideals. But then, who really ever has? I say yes. But . . ."

"No speeches, please," the President said. He smiled slightly. "Unless I make them. Your motives don't really matter, gentlemen, as long as your decisions are for the good of the American public. Which they are. And for the good of the world, too, because all other nations are going to follow our example. As I said, this means the death of capitalism, but it also means the death of socialism and communism, too."

He looked at his watch again. "I thank you, gentlemen."

They looked as if they would like to continue talking, but they left. There was a delay of a few seconds before the next group entered.

He felt weary, even though he knew that he would win out. The years ahead would be times of trouble, of crises, of pain and agony, of successes and failures. At least, mankind would no longer be drifting towards anarchy. Man would be deliberately shaping—reshaping—his society, turning topsyturvy an ancient and obsolete economy, good enough in its time but no longer applicable. At the same time, he would be tearing down the old cities and restoring Nature to something of its pristine condition, healing savage wounds inflicted by senseless selfish men in the past, cleansing the air, the poisoned rivers and lakes, growing new forests, permitting the wild creatures to flourish in their redeemed land. Man, the greedy savage child, had stripped the earth, killed the wild, fouled his own nest.

His anger, he suddenly realized, had been to divert him from that other feeling. Somehow, he had betrayed an ideal. He could not define the betrayal, because he knew that he was doing what had to be done and that that way was the only way. But he, and Kingbrook, Corrigan, and Beaucamp, had also felt this. He had seen it on their faces, like ectoplasm escaping the grasp of their minds.

A man had to be realistic. To gain one thing, you had to give up another. Life—the universe—was give and take, input and output, energy surrendered to conquer energy.

In short, politics. Compromises.

The door slid into the recess in the walls. Five men single-filed in. The President weighed each in the balance, anticipating his arguments and visualizing the bait which he would grab even if he saw the hook.

He said, "Gentlemen, be seated if you wish."

He looked at his watch and began to talk.

GETTING INTO WEDNESDAY was almost impossible.

Tom Pym had thought about living on other days of the week. Almost everybody with any imagination did. There were even TV shows speculating on this. Tom Pym had even acted in two of these. But he had no genuine desire to move out of his own world. Then his house burned down.

This was on the last day of the eight days of spring. He awoke to look out the door at the ashes and the firemen. A man in a white asbestos suit motioned for him to stay inside. After fifteen minutes, another man in a suit gestured that it was safe. He pressed the button by the door, and it swung open. He sank down in the ashes to his ankles; they were a trifle warm under the inch-thick coat of water-soaked crust.

There was no need to ask what had happened, but he did, anyway.

The fireman said, "A short-circuit, I suppose. Actually, we don't know. It started shortly after midnight, between the time that Monday quit and we took over."

Tom Pym thought that it must be strange to be a fireman or a policeman. Their hours were so different, even though they were still limited by the walls of midnight.

By then the others were stepping out of their stoners or "coffins" as they were often called. That left sixty still occupied.

They were due for work at 08:00. The problem of getting new clothes and a place to live would have to be put off until off-hours, because the TV studio where they worked was behind in the big special it was due to put on in 144 days.

They ate breakfast at an emergency center. Tom Pym asked a

grip if he knew of any place he could stay. Though the government would find one for him, it might not look very hard for a convenient place.

The grip told him about a house only six blocks from his former house. A makeup man had died, and as far as he knew the vacancy had not been filled. Tom got onto the phone at once, since he wasn't needed at that moment, but the office wouldn't be open until ten, as the recording informed him. The recording was a very pretty girl with red hair, tourmaline eyes, and a very sexy voice. Tom would have been more impressed if he had not known her. She had played in some small parts in two of his shows, and the maddening voice was not hers. Neither was the color of her eyes.

At noon he called again, got through after a ten-minute wait, and asked Mrs. Bellefield if she would put through a request for him. Mrs. Bellefield reprimanded him for not having phoned sooner; she was not sure that anything could be done today. He tried to tell her his circumstances and then gave up. Bureaucrats! That evening he went to a public emergency place, slept for the required four hours while the inductive field speeded up his dreaming, woke up, and got into the upright cylinder of eternium. He stood for ten seconds, gazing out through the transparent door at other cylinders with their still figures, and then he pressed the button. Approximately fifteen seconds later he became unconscious.

He had to spend three more nights in the public stoner. Three days of fall were gone; only five left. Not that that mattered in California so much. When he had lived in Chicago, winter was like a white blanket being shaken by a madwoman. Spring was a green explosion. Summer was a bright roar and a hot breath. Fall was the topple of a drunken jester in garish motley.

The fourth day, he received notice that he could move into the very house he had picked. This surprised and pleased him. He knew of a dozen who had spent a whole year—forty-eight days or so—in a public station while waiting. He moved in the fifth day with three days of spring to enjoy. But he would have to use up his two days off to shop for clothes, bring in groceries and other goods, and get acquainted with his housemates. Sometimes, he wished he had not been born with the compulsion to act. TV'ers worked five days at a stretch, sometimes six, while a plumber, for instance, only put in three days out of seven.

The house was as large as the other, and the six extra blocks to walk would be good for him. It held eight people per day, counting himself. He moved in that evening, introduced himself, and got Mabel Curta, who worked as a secretary for a producer, to fill him in on the household routine. After he made sure that his stoner had been moved into the stoner room, he could relax somewhat.

Mabel Curta had accompanied him into the stoner room, since she had appointed herself his guide. She was a short, overly curved woman of about thirty-five (Tuesday time). She had been divorced three times, and marriage was no more for her unless, of course, Mr. Right came along. Tom was between marriages himself, but he did not tell her so.

"We'll take a look at your bedroom," Mabel said. "It's small but it's soundproofed, thank God."

He started after her, then stopped. She looked back through the doorway and said, "What is it?"

"This girl . . ."

There were sixty-three of the tall gray eternium cylinders. He was looking through the door of the nearest at the girl within.

"Wow! Really beautiful!"

If Mabel felt any jealousy, she suppressed it.

"Yes, isn't she!"

The girl had long, black, slightly curly hair, a face that could have launched him a thousand times times a thousand times, a figure that had enough but not too much, and long legs. Her eyes were open; in the dim light they looked a purplish-blue. She wore a thin silvery dress.

The plate by the top of the door gave her vital data. Jennie Marlowe. Born 2031 A.D., San Marino, California. She would be twenty-four years old. Actress. Unmarried. Wednesday's child.

"What's the matter?" Mabel said.

"Nothing."

How could he tell her that he felt sick in his stomach from a desire that could never be satisfied? Sick from beauty?

For will in us is over-ruled by fate.
Who ever loved, that loved not at first sight?

"What?" Mabel said, and then, after laughing, "You must be kidding?"

She wasn't angry. She realized that Jennie Marlowe was no more competition than if she were dead. She was right. Better for him to busy himself with the living of this world. Mabel wasn't too bad, cuddly, really, and, after a few drinks, rather stimulating.

They went downstairs afterward after 18:00 to the TV room. Most of the others were there, too. Some had their ear plugs in; some were looking at the screen but talking. The newscast was on, of course. Everybody was filling up on what had happened last Tuesday and today. The Speaker of the House was retiring after his term was up. His days of usefulness were over and his recent ill health showed no signs of disappearing. There was a shot of the family graveyard in Mississippi with the pedestal reserved for him. When science someday learned how to rejuvenate, he would come out of stonerment.

"That'll be the day!" Mabel said. She squirmed on his lap.

"Oh, I think they'll crack it," he said. "They're already on the track; they've succeeded in stopping the aging of rabbits."

"I don't mean that," she said. "Sure, they'll find out how to rejuvenate people. But then what? You think they're going to bring them all back? With all the people they got now and then they'll double, maybe triple, maybe quadruple, the population? You think they won't just leave them standing there?" She giggled, and said, "What would the pigeons do without them?"

He squeezed her waist. At the same time, he had a vision of himself squeezing *that* girl's waist. Hers would be soft enough but with no hint of fat.

Forget about her. Think of now. Watch the news.

A Mrs. Wilder had stabbed her husband and then herself with a kitchen knife. Both had been stoned immediately after the police arrived, and they had been taken to the hospital. An investigation of a work slowdown in the county government offices was taking place. The complaints were that Monday's people were not setting up the computers for Tuesday's. The case was being referred to the proper authorities of both days. The Ganymede base reported that the Great Red Spot of Jupiter was emitting weak but definite pulses that did not seem to be random.

The last five minutes of the program was a precis devoted to outstanding events of the other days. Mrs. Cuthmar, the housemother, turned the channel to a situation comedy with no protests from anybody.

Tom left the room, after telling Mabel that he was going to bed early—alone, and to sleep. He had a hard day tomorrow.

He tiptoed down the hall and the stairs and into the stoner room. The lights were soft, there were many shadows, and it was quiet. The sixty-three cylinders were like ancient granite columns of an underground chamber of a buried city. Fifty-five faces were white blurs behind the clear metal. Some had their eyes open; most had closed them while waiting for the field radiated from the machine in the base. He looked through Jennie Marlowe's door. He felt sick again. Out of his reach; never for him. Wednesday was only a day away. No, it was only a little less than four and a half hours away.

He touched the door. It was slick and only a little cold. She stared at him. Her right forearm was bent to hold the strap of a large purse. When the door opened, she would step out, ready to go. Some people took their showers and fixed their faces as soon as they got up from their sleep and then went directly into the stoner. When the field was automatically radiated at 05:00, they stepped out a minute later, ready for the day.

He would like to step out of his "coffin," too, at the same time.

But he was barred by Wednesday.

He turned away. He was acting like a sixteen-year-old kid. He had been sixteen about one hundred and six years ago, not that that made any difference. Physiologically, he was thirty.

As he started up to the second floor, he almost turned around and went back for another look. But he took himself by his neck-collar and pulled himself up to his room. There he decided he would get to sleep at once. Perhaps he would dream about her. If dreams were wish-fulfillments, they would bring her to him. It still had not been "proved" that dreams always expressed wishes, but it had been proved that man deprived of dreaming did go mad. And so the somniums radiated a field that put man into a state in which he got all the sleep, and all the dreams, that he needed within a four-hour period. Then he was awakened and a little later went into the stoner where the field suspended all atomic and subatomic activity. He would remain in that state forever unless the activating field came on.

He slept, and Jennie Marlowe did not come to him. Or, if she did, he did not remember. He awoke, washed his face, went down eagerly to the stoner, where he found the entire household standing around, getting in one last smoke, talking, laughing. Then they would step into their cylinders, and a silence like that at the heart of a mountain would fall.

He had often wondered what would happen if he did not go into the stoner. How would he feel? Would he be panicked? All his life, he had known only Tuesdays. Would Wednesday rush at him, roaring, like a tidal wave? Pick him up and hurl him against the reefs of a strange time?

What if he made some excuse and went back upstairs and did not go back down until the field had come on? By then, he could not enter. The door to his cylinder would not open again until the proper time. He could still run down to the public emergency stoners only three blocks away. But if he stayed in his room, waiting for Wednesday?

Such things happened. If the breaker of the law did not have a reasonable excuse, he was put on trial. It was a felony second only to murder to "break time," and the unexcused were stonered. All felons, sane or insane, were stonered. Or *mañanaed*, as some said. The *mañanaed* criminal waited in immobility and unconsciousness, preserved unharmed until science had techniques to cure the insane, the neurotic, the criminal, the sick. *Mañana.*

"What was it like in Wednesday?" Tom had asked a man who had been unavoidably left behind because of an accident.

"How would I know? I was knocked out except for about fifteen minutes. I was in the same city, and I had never seen the faces of the ambulance men, of course, but then I've never seen them here. They stonered me and left me in the hospital for Tuesday to take care of."

He must have it bad, he thought. Bad. Even to think of such a thing was crazy. Getting into Wednesday was almost impossible. Almost. But it could be done. It would take time and patience, but it could be done.

He stood in front of his stoner for a moment. The others said, "See you! So long! Next Tuesday!" Mabel called, "Good night, lover!"

"Good night," he muttered.

"What?" she shouted.

"Good night!"

He glanced at the beautiful face behind the door. Then he smiled. He had been afraid that she might hear him say good night to a woman who called him lover.

He had ten minutes yet. The intercom alarms were whooping. Get going, everybody! Time to take the six-day trip! Run! Remember the penalties!

He remembered, but he wanted to leave a message. The recorder was on a table. He activated it, and said, "Dear *Miss* Jennie Marlowe. My name is Tom Pym, and my stoner is next to yours. I am an actor, too; in fact, I work at the same studio as you. I know this is presumptuous of me, but I have never seen anybody so beautiful. Do you have a talent to match your beauty? I would like to see some run-offs of your shows. Would you please leave some in room five? I'm sure the occupant won't mind. Yours, Tom Pym."

He ran it back. It was certainly bald enough, and that might be just what was needed. Too flowery or too pressing would have made her leery. He had commented on her beauty twice but not overstressed it. And the appeal to her pride in her acting would be difficult to resist. Nobody knew better than he about that.

He whistled a little on his way to the cylinder. Inside, he pressed the button and looked at his watch. Five minutes to midnight. The light on the huge screen above the computer in the police station would not be flashing for him. Ten minutes from now, Wednesday's police would step out of their stoners in the precinct station, and they would take over their duties.

There was a ten-minute hiatus between the two days in the police station. All hell could break loose in these few minutes and it sometimes did. But a price had to be paid to maintain the walls of time.

He opened his eyes. His knees sagged a little and his head bent. The activation was a million microseconds fast—from eternium to flesh and blood almost instantaneously and the heart never knew that it had been stopped for such a long time. Even so, there was a little delay in the muscles' response to a standing position.

He pressed the button, opened the door, and it was as if his button had launched the day. Mabel had made herself up last night so that she looked dawn-fresh. He complimented her and she smiled happily. But he told her he would meet her for breakfast. Halfway up the staircase, he stopped, and waited until the hall was empty. Then he sneaked back down and into the stoner room. He turned on the recorder.

A voice, husky but also melodious, said, "Dear Mister Pym. I've had a few messages from other days. It was fun to talk back and forth across the abyss between the worlds, if you don't mind my exaggerating a little. But there is really no sense in it, once the novelty has worn off. If you become interested in the other person, you're frustrating yourself. That person can only be a voice in a recorder and a cold waxy face in a metal coffin. I wax poetic. Pardon me. If the person doesn't interest you, why continue to communicate? There is no sense in either case. And I *may* be beautiful. Anyway, I thank you for the compliment, but I am also sensible.

"I should have just not bothered to reply. But I want to be nice; I didn't want to hurt your feelings. So please don't leave any more messages."

He waited while silence was played. Maybe she was pausing for effect. Now would come a chuckle or a low honey-throated laugh, and she would say, "However, I don't like to disappoint my public. The run-offs are in your room."

The silence stretched out. He turned off the machine and went to the dining room for breakfast.

Siesta time at work was from 14:40 to 14:45. He lay down on the bunk and pressed the button. Within a minute he was asleep. He did dream of Jennie this time; she was a white shimmering figure solidifying out of the darkness and floating toward him. She was even more beautiful than she had been in her stoner.

The shooting ran overtime that afternoon so that he got home just in time for supper. Even the studio would not dare keep a man past his supper hour, especially since the studio was authorized to serve food only at noon.

He had time to look at Jennie for a minute before Mrs. Cuthmar's voice screeched over the intercom. As he walked down the hall, he thought, "I'm getting barnacled on her. It's ridiculous. I'm a grown man. Maybe . . . maybe I should see a psycher."

Sure, make your petition, and wait until a psycher has time for you. Say about three hundred days from now, if you are lucky. And if the psycher doesn't work out for you, then petition for another, and wait six hundred days.

Petition. He slowed down. Petition. What about a request, not to see a psycher, but to move? Why not? What did he have to lose? It would probably be turned down, but he could at least try.

Even obtaining a form for the request was not easy. He spent two nonwork days standing in line at the Center City Bureau before he got the proper forms. The first time, he was handed the wrong form and had to start all over again. There was no line set aside for those who wanted to change their days. There were not enough who wished to do this to justify such a line. So he had to queue up before the Miscellaneous Office counter of the Mobility Section of the Vital Exchange Department of the Interchange and Cross Transfer Bureau. None of these titles had anything to do with emigration to another day.

When he got his form the second time, he refused to move from the office window until he had checked the number of the form and asked the clerk to double-check. He ignored the cries and the mutterings behind him. Then he went to one side of the vast room and stood in line before the punch machines. After two hours, he got to sit down at a small rolltop desk-shaped machine, above which was a large screen. He inserted the form into the slot, looked at the projection of the form, and punched buttons to mark the proper spaces opposite the proper questions. After that, all he had to do was to drop the form into a slot and hope it did not get lost. Or hope he would not have to go through the same procedure because he had improperly punched the form.

That evening, he put his head against the hard metal and murmured to the rigid face behind the door, "I must really love you to go through all this. And you don't even know it. And, worse, if you did, you might not care one bit."

To prove to himself that he had kept his gray stuff, he went out with Mabel that evening to a party given by Sol Voremwolf, a producer. Voremwolf had just passed a civil service examination giving him an A-13 rating. This meant that, in time, with some luck and the proper pull, he would become an executive vice-president of the studio.

The party was a qualified success. Tom and Mabel returned about half an hour before stoner time. Tom had managed to refrain from too many blowminds and liquor, so he was not tempted by Mabel. Even so, he knew that when he became un-stonered, he would be half-loaded and he'd have to take some dreadful counter-actives. He would look and feel like hell at work, since he had missed his sleep.

He put Mabel off with an excuse, and went down to the stoner room ahead of the others. Not that that would do him any good if he wanted to get stonered early. The stoners only activated within narrow time limits.

He leaned against the cylinder and patted the door. "I tried not to think about you all evening. I wanted to be fair to Mabel, it's not fair to go out with her and think about you all the time."

All's fair in love . . .

He left another message for her, then wiped it out. What was the use? Besides, he knew that his speech was a little thick. He wanted to appear at his best for her.

Why should he? What did she care for him?

The answer was, he did care, and there was no reason or logic connected with it. He loved this forbidden, untouchable, far-away-in-time, yet-so-near woman.

Mabel had come in silently. She said, "You're sick!"

Tom jumped away. Now why had he done that? He had

nothing to be ashamed of. Then why was he so angry with her? His embarrassment was understandable but his anger was not.

Mabel laughed at him, and he was glad. Now he could snarl at her. He did so, and she turned away and walked out. But she was back in a few minutes with the others. It would soon be midnight.

By then he was standing inside the cylinder. A few seconds later, he left it, pushed Jennie's backward on its wheels, and pushed his around so that it faced hers. He went back in, pressed the button, and stood there. The double doors only slightly distorted his view. But she seemed even more removed in distance, in time, and in unattainability.

Three days later, well into winter, he received a letter. The box inside the entrance hall buzzed just as he entered the front door. He went back and waited until the letter was printed and had dropped out from the slot. It was the reply to his request to move to Wednesday.

Denied. Reason: he had no reasonable reason to move.

That was true. But he could not give his real motive. It would have been even less impressive than the one he had given. He had punched the box opposite No. 12. REASON: TO GET INTO AN ENVIRONMENT WHERE MY TALENTS WILL BE MORE LIKELY TO BE ENCOURAGED.

He cursed and he raged. It was his human, his civil right to move into any day he pleased. That is, it should be his right. What if a move did cause much effort? What if it required a transfer of his I.D. and all the records connected with him from the moment of his birth? What if . . . ?

He could rage all he wanted to, but it would not change a thing. He was stuck in the world of Tuesday.

Not yet, he muttered. Not yet. Fortunately, there is no limit to the number of requests I can make in my own day. I'll send out another. They think they can wear me out, huh? Well, I'll wear them out. Man against the machine. Man against the system. Man against the bureaucracy and the hard cold rules.

Winter's twenty days had sped by. Spring's eight days rocketed by. It was summer again. On the second day of the twelve days of summer, he received a reply to his second request.

It was neither a denial nor an acceptance. It stated that if he thought he would be better off psychologically in Wednesday because his astrologer said so, then he would have to get a psycher's critique of the astrologer's analysis. Tom Pym jumped into the air and clicked his sandaled heels together. Thank God that he lived in an age that did not classify astrologers as charlatans! The people—the masses—had protested that astrology was a necessity and that it should be legalized and honored. So laws were passed, and because of that, Tom Pym had a chance.

He went down to the stoner room and kissed the door of the cylinder and told Jennie Marlowe the good news. She did not respond, though he thought he saw her eyes brighten just a little. That was, of course, only his imagination, but he liked his imagination.

Getting a psycher for a consultation and getting through the three sessions took another year, another forty-eight days. Doctor Sigmund Traurig was a friend of Doctor Stelhela, the astrologer, and so that made things easier for Tom.

"I've studied Doctor Stelhela's chart carefully and analyzed carefully your obsession for this woman," he said. "I agree with Doctor Stelhela that you will always be unhappy in Tuesday, but I don't quite agree with him that you will be happier in Wednesday. However, you have this thing going for this Miss Marlowe, so I think you should go to Wednesday. But only if you sign papers agreeing to see a psycher there for extended therapy."

Only later did Tom Pym realize that Doctor Traurig might have wanted to get rid of him because he had too many patients. But that was an uncharitable thought.

He had to wait while the proper papers were transmitted to Wednesday's authorities. His battle was only half-won. The other officials could turn him down. And if he did get to his goal, then what? She could reject him without giving him a second chance.

It was unthinkable, but she could.

He caressed the door and then pressed his lips against it.

"Pygmalion could at least touch Galatea," he said. "Surely, the gods—the big dumb bureaucrats—will take pity on me, who can't even touch you. Surely."

The psycher had said that he was incapable of a true and lasting bond with a woman, as so many men were in this world of easy-come-easy-go liaisons. He had fallen in love with Jennie Marlowe for several reasons. She may have resembled somebody he had loved when he was very young. His mother, perhaps? No? Well, never mind. He would find out in Wednesday—perhaps. The deep, the important, truth was that he loved Miss Marlowe because she could never reject him, kick him out, or become tiresome, complain, weep, yell, insult, and so forth. He loved her because she was unattainable and silent.

"I love her as Achilles must have loved Helen when he saw her on top of the walls of Troy," Tom said.

"I wasn't aware that Achilles was ever in love with Helen of Troy," Doctor Traurig said drily.

"Homer never said so, but I *know* that he must have been! Who could see her and *not* love her?"

"How the hell would I know? I never saw her! If I had suspected these delusions would intensify . . ."

"I am a poet!" Tom said.

"Overimaginative, you mean! Hmmm. She must be a douser! I don't have anything particular to do this evening. I'll tell you what . . . my curiosity is aroused . . . I'll come down to your place tonight and take a look at this fabulous beauty, your Helen of Troy."

Doctor Traurig appeared immediately after supper, and Tom Pym ushered him down the hall and into the stoner room at the rear of the big house as if he were a guide conducting a famous critic to a just-discovered Rembrandt.

The doctor stood for a long time in front of the cylinder. He hmmmed several times and checked her vital-data plate several times. Then he turned and said, "I see what you mean, Mr. Pym. Very well. I'll give the go-ahead."

"Ain't she something?" Tom said on the porch. "She's out of this world, literally and figuratively, of course."

"Very beautiful. But I believe that you are facing a great disappointment, perhaps heartbreak, perhaps, who knows, even madness, much as I hate to use that unscientific term."

"I'll take the chance," Tom said. "I know I sound nuts, but where would we be if it weren't for nuts? Look at the man who invented the wheel, at Columbus, at James Watt, at the Wright brothers, at Pasteur, you name them."

"You can scarcely compare these pioneers of science with their passion for truth with you and your desire to marry a woman. But, as I have observed, she is strikingly beautiful. Still, that makes me exceedingly cautious. Why isn't she married? What's wrong with her?"

"For all I know, she may have been married a dozen times!" Tom said. "The point is, she isn't now! Maybe she's disappointed and she's sworn to wait until the right man comes along. Maybe..."

"There's no maybe about it, you're neurotic," Traurig said. "But I actually believe that it would be more dangerous for you *not* to go to Wednesday than it would be *to* go."

"Then you'll say yes!" Tom said, grabbing the doctor's hand and shaking it.

"Perhaps. I have some doubts."

The doctor had a faraway look. Tom laughed and released the hand and slapped the doctor on the shoulder. "Admit it! You were really struck by her! You'd have to be dead not to!"

"She's all right," the doctor said. "But you must think this over. If you do go there and she turns you down, you might go off the deep end, much as I hate to use such a poetical term."

"No, I won't. I wouldn't be a bit the worse off. Better off, in fact. I'll at least get to see her in the flesh."

Spring and summer zipped by. Then, a morning he would never forget, the letter of acceptance. With it, instructions on how to get to Wednesday. These were simple enough. He was to make sure that the technicians came to his stoner sometime during the day and readjusted the timer within the base. He could not figure out why he could not just stay out of the stoner and let Wednesday catch up to him, but by now he was past trying to fathom the bureaucratic mind.

He did not intend to tell anyone at the house, mainly because of Mabel. But Mabel found out from someone at the studio. She wept when she saw him at supper time, and she ran upstairs to her room. He felt badly, but he did not follow to console her.

That evening, his heart beating hard, he opened the door to

his stoner. The others had found out by then; he had been unable to keep the business to himself. Actually, he was glad that he had told them. They seemed happy for him, and they brought in drinks and had many rounds of toasts. Finally, Mabel came downstairs, wiping her eyes, and she said she wished him luck, too. She had known that he was not really in love with her. But she did wish someone would fall in love with her just by looking inside her stoner.

When she found out that he had gone to see Doctor Traurig, she said, "He's a very influential man. Sol Voremwolf had him for his analyst. He says he's even got influence on other days. He edits the *Psyche Crosscurrents*, you know, one of the few periodicals read by other people."

Other, of course, meant those who lived in Wednesdays through Mondays.

Tom said he was glad he had gotten Traurig. Perhaps he had used his influence to get the Wednesday authorities to push through his request so swiftly. The walls between the worlds were seldom broken, but it was suspected that the very influential did it when they pleased.

Now, quivering, he stood before Jennie's cylinder again. The last time, he thought, that I'll see her stonered. Next time, she'll be warm, colorful, touchable flesh.

"*Ave atque vale!*" he said aloud. The others cheered. Mabel said, "How corny!" They thought he was addressing them, and perhaps he had included them.

He stepped inside the cylinder, closed the door, and pressed the button. He would keep his eyes open, so that . . .

And today was Wednesday. Though the view was exactly the same, it was like being on Mars.

He pushed open the door and stepped out. The seven people had faces he knew and names he had read on their plates. But he did not know them.

He started to say hello, and then he stopped.

Jennie Marlowe's cylinder was gone.

He seized the nearest man by the arm.

"Where's Jennie Marlowe?"

"Let go. You're hurting me. She's gone. To Tuesday."

"Tuesday! Tuesday?"

"Sure. She'd been trying to get out of here for a long time. She had something about this day being unlucky for her. She was unhappy, that's for sure. Just two days ago, she said her application had finally been accepted. Apparently, some Tuesday psycher had used his influence. He came down and saw her in her stoner and that was it, brother."

The walls and the people and the stoners seemed to be distorted. Time was bending itself this way and that. He wasn't in Wednesday; he wasn't in Tuesday. He wasn't in *any* day. He was stuck inside himself at some crazy date that should never have existed.

"She can't do that!"

"Oh, no! She just did that!"

"But . . . you can't transfer more than once!"

"That's her problem."

It was his, too.

"I should never have brought him down to look at her!" Tom said. "The swine! The unethical swine!"

Tom Pym stood there for a long time, and then he went into the kitchen. It was the same environment, if you discounted the people. Later, he went to the studio and got a part in a situation play which was, really, just like all those in Tuesday. He watched the newscaster that night. The President of the U.S.A. had a different name and face, but the words of his speech could have been those of Tuesday's President. He was introduced to a secretary of a producer; her name wasn't Mabel, but it might as well have been.

The difference here was that Jennie was gone, and oh, what a world of difference it made to him.

1973

1

*J*une 1, 1980
It is now 11:00 P.M., and I am afraid to go to bed. I am not alone. The whole world is afraid of sleep.

This morning I got up at 6:30 A.M., as I do every Wednesday. While I shaved and showered, I considered the case of the state of Illinois against Joseph Lankers, accused of murder. It was beginning to stink as if it were a three-day-old fish. My star witness would undoubtedly be charged with perjury.

I dressed, went downstairs, and kissed Carole good morning. She poured me a cup of coffee and said, "The paper's late."

That put me in a bad temper. I need both coffee and the morning newspaper to get me started.

Twice during breakfast, I left the table to look outside. Neither paper nor newsboy had appeared.

At seven, Carole went upstairs to wake up Mike and Tom, aged ten and eight respectively. Saturdays and Sundays they rise early even though I'd like them to stay in bed so their horsing around won't wake me. School days they have to be dragged out.

The third time I looked out of the door, Joe Gale, the paperboy, was next door. My paper lay on the stoop.

I felt disorientated, as if I'd walked into the wrong courtroom or the judge had given my client, a shoplifter, a life sentence. I was out of phase with the world. This couldn't be Sunday. So what was the Sunday issue, bright in its covering of the colored comic section, doing here? Today was Wednesday.

I stepped out to pick it up and saw old Mrs. Douglas, my neighbor to the left. She was looking at the front page of her paper as if she could not believe it.

The world rearranged itself into the correct lines of polarization. My thin panic dwindled into nothing. I thought, the *Star* has really goofed this time. That's what comes from depending so much on a computer to put it together. One little short circuit, and Wednesday's paper comes out in Sunday's format.

The *Star*'s night shift must have decided to let it go through; it was too late for them to rectify the error.

I said, "Good morning, Mrs. Douglas! Tell me, what day is it?"

"The twenty-eighth of May," she said. "I think . . ."

I walked out into the yard and shouted after Joe. Reluctantly, he wheeled his bike around.

"What is this?" I said, shaking the paper at him. "Did the *Star* screw up?"

"I don't know, Mr. Franham," he said. "None of us knows, honest to God."

By "us" he must have meant the other boys he met in the morning at the paper drop.

"We all thought it was Wednesday. That's why I'm late. We couldn't understand what was happening, so we talked a long time and then Bill Ambers called the office. Gates, he's the circulation manager, was just as bongo as we was."

"Were," I said.

"What?" he said.

"We *were*, not *was*, just as bongo, whatever that means," I said.

"For God's sake, Mr. Franham, who cares!" he said.

"Some of us still do," I said. "All right, what did Gates say?"

"He was upset as hell," Joe said. "He said heads were gonna roll. The night staff had fallen asleep for a couple of hours, and some joker had diddled up the computers, or . . ."

"That's all it is?" I said. I felt relieved.

When I went inside, I got out the papers for the last four days from the cycler. I sat down on the sofa and scanned them.

I didn't remember reading them. I didn't remember the past four days at all!

Wednesday's headline was: MYSTERIOUS OBJECT ORBITS EARTH.

I did remember Tuesday's articles, which stated that the big round object was heading for a point between the Earth and the moon. It had been detected three weeks ago when it was passing through the so-called asteroid belt. It was at that time traveling approximately 57,000 kilometers per hour, relative to the sun. Then it had slowed down, had changed course several times, and it became obvious that, unless it changed course again, it was going to come near Earth.

By the time it was eleven million miles away, the radars had defined its size and shape, though not its material composition. It was perfectly spherical and exactly half a kilometer in diameter. It did not reflect much light. Since it had altered its path so often, it had to be artificial. Strange hands, or strange somethings, had built it.

I remembered the panic and the many wild articles in the papers and magazines and the TV specials made overnight to discuss its implications.

It had failed to make any response whatever to the radio and laser signals sent from Earth. Many scientists said that it probably contained no living passengers. It had to be of interstellar origin. The sentient beings of some planet circling some star had sent it out equipped with automatic equipment of some sort. No being could live long enough to travel between the stars. It would take over four years to get from the nearest star to Earth even if the object could travel at the speed of light, and that was impossible. Even one-sixteenth the speed of light seemed incredible because of the vast energy requirements. No, this thing had been launched with only electromechanical devices as passengers, had attained its top speed, turned off its power, and coasted until it came within the outer reaches of our solar system.

According to the experts, it must be unable to land on Earth because of its size and weight. It was probably just a surveying vessel, and after it had taken some photographs and made some radar/laser sweeps, it would proceed to wherever it was supposed to go, probably back to an orbit around its home planet.

2

Last Wednesday night, the president had told us that we had nothing to fear. And he'd tried to end on an optimistic note. At least, that's what Wednesday's paper said. The beings who had sent The Ball must be more advanced than we, and they must have many good things to give us. And we might be able to make beneficial contributions to them. Like what? I thought.

Some photographs of The Ball, taken from one of the manned orbiting laboratories, were on the second page. It looked just like a giant black billiard ball. One TV comic had suggested that the other side might bear a big white 8. I may have thought that this was funny last Wednesday, but I didn't think so now. It seemed highly probable to me that The Ball was connected with the four-days' loss of memory. How, I had no idea.

I turned on the 7:30 news channels, but they weren't much help except in telling us that the same thing had happened to everybody all over the world. Even those in the deepest diamond mines or submarines had been affected. The president was in conference, but he'd be making a statement over the networks sometime today. Meantime, it was known that no radiation of any sort had been detected emanating from The Ball. There was no evidence whatsoever that the object had caused the loss of memory. Or, as the jargon-crazy casters were already calling it, "memloss."

I'm a lawyer, and I like to think logically, not only about what has happened but what might happen. So I extrapolated on the basis of what little evidence, or data, there was.

On the first of June, a Sunday, we woke up with all memory of May 31 back through May 28 completely gone. We had thought that yesterday was the twenty-seventh and that this morning was that of the twenty-eighth.

If The Ball had caused this, why had it only taken four days of our memory? I didn't know. Nobody knew. But perhaps The Ball, its devices, that is, were limited in scope. Perhaps they couldn't strip off more than four days of memory at a time from everybody on Earth.

Postulate that this is the case. Then, what if the same thing happens tomorrow? We'll wake up tomorrow, June 2, with all memory of yesterday, June 1, and three more days of May, the twenty-seventh through the twenty-fifth, gone. Eight days in one solid stretch.

And if this ghastly thing should occur the following day, June 3, we'll lose another four days. All memory of June 2 will have disappeared. With it will go the memory of three more days, from May twenty-fourth through the twenty-second. Twelve days in all from June 2 backward!

And the next day? June 3 lost, too, along with May 21 through May 19. Sixteen days of a total blank. And the next day? And the next?

No, it's too hideous, and too fantastic, to think about.

While we were watching TV, Carole and the boys besieged me with questions. She was frantic. The boys seemed to be enjoying the mystery. They'd awakened expecting to go to school, and now they were having a holiday.

To all their questions, I said, "I don't know. Nobody knows."

I wasn't going to frighten them with my extrapolations. Besides, I didn't believe them myself.

"You'd better call up your office and tell them you can't come in today," Carole said. "Surely Judge Payne'll call off the session today."

"Carole, it's Sunday, not Wednesday, remember?" I said.

She cried for a minute. After she'd wiped away the tears, she said, "That's just it! I *don't* remember! My God, what's happening?"

The newscasters also reported that the White House was flooded with telegrams and phone calls demanding that rockets with H-bomb warheads be launched against The Ball. The specials, which came on after the news, were devoted to The Ball. These had various authorities, scientists, military men, ministers, and a few science-fiction authors. None of them radiated confidence, but they were all temperate in their approach to the problem. I suppose they had been picked for their level-headedness. The networks had screened out the hotheads and the crackpots. They didn't want to be generating any more hysteria.

But Anel Robertson, a fundamentalist faith healer with a

powerful radio/TV station of his own, had already declared that
The Ball was a judgment of God on a sinful planet. It was The
Destroying Angel. I knew that because Mrs. Douglas, no fanatic
but certainly a zealot, had phoned me and told me to dial him in.
Robertson had been speaking for an hour, she said, and he was
going to talk all day.

She sounded frightened, and yet, beneath the fear was a note
of joy. Obviously, she didn't think that she was going to be among
the goats when the last days arrived. She'd be right in there with
the whitest of the sheep. My curiosity finally overcame my repug-
nance for Robertson. I dialed the correct number but got nothing
except a pattern. Later today, I found out his station had been
shut down for some infraction of FCC regulations. At least, that
was the explanation given on the news, but I suspected that the
government regarded him as a hysteria monger.

At eleven, Carole reminded me that it was Sunday and that if
we didn't hurry, we'd miss church.

The Forrest Hill Presbyterian has a good attendance, but its
huge parking lot has always been adequate. This morning, we had
to park two blocks up the street and walk to church. Every seat
was filled. We had to stand in the anteroom near the front door.
The crowd stank of fear. Their faces were pale and set; their eyes,
big. The air conditioning labored unsuccessfully to carry away the
heat and humidity of the packed and sweating bodies. The choir
was loud but quavering; their "Rock of Ages" was crumbling.

Dr. Boynton would have prepared his sermon on Saturday afternoon, as he always did. But today he spoke impromptu. Perhaps, he said, this loss of memory *had* been caused by The Ball.
Perhaps there were living beings in it who had taken four days
away from us, not as a hostile move but merely to demonstrate
their immense powers. There was no reason to anticipate that we
would suffer another loss of memory. These beings merely wanted
to show us that we were hopelessly inferior in science and that we
could not launch a successful attack against them.

"What the hell's he doing?" I thought. "Is he trying to scare
us to death?"

Boynton hastened then to say that beings with such powers,
of such obvious advancement, would not, could not, be hostile.

They would be on too high an ethical plane for such evil things as war, unless they were attacked, of course. They would regard us as beings who had not yet progressed to their level but had the potentiality, the God-given potentiality, to be brought up to a high level. He was sure that, when they made contact with us, they would tell us that all was for the best.

They would tell us that we must, like it or not, become true Christians. At least, we must all, Buddhists, Moslems and so forth, become Christian in spirit, whatever our religion or lack thereof. They would teach us how to live as brothers and sisters, how to be happy, how to truly love. Assuredly, God had sent The Ball, since nothing happened without His knowledge and consent. He had sent these beings, whoever they were, not as Destroying Angels but as Sharers of Peace, Love and Prosperity.

That last, with the big P, seemed to settle down most of the congregation. Boynton had not forgotten that most of his flock were of the big-business and professional classes. Nor had he forgotten that, inscribed on the arch above the church entrance was, THEY SHALL PROSPER WHO LOVE THEE.

3

We poured out into a bright warm June afternoon. I looked up into the sky but could see no Ball, of course. The news media had said that, despite its great distance from Earth, it was circling Earth every sixty-five minutes. It wasn't in a free fall orbit. It was applying continuous power to keep it on its path, although there were no detectable emanations of energy from it.

The memory loss had occurred all over the world between 1:00 A.M. and 2:00 A.M. Central Standard Time. Those who were not already asleep fell asleep for a minimum of an hour. This had, of course, caused hundreds of thousands of accidents. Planes not on automatic pilot had crashed, trains had collided or been derailed, ships had sunk, and more·than two hundred thousand had been killed or seriously injured. At least a million vehicle drivers and passengers had been injured. The ambulance and hospital services had found it impossible to handle the situation. The fact that their personnel had been asleep for at least an hour and that it had taken them some time to recover from their confusion on awakening had aggravated the situation considerably. Many had died who might have lived if immediate service had been available.

There were many fires, too, the largest of which were still raging in Tokyo, Athens, Naples, Harlem, and Baltimore.

I thought, Would beings on a high ethical plane have put us to sleep knowing that so many people would be killed and badly hurt?

One curious item was about two rangers who had been thinning a herd of elephants in Kenya. While sleeping, they had been trampled to death. Whatever it is that's causing this, it's very specific. Only human beings are affected.

The optimism, which Boynton had given us in the church, melted in the sun. Many must have been thinking, as I was, that if Boynton's words were prophetic, we were helpless. Whatever the things in The Ball, whether living or mechanical, decided to do for us, or to us, we were no longer masters of our own fate. Some of them must have been thinking about what the technologically superior whites had done to various aboriginal cultures. All in the name of progress and God.

But this would be, must be, different, I thought. Boynton must be right. Surely such an advanced people would not be as we were. Even we are not what we were in the bad old days. We have learned.

But then an advanced technology does not necessarily accompany an advanced ethics.

"Or whatever," I murmured.

"What did you say, dear?" Carole said.

I said, "Nothing," and shook her hand off my arm. She had clung to it tightly all through the services, as if I were the rock of the ages. I walked over to Judge Payne, who's sixty years old but looked this morning as if he were eighty. The many broken veins on his face were red, but underneath them was a grayishness.

I said hello and then asked him if things would be normal tomorrow. He didn't seem to know what I was getting at, so I said, "The trial will start on time tomorrow?"

"Oh, yes, the trial," he said. "Of course, Mark."

He laughed whinnyingly and said, "Provided that we all haven't forgotten today when we wake up tomorrow."

That seemed incredible, and I told him so.

"It's not law school that makes good lawyers," he said. "It's experience. And experience tells us that the same damned thing, with some trifling variations, occurs over and over, day after day. So what makes you think this evil thing won't happen again? And if it does, how're you going to learn from it when you can't remember it?"

I had no logical argument, and he didn't want to talk any more. He grabbed his wife by the arm, and they waded through the crowd as if they thought they were going to step in a sinkhole and drown in a sea of bodies.

This evening, I decided to record on tape what's happened today. Now I lay me down to sleep, I pray the Lord my memory to keep, if I forget while I sleep . . .

Most of the rest of today, I've spent before the TV. Carole wasted hours trying to get through the lines to her friends for phone conversations. Three-fourths of the time, she got a busy signal. There were bulletins on the TV asking people not to use the phone except for emergencies, but she paid no attention to it until eight o'clock. A TV bulletin, for the sixth time in an hour, asked that the lines be kept open. About twenty fires had broken out over the town, and the firemen couldn't be informed of them because of the tie-up. Calls to hospitals had been similarly blocked.

I told Carole to knock it off, and we quarreled. Our suppressed hysteria broke loose, and the boys retreated upstairs to their room behind a closed door. Eventually, Carole started crying and threw herself into my arms, and then I cried. We kissed and made up. The boys came down looking as if we had failed them, which we had. For them, it was no longer a fun-adventure from some science-fiction story.

Mike said, "Dad, could you help me go over my arithmetic lessons?"

I didn't feel like it, but I wanted to make it up to him for that savage scene. I said sure and then, when I saw what he had to do,

I said, "But all this? What's the matter with your teacher? I never saw so much . . ."

I stopped. Of course, he had forgotten all he'd learned in the last three days of school. He had to do his lessons all over again.

This took us until eleven, though we might have gone faster if I hadn't insisted on watching the news every half-hour for at least ten minutes. A full thirty minutes were used listening to the president, who came on at 9:30. He had nothing to add to what the newsmen had said except that, within thirty days, The Ball would be completely dealt with—one way or another. If it didn't make some response to our signals within two days, then we would send up a four-man expedition, which would explore The Ball.

If it can get inside, I thought.

If, however, The Ball should commit any more hostile acts, then the United States would immediately launch, in conjunction with other nations, rockets armed with H-bombs.

Meanwhile, would we all join the president in an interdenominational prayer?

We certainly would.

At eleven, we put the kids to bed. Tom went to sleep before we were out of the room. But about half an hour later, as I passed their door, I heard a low voice from the TV. I didn't say anything to Mike, even if he did have to go to school next day.

At twelve, I made the first part of this tape.

But here it is, one minute to one o'clock in the morning. If the same thing happens tonight as happened yesterday, then the nightside hemisphere will be affected first. People in the time zone which bisects the South and North Atlantic oceans and covers the eastern half of Greenland, will fall asleep. Just in case it does happen again, all airplanes have been grounded. Right now, the TV is showing the bridge and the salon of the trans-Atlantic liner *Pax*. It's five o'clock there, but the salon is crowded. The passengers are wearing party hats and confetti, and balloons are floating everywhere. I don't know what they could be celebrating. The captain said a little while ago that the ship's on automatic, but he doesn't expect a repetition of last night. The interviewer said that the governments of the dayside nations have not been successful keeping people home. We've been getting shots from everywhere, the sirens are wailing all over the world, but, except for the totalitarian nations, the streets of the daytime world are filled with cars. The damned fools just didn't believe it would happen again.

Back to the bridge and the salon of the ship. My God! They *are* falling asleep!

The announcers are repeating warnings. Everybody lie down so they won't get hurt by falling. Make sure all home appliances, which might cause fires, are turned off. And so on and so on.

I'm sitting in a chair with a tilted back. Carole is on the sofa.

Now I'm on the sofa. Carole just said she wanted to be holding on to me when this horrible thing comes.

The announcers are getting hysterical. In a few minutes, New York will be hit. The eastern half of South America is under. The central section is going under.

4

True date: June 2, 1980. Subjective date: May 25, 1980

My God! How many times have I said, "My God!" in the last two days?

I awoke on the sofa beside Carole and Mike. The clock indicated three in the morning. Chris Turner was on the TV. I didn't know what he was talking about. All I could understand was that he was trying to reassure his viewers that everything was all right and that everything would be explained shortly.

What was I doing on the sofa? I'd gone to bed about eleven the night of May 24, a Saturday. Carole and I had had a little quarrel because I'd spent all day working on the Lankers case, and she said that I'd promised to take her to see *Nova Express*. And so I had—if I finished work before eight, which I obviously had not done. So what were we doing on the sofa, where had Mike come from, and what did Turner mean by saying that today was June 2?

The tape recorder was on the table near me, but it didn't occur to me to turn it on.

I shook Carole awake, and we confusedly asked each other

what had happened. Finally, Turner's insistent voice got our attention, and he explained the situation for about the fifth time so far. Later, he said that an alarm clock placed by his ear had awakened him at two-thirty.

Carole made some coffee, and we drank four cups apiece. We talked wildly, with occasional breaks to listen to Turner, before we became half-convinced that we had indeed lost all memory of the last eight days. Mike slept on through it, and finally I carried him up to his bed. His TV was still on. Nate Frobisher, Mike's favorite spieler, was talking hysterically. I turned him off and went back downstairs. I figured out later that Mike had gotten scared and come downstairs to sit with us.

Dawn found us rereading the papers from May 24 through June 1. It was like getting news from Mars. Carole took a tranquilizer to quiet herself down, but I preferred Wild Turkey. After she'd seen me down six ounces, Carole said I should lay off the bourbon. I wouldn't be fit to go to work. I told her that if she thought anybody'd be working today, she was out of her mind.

At seven, I went out to pick up the paper. It wasn't there. At a quarter to eight, Joe delivered it. I tried to talk to him, but he wouldn't stop. All he said, as he pedaled away, was, "It ain't Saturday!"

I went back in. The entire front page was devoted to The Ball and this morning's events up to four o'clock. Part of the paper had been set up before one o'clock. According to a notice at the bottom of the page, the staff had awakened about three. It took them an hour to straighten themselves out, and then they'd gotten together the latest news and made up the front page and some of section C. They'd have never made it when they did if it wasn't for the computer, which printed justified lines from voice input.

Despite what I'd said earlier, I decided to go to work. First, I had to straighten the boys out. At ten, they went off to school. It seemed to me that it was useless for them to do so. But they were eager to talk with their classmates about this situation. To tell the truth, I wanted to get down to the office and the courthouse for the same reason. I wanted to talk this over with my colleagues. Staying home all day with Carole seemed a waste of time. We just kept saying the same thing over and over again.

Carole didn't want me to leave. She was too frightened to stay home by herself. Both our parents are dead, but she does have a sister who lives in Hannah, a small town nearby. I told her it'd do her good to get out of the house. And I just had to get to the courthouse. I couldn't find out what was happening there because the phone lines were tied up.

When I went outside to get into my car, Carole ran down after me. Her long blonde hair was straggling; she had big bags under her eyes; she looked like a witch.

"Mark! Mark!" she said.

I took my finger off the starter button and said, "What is it?"

"I know you'll think I'm crazy, Mark," she said. "But I'm about to fall apart!"

"Who isn't?" I said.

"Mark," she said, "what if I go out to my sister's and then forget how to get back? What if I forgot *you?*"

"This thing only happens at night," I said.

"So far!" she screamed. "So far!"

"Honey," I said, "I'll be home early, I promise. If you don't want to go, stay here. Go over and talk to Mrs. Knight. I see her looking out her window. She'll talk your leg off all day."

I didn't tell her to visit any of her close friends, because she didn't have any. Her best friend had died of cancer last year, and two others with whom she was familiar had moved away.

"If you do go to your sister's," I said, "make a note on a map reminding you where you live and stick it on top of the dashboard, where you can see it."

"You son of a bitch," she said. "It isn't funny!"

"I'm not being funny," I said. "I got a feeling . . ."

"What about?" she said.

"Well, we'll be making notes to ourselves soon. If this keeps up," I said.

I thought I was kidding then. Thinking about it later today I see that that is the only way to get orientated in the morning. Well, not the only way, but it'll have to be the way to get started when you wake up. Put a note where you can't overlook it, and it'll tell you to turn on a recording, which will, in turn, summarize the situation. Then you turn on the TV and get some more information.

I might as well have stayed home. Only half of the courthouse personnel showed up, and they were hopelessly inefficient. Judge Payne wasn't there and never will be. He'd had a fatal stroke at six that morning while listening to the TV. Walter Barbindale, my partner, said that the judge probably would have had a stroke sometime in the near future, anyway. But this situation must certainly have hastened it.

"The stock market's about hit bottom," he said. "One more day of this, and we'll have another world-wide depression. Nineteen twenty-nine won't hold a candle to it. And I can't even get through to my brother to tell him to sell everything."

"If everybody sells, then the market *will* crash," I said.

"Are you hanging onto your stocks?" he said.

"I've been too busy to even think about it," I said. "You might say I forgot."

"That isn't funny," he said.

"That's what my wife said," I answered. "But I'm not trying to be funny, though God knows I could use a good laugh. Well, what're we going to do about Lankers?"

"I went over some of the records," he said. "We haven't got a chance. I tell you, it was a shock finding out, for the second time, mind you, though I don't remember the first, that our star witness is in jail on a perjury charge."

Since all was chaos in the courthouse, it wasn't much use trying to find out who the judge would be for the new trial for Lankers. To tell the truth, I didn't much care. There were far more important things to worry about than the fate of an undoubtedly guilty murderer.

I went to Grover's Rover Bar, which is a block from the courthouse. As an aside, for my reference or for whoever might be listening to this someday, why am I telling myself things I know perfectly well, like the location of Grover's? Maybe it's because I think I might forget them some day.

Grover's, at least, I remembered well, as I should, since I'd been going there ever since it was built, five years ago. The air was thick with tobacco and pot smoke and the odors of pot, beer and booze. And noisy. Everybody was talking fast and loud, which is to be expected in a place filled with members of the legal profession. I bellied up to the bar and bought the D.A. a shot of Wild Turkey. We talked about what we'd done that morning, and then he told me he had to release two burglars that day. They'd been caught and jailed two days before. The arresting officers had, of course, filed their reports. But that wasn't going to be enough when the trial came up. Neither the burglars nor the victims and the officers remembered a thing about the case.

"Also," the D.A. said, "at two-ten this morning, the police got a call from the Black Shadow Tavern on Washington Street. They didn't get there until three-thirty because they were too disorientated to do anything for an hour or more. When they did get to the tavern, they found a dead man. He'd been beaten badly and then stabbed in the stomach. Nobody remembered anything, of course. But from what we could piece together, the dead man must've gotten into a drunken brawl with a person or persons unknown shortly before 1:00 A.M. Thirty people must've witnessed the murder. So we have a murderer or murderers walking the streets today who don't even remember the killing or anything leading up to it."

"They might know they're guilty if they'd been planning it for a long time," I said.

He grinned and said, "But he, or they, won't be telling anybody. No one except the corpse had blood on him nor did anybody have bruised knuckles. Two were arrested for carrying saps, but so what? They'll be out soon, and nobody, but nobody, can prove they used the saps. The knife was still half-sticking in the deceased's belly, and his efforts to pull it out destroyed any fingerprints."

5

We talked and drank a lot, and suddenly it was 6:00 P.M. I was in no condition to drive and had sense enough to know it. I tried calling Carole to come down and get me, but I couldn't get through. At 6:30 and 7:00, I tried again without success. I decided to take a taxi. But after another drink, I tried again and this time got through.

"Where've you been?" she said. "I called your office, but nobody answered. I was thinking about calling the police."

"As if they haven't got enough to do," I said. "When did *you* get home?"

"You're slurring," she said coldly.

I repeated the question.

"Two hours ago," she said.

"The lines were tied up," I said. "I tried."

"You knew how scared I was, and you didn't even care," she said.

"Can I help it if the D.A. insisted on conducting business at the Rover?" I said. "Besides, I was trying to forget."

"Forget what?" she said.

"Whatever it was I forgot," I said.

"You ass!" she screamed. "Take a taxi!"

The phone clicked off.

She didn't make a scene when I got home. She'd decided to play it cool because of the kids, I suppose. She was drinking gin and tonic when I entered, and she said, in a level voice, "*You'll* have some coffee. And after a while you can listen to the tape you made yesterday. It's interesting, but spooky."

"What tape?" I said.

"Mike was fooling around with it," she said. "And he found out you'd recorded what happened yesterday."

"That kid!" I said. "He's always snooping around. I told him to leave my stuff alone. Can't a man have any privacy around here?"

"Well, don't say anything to him," she said. "He's upset as it is. Anyway, it's a good thing he did turn it on. Otherwise, you'd have forgotten all about it. I think you should make a daily record."

"So you think it'll happen again?" I said.

She burst into tears. After a moment, I put my arms around her. I felt like crying, too. But she pushed me away, saying, "You stink of rotten whiskey!"

"That's because it's mostly bar whiskey," I said. "I can't afford Wild Turkey at three dollars a shot."

I drank four cups of black coffee and munched on some shrimp dip. As an aside, I can't really afford that, either, since I only make forty-five thousand dollars a year.

When we went to bed, we went to bed. Afterward, Carole said, "I'm sorry, darling, but my heart wasn't really in it."

"That wasn't all," I said.

"You've got a dirty mind," she said. "What I meant was I couldn't stop thinking, even while we were doing it, that it wasn't any good doing it. We won't remember it tomorrow, I thought."

"How many do we really remember?" I said. "Sufficient unto the day is the, uh, good thereof."

"It's a good thing you didn't try to fulfill your childhood dream of becoming a preacher," she said. "You're a born shyster. You'd have made a lousy minister."

"Look," I said, "I remember the especially good ones. And I'll never forget our honeymoon. But we need sleep. We haven't had any to speak of for twenty-four hours. Let's hit the hay and forget everything until tomorrow. In which case . . ."

She stared at me and then said, "Poor dear, no wonder you're so belligerently flippant! It's a defense against fear!"

I slammed my fist into my palm and shouted, "I know! I know! For God's sake, how long is this going on?"

I went into the bathroom. The face in the mirror looked as if it were trying to flirt with me. The left eye wouldn't stop winking.

When I returned to the bedroom, Carole reminded me that I'd not made today's recording. I didn't want to do it because I was so tired. But the possibility of losing another day's memory spurred me. No, not another day, I thought. It this occurs tomorrow, I'll lose another four days. Tomorrow and the three preceding May 25. I'll wake up June 3 and think it's the morning of the twenty-second.

I'm making this downstairs in my study. I wouldn't want Carole to hear some of my comments.

Until tomorrow then. It's not tomorrow but yesterday that won't come. I'll make a note to myself and stick it in a corner of the case which holds my glasses.

6

True date: June 3, 1980

I woke up thinking that today was my birthday, May 22. I rolled over, saw the piece of paper half-stuck from my glasses case, put on my glasses and read the note.

It didn't enlighten me. I didn't remember writing the note. And why should I go downstairs and turn on the recorder? But I did so.

As I listened to the machine, my heart thudded as if it were a judge's gavel. My voice kept fading in and out. Was I going to faint?

And so half of today was wasted trying to regain twelve days in my mind. I didn't go to the office, and the kids went to school late. And what about the kids in school on the dayside of Earth? If they sleep during their geometry class, say, then they have to go through that class again on the same day. And that shoves the schedule forward, or is it backward, for that day. And then there's the time workers will lose on their jobs. They have to make it up, which means they get out an hour later. Only it takes more than an hour to recover from the confusion and get orientated. What a mess it has been! What a mess it'll be if this keeps on!

At eleven, Carole and I were straightened out enough to go to the supermarket. It was Tuesday, but Carole wanted me to be with her, so I tried to phone in and tell my secretary I'd be absent. The lines were tied up, and I doubt that she was at work. So I said to hell with it.

Our supermarket usually opens at eight. Not today. We had to stand in a long line, which kept getting longer. The doors opened at twelve. The manager, clerks and boys had had just as much trouble as we did unconfusing themselves, of course. Some didn't show at all. And some of the trucks which were to bring fresh stores never appeared.

By the time Carole and I got inside, those ahead of us had cleaned out half the supplies. They had the same idea we had. Load up now so there wouldn't be any standing in line so many times. The fresh milk was all gone, and the powdered milk shelf had one box left. I started for it but some teen-ager beat me to it. I felt like hitting him, but I didn't, of course.

The prices for everything were being upped by a fourth even as we shopped. Some of the stuff was being marked upward once more while we stood in line at the checkout counter. From the time we entered the line until we pushed out three overflowing carts, four hours had passed.

While Carole put away the groceries, I drove to another supermarket. The line there was a block long; it would be emptied and closed up before I ever got to its doors.

The next two supermarkets and a corner grocery store were just as hopeless. And the three liquor stores I went to were no better. The fourth only had about thirty men in line, so I tried that. When I got inside, all the beer was gone, which didn't bother me any, but the only hard stuff left was a fifth of rotgut. I drank it when I went to college because I couldn't afford anything better. I put the terrible stuff and a half-gallon of cheap muscatel on the counter. Anything was better than nothing, even though the prices had been doubled.

I started to make out the check, but the clerk said, "Sorry, sir. Cash only."

"What?" I said.

"Haven't you heard, sir?" he said. "The banks were closed at 2:00 P.M. today."

"The banks are closed?" I said. I sounded stupid even to myself.

"Yes, sir," he said. "By the federal government. It's only temporary, sir, at least that's what the TV said. They'll be reopened after the stock market mess is cleared up."

"But . . ." I said.

"It's destructed," he said.

"Destroyed," I said automatically. "You mean, it's another Black Friday?"

"It's Tuesday today," he said.

"You're too young to know the reference," I said. And too uneducated, too, I thought.

"The president is going to set up a rationing system," he said.

"For The Interim. And price controls, too. Turner said so on TV an hour ago. The president is going to lay it all out at six tonight."

When I came home, I found Carole in front of the TV. She was pale and wide-eyed.

"There's going to be another depression!" she said. "Oh, Mark, what are we going to do?"

"I don't know," I said. "I'm not the president, you know." And I slumped down onto the sofa. I had lost my flippancy.

Neither of us, having been born in 1945, knew what a Depression, with a big capital D, was; that is, we hadn't experienced it personally. But we'd heard our parents, who were kids when it happened, talk about it. Carole's parents had gotten along, though they didn't live well, but my father used to tell me about days when he had nothing but stale bread and turnips to eat and was happy to get them.

The president's TV speech was mostly about the depression, which he claimed would be temporary. At the end of half an hour of optimistic talk, he revealed why he thought the situation wouldn't last. The federal government wasn't going to wait for the sentients in The Ball—if there were any there—to communicate with us. Obviously, The Ball was hostile. So the survey expedition had been canceled. Tomorrow, the USA, the USSR, France, West Germany, Israel, India, Japan and China would send up an armada of rockets tipped with H-bombs. The orbits and the order of battle were determined this morning by computers; one after the other, the missiles would zero in until The Ball was completely destroyed. It would be over-kill with a vengeance.

"That ought to bring up the stock market!" I said.

And so, after I've finished recording, to bed. Tomorrow, we'll follow our instructions on the notes, relisten to the tapes, reread certain sections of the newspapers and await the news on the TV. To hell with going to the courthouse; nobody's going to be there anyway.

Oh, yes. With all this confusion and excitement, everybody, myself included, forgot that today was my birthday. Wait a minute! It's *not* my birthday!

True date: June 5, 1980. Subjective date: May 16, 1980

I woke up mad at Carole because of our argument the previous day. Not that of June 4, of course, but our brawl of May 15. We'd been at a party given by the Burlingtons, where I met a beautiful young artist, Roberta Gardner. Carole thought I was paying too much attention to her because she looked like Myrna. Maybe I was. On the other hand, I really was interested in her paintings. It seemed to me that she had a genuine talent. When we got home, Carole tore into me, accused me of still being in love with Myrna. My protests did no good whatsoever. Finally, I told her we might as well get a divorce if she couldn't forgive and forget. She ran crying out of the room and slept on the sofa downstairs.

I don't remember what reconciled us, of course, but we must have worked it out, otherwise we wouldn't still be married.

Anyway, I woke up determined to see a divorce lawyer today. I was sick about what Mike and Tom would have to go through. But it would be better for them to be spared our terrible quarrels. I can remember my reactions when I was an adolescent and overheard my parents fighting. It was a relief, though a sad one, when they separated.

Thinking this, I reached for my glasses. And I found the note. And so another voyage into confusion, disbelief and horror.

Now that the panic has eased off somewhat, May 16 is back in the saddle—somewhat. Carole and I are, in a sense, still in that day, and things are a bit cool.

It's 1:00 P.M. now. We just watched the first rockets take off. Ten of them, one after the other.

It's 1:35 P.M. Via satellite, we watched the Japanese missiles.

We just heard that the Chinese and Russian rockets are being launched. When the other nations send theirs up, there will be thirty-seven in all.

No news at 12:30 A.M., June 5. In this case, no news must be bad news. But what could have happened? The newscasters won't say; they just talk around the subject.

7

True date: June 6, 1980. Subjective date: May 13, 1980

My records say that this morning was just like the other four. Hell.

One o'clock. The president, looking like a sad old man, though he's only forty-four, reported the catastrophe. All thirty-seven rockets were blown up by their own H-bombs about three thousand miles from The Ball. We saw some photographs of them taken from the orbiting labs. They weren't very impressive. No mushroom clouds, of course, and not even much light.

The Ball has weapons we can't hope to match. And if it can activate our H-bombs out in space, it should be able to do the same to those on Earth's surface. My God! It could wipe out all life if it wished to do so!

Near the end of the speech, the president did throw out a line of hope. With a weak smile—he was trying desperately to give us his big vote-winning one—he said that all was not lost by any means. A new plan, called Project Toro, was being drawn up even as he spoke.

Toro was Spanish for bull, I thought, but I didn't say so. Carole and the kids wouldn't have thought it funny, and I didn't think it was so funny myself. Anyway, I thought, maybe it's a Japanese word meaning *victory* or *destruction* or something like that.

Toro, as it turned out, was the name of a small irregularly shaped asteroid about 2.413 kilometers long and 1.609 kilometers wide. Its peculiar orbit had been calculated in 1972 by an L. Danielsson of the Swedish Royal Institute of Technology and a W. H. Ip of the University of California at San Diego. Toro, the president said, was bound into a resonant orbit with the Earth. Each time Toro came near the Earth—"near" was sometimes 12.6 million miles—it got exactly enough energy or "kick" from the Earth to push it on around so that it would come back for another near passage.

But the orbit was unstable, which meant that both Earth and Venus take turns controlling the asteroid. For a few centuries, Earth governs Toro; then Venus takes over. Earth has controlled

Toro since A.D. 1580, Venus will take over in 2200. Earth grabs it again in 2350; Venus gets it back in 2800.

I was wondering what all this stuff about this celestial Ping-pong game was about. Then the president said that it was possible to land rockets on Toro. In fact, the plan called for many shuttles to land there carrying parts of huge rocket motors, which would be assembled on Toro.

When the motors were erected on massive and deep stands, power would be applied to nudge Toro out of its orbit. This would require many trips by many rockets with cargoes of fuel and spare parts for the motors. The motors would burn out a number of times. Eventually, though, the asteroid would be placed in an orbit that would end in a direct collision with The Ball. Toro's millions of tons of hard rock and nickel-steel would destroy The Ball utterly, would turn it into pure energy.

"Yes," I said aloud, "but what's to keep The Ball from just changing its orbit? Its sensors will detect the asteroid; it'll change course; Toro will go on by it, like a train on a track."

This was the next point of the president's speech. The failure of the attack had revealed at least one item of information, or, rather, verified it. The radiation of the H-bombs had blocked off, disrupted, all control and observation of the rockets by radar and laser. In their final approach, the rockets had gone in blind, as it were, unable to be regulated from Earth. But if the bombs did this to our sensors, they must be doing the same to The Ball's.

So, just before Toro's course is altered to send it into its final path, H-bombs will be set off all around The Ball. In effect, it will be enclosed in a sphere of radiation. It will have no sensor capabilities. Nor will The Ball *believe* that it will have to alter its orbit to dodge Toro. It will have calculated that Toro's orbit won't endanger it. After the radiation fills the space around it, it won't be able to *see* that Toro is being given a final series of nudges to push it into a collision course.

The project is going to require immense amounts of materials and manpower. The USA can't handle it alone; Toro is going to be a completely international job. What one nation can't provide, the other will.

The president ended with a few words about how Project

Toro, plus the situation of memory loss, is going to bring about a radical revision of the economic setup. He's going to announce the outlines of the new structure—not just policy but structure— two days from now. It'll be designed, so he says, to restore prosperity and, not incidentally, rid society of many problems plaguing it since the industrial revolution.

"Yes, but how long will Project Toro take?" I said. "Oh, Lord, how long?"

Six years, the president said, as if he'd heard me. Perhaps longer.

Six years!

I didn't tell Carole what I could see coming. But she's no dummy. She could figure out some of the things that were bound to happen in six years, and none of them were good.

I never felt so hopeless in my life, and neither did she. But we do have each other, and so we clung tightly for a while. May 16 isn't forgotten, but it seems so unimportant. Mike and Tom cried, I suppose because they knew that this exhibition of love meant something terrible for all of us. Poor kids! They get upset by our hatreds and then become even more upset by our love.

When we realized what we were doing to them, we tried to be jolly. But we couldn't get them to smile.

True date: middle of 1981. Subjective date: middle of 1977

I'm writing this, since I couldn't get any new tapes today. The shortage is only temporary, I'm told. I could erase part of the old ones and use them, but it'd be like losing a vital part of myself. And God knows I've lost enough.

Old Mrs. Douglas next door is dead. Killed herself, according to my note on the calendar, April 2 of this year. I never would have thought she'd do it. She was such a strong fundamentalist, and these believe as strongly as the Roman Catholics that suicide is well-nigh unforgivable. I suspect that the double shock of her husband's death caused her to take her own life. April 2 of 1976 was the day he died. She had to be hospitalized because of the shock and grief for two weeks after his death. Carole and I had her over to dinner a few times after she came home, and all she could talk about was her dead husband. So I presume that, as she traveled backward to the day of his death, the grief became daily more unbearable. She couldn't face the arrival of the day he died.

Hers is not the only empty house on the block. Jack Bridger killed his wife and his three kids and his mother-in-law and himself last month—according to my records. Nobody knows why, but I suspect that he couldn't stand seeing his three-year-old girl become no more than an idiot. She'd retrogressed to the day of her birth and perhaps beyond. She'd lost her language abilities and could no longer feed herself. Strangely, she could still walk, and her intelligence potential was high. She had the brain of a three-year-old, fully developed, but lacking all postbirth experience. It would have been better if she hadn't been able to walk. Confined to a cradle, she would at least not have had to be watched every minute.

Little Ann's fate is going to be Tom's. He talks like a five-year-old now. And Mike's fate . . . my fate . . . Carole's . . . God! We'll end up like Ann! I can't stand thinking about it.

Poor Carole. She has the toughest job. I'm away part of the day, but she has to take care of what are, in effect, a five-year-old and an eight-year-old, getting younger every day. There is no relief for her, since they're always home. All educational institutions, except for certain research laboratories, are closed.

The president says we're going to convert ninety percent of all industries to cybernation. In fact, anything that can be cybernated will be. They have to be. Almost everything, from the mines to the loading equipment to the railroads and trucks and the unloading equipment and the arrangement and dispersal of the final goods at central distribution points.

Are six years enough to do this?

And who's going to pay for this? Never mind, he says. Money is on its way out. The president is a goddamned radical. He's taking advantage of this situation to put over his own ideas, which he sure as hell never revealed during his campaign for election. Sometimes I wonder *who* put The Ball up there. But that idea is sheer paranoia. At least, this gigantic WPA project is giving work to those who are able to work. The rest are on, or going to be on, a minimum guaranteed income, and I mean minimum. But the president says that, in time, everybody will have all he needs, and more, in the way of food, housing, schooling, clothing, etc. *He* says! What if Project Toro doesn't work? And what if it does work? Are we then going to return to the old economy? Of course not! It'll be impossible to abandon everything we've worked on; the new establishment will see to that.

I tried to find out where Myrna lived. I'm making this record in my office, so Carole isn't going to get hold of it. I love her— Myrna, I mean—passionately. I hired her two weeks ago and fell headlong, burningly, in love with her. All this was in 1977 of course, but today, inside of *me, is* 1977.

Carole doesn't know about this, of course. According to the letters and notes from Myrna, which I should have destroyed but, thank God, never had the heart to do, Carole didn't find out about Myrna until two years later. At least that's what this letter from Myrna says. She was away visiting her sister then and wrote to me in answer to my letter. A good thing, too, otherwise I wouldn't know what went on then.

My reason tells me to forget about Myrna. And so I will.

I've traveled backward in our affair, from our final bitter parting, to this state, when I was most in love with her. I know this because I've just reread the records of our relationship. It began deteriorating about six months before we split up, but I don't feel those emotions now, of course. And in two weeks I won't feel anything for her. If I don't refer to the records, I won't even know she ever existed.

This thought is intolerable. I have to find her, but I've had no success at all so far. In fourteen days, no, five, since every day ahead takes three more of the past, I'll have no drive to locate her. Because I won't know what I'm missing.

I don't hate Carole. I love her, but with a cool much-married love. Myrna makes me feel like a boy again. I burn exquisitely.

But where is Myrna?

True date: October 30, 1981

I ran into Brackwell Lee, the old mystery story writer today. Like most writers who haven't gone to work for the government propaganda office, he's in a bad way financially. He's surviving on his GMI, but for him there are no more first editions of rare books, new sports cars, Western Reserve or young girls. I stood him three shots of the rotgut which is the only whiskey now served at Grover's and listened to the funny stories he told to pay me for the drinks. But I also had to listen to his tales of woe.

Nobody buys fiction or, in fact, any long works of any kind anymore. Even if you're a speed reader and go through a whole novel in one day, you have to start all over again the next time you pick it up. TV writing, except for the propaganda shows, is no alternative. The same old shows are shown every day and enjoyed just as much as yesterday or last year. According to my records, I've seen the hilarious pilot movie of the "Soap Opera Blues" series fifty times.

When old Lee talked about how he had been dropped by the young girls, he got obnoxiously weepy. I told him that that didn't say much for him or the girls either. But if he didn't want to be hurt, why didn't he erase those records that noted his rejections?

He didn't want to do that, though he could give me no logical reason why he shouldn't.

"Listen," I said with a sudden drunken inspiration, "why don't you erase the old records and make some new ones? How you laid this and that beautiful young thing. Describe your conquests in detail. You'll think you're the greatest Casanova that ever lived."

"But that wouldn't be true!" he said.

"You, a writer of lies, say that?" I said. "Anyway, you wouldn't know that they weren't the truth."

"Yeah," he said, "but if I get all charged up and come barreling down here to pick up some tail, I'll be rejected and so'll be right back where I was."

"Leave a stern note to yourself to listen to them only late at night, say, an hour before The Ball puts all to sleep. That way, you won't ever get hurt."

George Palmer wandered in then. I asked him how things were doing.

"I'm up to here handling cases for kids who can't get drivers' licenses," he said. "It's true you can teach anybody how to drive in a day, but the lessons are forgotten the next day. Anyway, it's experience that makes a good driver, and . . . need I explain more? The kids have to have cars, so they drive them regardless. Hence, as you no doubt have forgotten, the traffic accidents and violations are going up and up."

"Is that right?" I said.

"Yeah. There aren't too many in the mornings, since most people don't go to work until noon. However, the new transit system should take care of that when we get it, sometime in 1984 or 5."

"What new transit system?" I said.

"It's been in the papers," he said. "I reread some of last week's this morning. The city of Los Angeles is equipped with a model system now, and it's working so well it's going to be extended throughout Los Angeles County. Eventually, every city of any size in the country'll have it. Nobody'll have to walk more than four blocks to get to a line. It'll cut air pollution by half and the traffic load by three-thirds. Of course, it'll be compulsory; you'll have to show cause to drive a car. And I hate to think about the mess *that's* going to be, the paperwork, the pile-up in the courts and so forth. But after the way the government handled the L.A. riot, the rest of the country should get in line."

"How will the rest of the country know how the government handled it unless they're told?" I said.

"They'll be told. Every day," he said.

"Eventually, there won't be enough time in the day for the news channels to tell us all we'll need to know," I said. "And even if there were enough time, we'd have to spend all day watching TV. So who's going to get the work done?"

"Each person will have to develop his own viewing specialty," he said. "They'll just have to watch the news that concerns them and ignore the rest."

"And how can they do that if they won't know what concerns them until they've run through everything?" I said. "Day after day."

"I'll buy a drink," he said. "Liquor's good for one thing. It makes you forget what you're afraid not to forget."

8

True date: late 1982. Subjective date: late 1974

She came into my office, and I knew at once that she was going to be more than just another client. I'd been suffering all day from the "mirror syndrome," but the sight of her stabilized me. I forgot the thirty-seven-year-old face my twenty-nine-year-old mind had seen in the bathroom that morning. She is a beautiful woman, only twenty-seven. I had trouble at first listening to her story; all I wanted to do was to look at her. I finally understood that she wanted me to get her husband out of jail on a murder rap. It seemed he'd been in since 1976 (real time). She wanted me to get the case reopened, to use the new plea of rehabilitation by retrogression.

I was supposed to know that, but I had to take a quick look through my resumé before I could tell her what chance she had. Under RBR was the definition of the term and a notation that a number of people had been released because of it. The main idea behind it is that criminals are not the same people they were before they became criminals, if they have lost all memory of the crime. They've traveled backward to goodness, you might say. Of course, RBR doesn't apply to hardened criminals or to someone who'd planned a crime a long time before it was actually committed.

I asked her why she would want to help a man who had killed his mistress in a fit of rage when he'd found her cheating on him?

"I love him," she said.

And I love you, I thought.

She gave me some documents from the big rec bag she carried. I looked through them and said, "But you divorced him in 1977?"

"Yes, he's really my ex-husband," she said. "But I think of him now as my husband."

No need to ask her why.

"I'll study the case," I said. "You make a note to see me tomorrow. Meantime, how about a drink at the Rover bar so we can discuss our strategy?"

That's how it all started—again.

It wasn't until a week later, when I was going over some old recs, that I discovered it was *again*. It made no difference. I love her. I also love Carole, rather, *a* Carole. The one who married me six years ago, that is, six years ago in my memory.

But there is the other Carole, the one existing today, the poor miserable wretch who can't get out of the house until I come home. And I can't come home until late evening because I can't get started to work until about twelve noon. It's true that I could come home earlier than I do if it weren't for Myrna. I try. No use. I have to see Myrna.

I tell myself I'm a bastard, which I am, because Carole and the children need me very much. Tom is ten and acts as if he's two. Mike is a four-year-old in a twelve-year-old body. I come home from Myrna to bedlam every day, according to my records, and every day must be like today.

That I feel both guilt and shame doesn't help. I become enraged; I try to suppress my anger, which is born out of my desperation and helplessness and guilt and shame. But it comes boiling out, and then bedlam becomes hell.

I tell myself that Carole and the kids need a tower of strength now. One who can be calm and reassuring and, above all, loving. One who can handle the thousand tedious and aggravating problems that infest every household in this world of diminishing memory. In short, a hero. Because the real heroes, and heroines, are those who deal heroically with the everyday cares of life, though God knows they've been multiplied enormously. It's not the guy who kills a dragon once in his lifetime and then retires that's a hero. It's the guy who kills cockroaches and rats every day, day after day, and doesn't rest on his laurels until he's an old man, if then.

What am I talking about? Maybe I could handle the problems if it weren't for this memory loss. I can't adjust because I can't ever get used to it. My whole being, body and mind, must get the same high-voltage jolt every morning.

The insurance companies have canceled all policies for anybody under twelve. The government's contemplated taking over these policies but has decided against it. It will, however, pay for the burials, since this service is necessary. I don't really think that many children are being "accidentally" killed because of the insurance money. Most fatalities are obviously just results of neglect or parents going berserk.

I'm getting away from Myrna, trying to, anyway, because I wish to forget my guilt. I love her, but if I didn't see her tomorrow, I'd forget her. But I *will* see her tomorrow. My notes will make sure of that. And each day is, for me, love at first sight. It's a wonderful feeling, and I wish it could go on forever.

If I just had the guts to destroy all reference to her tonight. But I won't. The thought of losing her makes me panic.

9

True date: middle of 1984. Subjective date: middle of 1968

I was surprised that I woke up so early.

Yesterday, Carole and I had been married at noon. We'd driven up to this classy motel near Lake Geneva. We'd spent most of our time in bed after we got there, naturally, though we did get up for dinner and champagne. We finally fell asleep about four in the morning. That was why I hadn't expected to wake up at dawn. I reached over to touch Carole, wondering if she would be too sleepy. But she wasn't there.

She's gone to the bathroom, I thought. I'll catch her on the way back.

Then I sat up, my heart beating as if it had suddenly discovered it was alive. The edges of the room got fuzzy, and then the fuzziness raced in toward me.

The dawn light was filtered by the blinds, but I had seen that the furniture was not familiar. I'd never been in this place before.

I sprang out of bed and did not, of course, notice the note sticking out of my glass case. Why should I? I didn't wear glasses then.

Bellowing, "Carole!" I ran down a long and utterly strange hall and past the bedroom door, which was open, and into the room at the end of the hall. Inside it, I stopped. This was a kids' bedroom: bunks, pennants, slogans, photographs of two young boys, posters and blowups of faces I'd never seen, except one of Laurel and Hardy, some science fiction and Tolkien and Tarzan books, some school texts, and a large flat piece of equipment hanging on the wall. I would not have known that it was a TV set if its controls had not made its purpose obvious.

The bunks had not been slept in. The first rays of the sun fell on thick dust on a table.

I ran back down the hall, looked into the bathroom again, though I knew no one was there, saw dirty towels, underwear and socks heaped in a corner, and ran back to my bedroom. The blinds did not let enough light in, so I looked for a light switch on the wall. There wasn't any, though there was a small round plate of brass where the switch should have been. I touched it, and the ceiling lights came on.

Carole's side of the bed had not been slept in.

The mirror over the bureau caught me, drew me and held me. Who was this haggard old man staring out from my twenty-three-year-old self? I had gray hair, big bags under my eyes, thickening and sagging features, and a long scar on my right cheek.

After a while, still dazed and trembling, I picked up a book from the bureau and looked at it. At this close distance, I could just barely make out the title, and, when I opened it, the print was a blur.

I put the book down, *Be Your Own Handyman Around Your House*, and proceeded to go through the house from attic to basement. Several times, I whimpered, "Carole! Carole!" Finding no one, I left the house and walked to the house next door and beat on its door. No one answered; no lights came on inside.

I ran to the next house and tried to wake up the people in it. But there weren't any.

A woman in a house across the street shouted at me. I ran to her, babbling. She was about fifty years old and also hysterical. A moment later, a man her age appeared behind her. Neither listened to me; they kept asking me questions, the same questions I was asking them. Then I saw a black and white police car of a model unknown to me come around the corner half a block away. I ran toward it, then stopped. The car was so silent that I knew even in my panic that it was electrically powered. The two cops wore strange uniforms, charcoal gray with white helmets topped by red panaches. Their aluminum badges were in the shape of a spread eagle.

I found out later that the police throughout the country had been federalized. These two were on the night shift and so had had enough time to get reorientated. Even so, one had such a case of the shakes that the other told him to get back into the car and take it easy for a while.

After he got us calmed down, he asked us why we hadn't listened to our tapes.

"What tapes?" we said.

"Where's your bedroom?" he said to the couple.

They led him to it, and he turned on a machine on the bedside table.

"Good morning," a voice said. I recognized it as the husband's. "Don't panic. Stay in bed and listen to me. Listen to everything I say."

The rest was a resumé, by no means short, of the main events since the first day of memory loss. It ended by directing the two to a notebook that would tell them personal things they needed to know, such as where their jobs were, how they could get to them, where the area central distributing stores were, how to use their I.D. cards and so on.

The policeman said, "You have the rec set to turn on at 6:30, but you woke up before then. Happens a lot."

I went back, reluctantly, to the house I'd fled. It was mine, but I felt as if I were a stranger. I ran off my own recs twice. Then I put my glasses on and started to put together my life. The daily rerun of "Narrative of an Old-Young Man Shipwrecked on the Shoals of Time."

I didn't go any place today. Why should I? I had no job. Who needs a lawyer who isn't through law school yet? I did have, I found out, an application in for a position on the police force. The police force was getting bigger and bigger but at the same time was having a large turnover. My recs said that I was to appear at the City Hall for an interview tomorrow.

If I feel tomorrow as I do today, and I will, I probably won't be able to make myself go to the interview. I'm too grief-stricken to do anything but sit and stare or, now and then, get up and pace back and forth, like a sick leopard in a cage made by Time. Even the tranquilizers haven't helped me much.

I have lost my bride the day after we were married. And I love Carole deeply. We were going to live a long happy life and have two children. We would raise them in a house filled with love.

But the recs say that the oldest boy escaped from the house and was killed by a car and Carole, in a fit of anguish and despair, killed the youngest boy and then herself.

They're buried in Springdale Cemetery.

I can't feel a retroactive grief for those strangers called Mike and Tom.

But Carole, lovely laughing Carole, lives in my mind.

Oh, God, why don't I just erase all my recs? Then I'd not have to suffer remorse for all I've done or failed to do. I wouldn't know what a bastard I'd been.

Why don't I do it? Take the past and shed its heartbreaks and its guilts as a snake sheds its skin. Or as the legislature cancels old laws. Press a button, fill the wastebasket, and you're clean and easy again, innocent again. That's the logical thing to do, and I'm a lawyer, dedicated to logic.

Why not? Why not?

But I can't. Maybe I like to suffer. I've liked to inflict suffering, and according to what I understand, those who like to inflict, unconsciously hope to be inflicted upon.

No, that can't be it. At least, not all of it. My main reason for hanging on to the recs is that I don't want to lose my identity. A major part of me, a unique person, is not in the neurons of my mind, where it belongs, but in an electro-mechanical device or in tracings of lead or ink on paper. The protein, the flesh for which I owe, can't hang on to *me*.

I'm becoming less and less, dwindling away, like the wicked witch on whom Dorothy poured water. I'll become a puddle, a wailing voice of hopeless despair, and then . . . nothing.

God, haven't I suffered enough! I said I owe for the flesh and

I'm down in Your books. Why do I have to struggle each day against becoming a dumb brute, a thing without memory? Why not rid myself of the struggle? Press the button, fill the wastebasket, discharge my grief in a chaos of magnetic lines and pulped paper?

Sufficient unto the day is the evil thereof.

I didn't realize, Lord, what that really meant.

10

I will marry Carole in three days. No, I would have. No, I did.

I remember reading a collection of Krazy Kat comic strips when I was twenty-one. One was captioned: COMA REIGNS. Coconing County was in the doldrums, comatose. Nobody, Krazy Kat, Ignatz Mouse, Officer Pupp, nobody had the energy to do anything. Mouse was too lazy even to think about hurling his brickbat. Strange how that sticks in my mind. Strange to think that it won't be long before it becomes forever unstuck.

Coma reigns today over the world.

Except for Project Toro, the TV says. And that is behind schedule. But the Earth, Ignatz Mouse, will not allow itself to forget that it must hurl the brickbat, the asteroid. But where Ignatz expressed his love, in a queer perverted fashion, by banging Kat in the back of the head with his brick, the world is expressing its hatred, and its desperation, by throwing Toro at The Ball.

I did manage today to go downtown to my appointment. I did it only to keep from going mad with grief. I was late, but Chief Moberly seemed to expect that I would be. Almost everybody is, he said. One reason for my tardiness was that I got lost. This residential area was nothing in 1968 but a forest out past the edge of town. I don't have a car, and the house is in the middle of the area, which has many winding streets. I do have a map of the area, which I forgot about. I kept going eastward and finally came to a main thoroughfare. This was Route 98, over which I've traveled many times since I was a child. But the road itself, and the houses along it, were strange. The private airport which should have been across the road was gone, replaced by a number of large industrial buildings.

A big sign near a roofed bench told me to wait there for the RTS bus. One would be along every ten minutes, the sign stated.

I waited an hour. The bus, when it came, was not the fully automated vehicle promised by the sign. It held a sleepy-looking driver and ten nervous passengers. The driver didn't ask me for money, so I didn't offer any. I sat down and watched him with an occasional look out of the window. He didn't have a steering wheel. When he wanted the bus to slow down or stop he pushed a lever forward. To speed it up, he pulled back on the lever. The bus was apparently following a single aluminum rail in the middle of the right-hand lane. My recs told me later that the automatic pilot and door-opening equipment had never been delivered and probably wouldn't be for some years—if ever. The grand plan of cybernating everything possible had failed. There aren't enough people who can provide the know-how or the man-hours. In fact, everything is going to hell.

The police chief, Adam Moberly, is fifty years old and looks as if he's sixty-five. He talked to me for about fifteen minutes and then had me put through a short physical and intelligence test. Three hours after I had walked into the station, I was sworn in. He suggested that I room with two other officers, one of whom was a sixty-year-old veteran, in the hotel across the street from the station. If I had company, I'd get over the morning disorientation more quickly. Besides, the policemen who lived in the central area of the city got preferential treatment in many things, including the rationed supplies.

I refused to move. I couldn't claim that my house was a home to me, but I feel that it's a link to the past, I mean the future, no, I mean the past. Leaving it would be cutting out one more part of me.

True date: late 1984. Subjective date: early 1967
My mother died today. That is, as far as I'm concerned, she did. The days ahead of me are going to be full of anxiety and grief.

She took a long time to die. She found out she had cancer two weeks after my father died. So I'll be voyaging backward in sorrow through my mother and then through my father, who was also sick for a long time.

Thank God I won't have to go through every day of that, though. Only a third of them. And these are the last words I'm going to record about their illnesses.

But how can I not record them unless I make a recording reminding me not to do so?

I found out from my recs how I'd gotten this big scar on my face. Myrna's ex-husband slashed me before I laid him out with a big ashtray. He was shipped off this time to a hospital for the criminally insane where he died a few months later in the fire that burned every prisoner in his building. I haven't the faintest idea what happened to Myrna after that. Apparently I decided not to record it.

I feel dead tired tonight, and, according to my recs, every night. It's no wonder, if every day is like today. Fires, murders, suicides, accidents and insane people. Babies up to fourteen years old abandoned. And a police department which is ninety percent composed, in effect, of raw rookies. The victims are taken to hospitals where the nurses are only half-trained, if that, and the doctors are mostly old geezers hauled out of retirement.

I'm going to bed soon even if it's only nine o'clock. I'm so exhausted that even Jayne Mansfield couldn't keep me awake. And I dread tomorrow. Besides the usual reasons for loathing it, I have one which I can hardly stand thinking about.

Tomorrow my memory will have slid past the day I met Carole. I won't remember her at all.

Why do I cry because I'll be relieved of a great sorrow?

11

True date: 1986. Subjective date: 1962

I'm nuts about Jean, and I'm way down because I can't find her. According to my recs, she went to Canada in 1965. Why?

We surely didn't fall in and then out of love? Our love would never die. Her parents must've moved to Canada. And so here we both are in 1962, in effect. Halfway in 1962, anyway. Amphibians of time. Is she thinking about me now? Is she unable to think about me, about anything, because she's dead or crazy? Tomorrow I'll start the official wheels grinding. The Canadian government should be able to find her through the International Information Computer Network, according to the recs. Meanwhile, I burn, though with a low flame. I'm so goddamn tired.

Even Marilyn Monroe couldn't get a rise out of me tonight. But Jean. Yeah, Jean. I see her as seventeen years old, tall, slim but full-busted, with creamy white skin and a high forehead and huge blue eyes and glossy black hair and the most kissable lips ever. And broadcasting sex waves so thick you can see them, like heat waves. Wow!

And so tired old Wow goes to bed.

February 6, 1987

While I was watching TV to get orientated this morning, a news flash interrupted the program. The president of the United States had died of a heart attack a few minutes before.

"My God!" I said. "Old Eisenhower is dead!"

But the picture of the president certainly wasn't that of Eisenhower. And the name was one I never heard, of course.

I can't feel bad for a guy I never knew.

I got to thinking about him, though. Was he as confused every morning as I was? Imagine a guy waking up, thinking he's a senator in Washington and then he finds he's the president? At least, he knows something about running the country. But it's no wonder the old pump conked out. The TV says we've had five prexies, mostly real old guys, in the last seven years. One was shot; one dived out of the White House window onto his head; two had heart attacks; one went crazy and almost caused a war, as if we didn't have grief enough, for crying out loud.

Even after the orientation, I really didn't get it. I guess I'm too dumb for anything to percolate through my dome.

A policeman called and told me I'd better get my ass down to work. I said I didn't feel up to it, besides, why would I want to be a cop? He said that if I didn't show, I might go to jail. So I showed.

True date: late 1988. Subjective date: 1956

Here I am, eleven years old, going on ten.

In one way, that is. The other way, here I am forty-three and going on about sixty. At least, that's what my face looks like to me. Sixty.

This place is just like a prison except some of us get treated like trusties. According to the work chart, I leave through the big iron gates every day at twelve noon with a demolition crew. We tore down five partly burned houses today. The gang chief, old Rogers, says it's just WPA work, whatever that is. Anyway, one of the guys I work with kept looking more and more familiar. Suddenly, I felt like I was going to pass out. I put down my sledgehammer and walked over to him, and I said, "Aren't you Stinky Davis?"

He looked funny and then he said, "Jesus! You're Gabby! Gabby Franham!"

I didn't like his using the Lord's name in vain, but I guess he can be excused.

Nothing would've tasted good the way I felt, but the sandwiches we got for breakfast, lunch and supper tasted like they had a dash of oil in them. Engine oil, I mean. The head honcho, he's eighty if he's a day, says his recs tell him they're derived from petroleum. The oil is converted into a kind of protein and then flavoring and stuff is added. Oil-burgers, they call them.

Tonight, before lights-out, we watched the prez give a speech. He said that, within a month, Project Toro will be finished. One way or the other. And all this memory loss should stop. I can't quite get it even if I was briefed this morning. Men on the moon, unmanned ships on Venus and Mars, all since I was eleven years old. And The Black Ball, the thing from outer space. And now we're pushing asteroids around. Talk about your science fiction!

12

September 4, 1988

Today's the day.

Actually, the big collision'll be tomorrow, ten minutes before 1:00 A.M. . . . but I think of it as today. Toro, going 15,000 miles an hour, will run head-on into The Ball. Maybe.

Here I am again, Mark Franham, recording just in case The Ball does dodge out of the way and I have to depend on my recs. It's 7:00 P.M. and after that raunchy supper of oil-burgers, potato soup and canned carrots, fifty of us gathered around set No. 8. There's a couple of scientists talking now, discussing theories about just what The Ball is and why it's been taking our memories away from us. Old Doctor Charles Presley—any relation to Elvis?—thinks The Ball is some sort of unmanned survey ship. When it finds a planet inhabited by sentient life, sentient means intelligent, it takes specimens. Specimens of the mind, that is. It unpeels people's minds four days' worth at a time, because that's all it's capable of. But it can do it to billions of specimens. It's like it was reading our minds but destroying the mind at the same time. Presley said it was like some sort of Heisenberg principle of the mind. The Ball can't observe our memories closely without disturbing them.

This Ball, Presley says, takes our memories and stores them. And when it's through with us, sucked us dry, it'll take off for another planet circling some far-off star. Someday, it'll return to its home planet, and the scientists there will study the recordings of our minds.

The other scientist, Dr. Marbles—he's still got his, ha! ha!—asked why any species advanced enough to be able to do this could be so callous? Surely, the extees must know what great damage they're doing to us. Wouldn't they be too ethical for this?

Doc Presley says maybe they think of us as animals, they are so far above us. Doc Marbles says that could be. But it could also be that whoever built The Ball have different brains than we do. Their mind-reading ray, or whatever it is, when used on themselves doesn't disturb the memory patterns. But we're different. The extees don't know this, of course. Not now, anyway. When The Ball goes home, and the extees read our minds, they'll be shocked at what they've done to us. But it'll be too late then.

Presley and Marbles got into an argument about how the extees would be able to interpret their recordings. How could they translate our languages when they have no references—I mean, referents? How're they going to translate *chair* and *recs* and *rock and roll* and *yucky* and so on when they don't have anybody to tell them their meanings. Marbles said they wouldn't have just words; they'd have mental images to associate with the words. And so on. Some of the stuff they spouted I didn't understand at all.

I do know one thing, though, and I'm sure those bigdomes do, too. But they wouldn't be allowed to say it over TV because we'd be even more gloomy and hopeless-feeling. That is, what if right now the computers in The Ball are translating our languages, reading our minds, as they're recorded? Then they know all about Project Toro. They'll be ready for the asteroid, destroy it if they have the weapons to do it, or, if they haven't, they'll just move The Ball into a different orbit.

I'm not going to say anything to the other guys about this. Why make them feel worse?

It's ten o'clock now. According to regulations posted up all over the place, it's time to go to bed. But nobody is. Not tonight. You don't sleep when the End of the World may be coming up.

I wish my Mom and Dad were here. I cried this morning when I found they weren't in this dump, and I asked the chief where they were. He said they were working in a city nearby, but they'd be visiting me soon. I think he lied.

Stinky saw me crying, but he didn't say anything. Why should he? I'll bet he's shed a few when he thought nobody was looking, too.

Twelve o'clock. Midnight. Less than an hour to go. Then, the big smash! Or, I hate to think about it, the big flop. We won't be able to see it directly because the skies are cloudy over most of North America. But we've got a system worked out so we can see it on TV. If there's a gigantic flash when the Toro and The Ball collide, that is.

What if there isn't? Then we'll soon be just like those grown-up kids, some of them twenty years old, that they keep locked up in the big building in the northwest corner of this place. Saying nothing but Da Da or Ma Ma, drooling, filling their diapers. If they got diapers, because old Rogers says he heard, today, of course, they don't wear nothing. The nurses come in once a day and hose them and the place down. The nurses don't have time to change and wash diapers and give personal baths. They got enough to do just spoon-feeding them.

Three and a half more hours to go, and I'll be just like them. Unless, before then, I flip, and they put me in that building old Rogers calls the puzzle factory. They're all completely out of their skulls, he says, and even if memloss stops tonight, they won't change any.

Old Rogers says there's fifty million less people in the United States than there were in 1980, according to the recs. And a good thing, too, he says, because it's all we can do to feed what we got.

Come on, Toro! You're our last chance!

If Toro doesn't make it, I'll kill myself! I will! I'm not going to let myself become an idiot. Anyway, by the time I do become one, there won't be enough food to go around for those that do have their minds. I'll be starving to death. I'd rather get it over with now than go through that.

God'll forgive me.

God, You know I want to be a minister of the gospel when I grow up and that I want to help people. I'll marry a good woman, and we'll have children that'll be brought up right. And we'll thank You every day for the good things of life and battle the bad things.

Love, that's what I got, Lord. Love for You and love for Your people. So don't make me hate You. Guide Toro right into The Ball, and get us started on the right path again.

I wish Mom and Dad were here.

Twelve-thirty. In twenty minutes, we'll know.

The TV says the H-bombs are still going off all around The Ball.

The TV says the people on the East Coast are falling asleep. The rays, or whatever The Ball uses, aren't being affected by the

H-bomb radiation. But that doesn't mean that its sensors aren't. I pray to God that they are cut off.

Ten minutes to go. Toro's got twenty-five thousand miles to go. Our sensors can't tell whether or not The Ball's still on its original orbit. I hope it is; I hope it is! If it's changed its path, then we're through! Done! Finished! Wiped out!

Five minutes to go; twelve thousand five hundred miles to go.

I can see in my mind's eyes The Ball, almost half a mile in diameter, hurtling on its orbit, blind as a bat, I hope and pray, the bombs, the last of the five thousand bombs, flashing, and Toro, a mile and a half long, a mile wide, millions of tons of rock and nickel-steel, charging toward its destined spot.

If it *is* destined.

But space *is* big, and even the Ball and Toro are small compared to all that emptiness out there. What if the mathematics of the scientists is just a little off, or the rocket motors on Toro aren't working just like they're supposed to, and Toro just tears on by The Ball? It's got to meet The Ball at the exact time and place, it's just *got* to!

I wish the radars and lasers could see what's going on.

Maybe it's better they can't. If we knew that The Ball had changed course . . . but this way we still got hope.

If Toro misses, I'll kill myself, I swear it.

Two minutes to go. One hundred and twenty seconds. The big room is silent except for kids like me praying or talking quietly into our recs or praying and talking and sobbing.

The TV says the bombs have quit exploding. No more flashes until Toro hits The Ball—if it does. Oh, God, let it hit, let it hit!

The unmanned satellites are going to open their camera lenses at the exact second of impact and take a quick shot. The cameras are encased in lead, the shutters are lead, and the equipment is special, mostly mechanical, not electrical, almost like a human eyeball. If the cameras see the big flash, they'll send an electrical impulse through circuits, also encased in lead, to a mechanism that'll shoot a big thin-shelled ball out. This is crammed with flashpowder, the same stuff photographers use, and mixed with oxygen pellets so the powder will ignite. There's to be three of the biggest flashes you ever saw. Three. Three for Victory.

If Toro misses, then only one flashball'll be set off.

Oh, Lord, don't let it happen!

Planes with automatic pilots'll be cruising above the clouds, and their equipment will see the flashes and transmit them to the ground TV equipment.

One minute to go.

Come on, God!

Don't let it happen, please don't let it happen, that some place way out there, some thousands of years from now, some weird-looking character reads this and finds out to his horror what his people have done to us. Will he feel bad about it? Lot of good that'll do. You, out there, I hate you! God, how I hate you!

Our Father which art in Heaven, fifteen seconds, Hallowed be Thy name, ten seconds, Thy will be done, five seconds, Thy will be done, but if it's thumbs, down, God, why? Why? What did I ever do to You?

The screen's blank! Oh, my God, the screen's blank! What happened? Transmission trouble? Or they're afraid to tell us the truth?

It's on! It's on!

YAAAAAAY!

13

July 4, A.D. *2002*

I may erase this. If I have any sense, I will. If I had any sense, I wouldn't make it in the first place.

Independence Day, and we're still under an iron rule. But old Dick the Dictator insists that when there's no longer a need for strict control, the Constitution will be restored, and we'll be a democracy again. He's ninety-five years old and can't last much longer. The vice-president is only eighty, but he's as tough an octogenarian as ever lived. And he's even more of a totalitarian than

Dick. And when have men ever voluntarily relinquished power?

I'm one of the elite, so I don't have it so bad. Just being fifty-seven years old makes me a candidate for that class. In addition, I have my Ph.D. in education and I'm a part-time minister. I don't know why I say part-time, since there aren't any full-time ministers outside of the executives of the North American Council of Churches. The People can't afford full-time divines. Everybody has to work at least ten hours a day. But I'm better off than many. I've been eating fresh beef and pork for three years now. I have a nice house I don't have to share with another family. The house isn't the one my recs say I once owned. The People took it over to pay for back taxes. It did me no good to protest that property taxes had been canceled during The Interim. That, say the People, ended when The Ball was destroyed.

But how could I pay taxes on it when I was only eleven years old, in effect?

I went out this afternoon, it being a holiday, with Leona to Springdale. We put flowers on her parents' and sisters' graves, none of whom she remembers, and on my parents' and Carole's and the children's graves, whom I know only through the recs. I prayed for the forgiveness of Carole and the boys.

Near Carole's grave was Stinky Davis's. Poor fellow, he went berserk the night The Ball was destroyed and had to be put in a padded cell. Still mad, he died five years later.

I sometimes wonder why I didn't go mad, too. The daily shocks and jars of memloss should have made everyone fall apart. But a certain number of us were very tough, tougher than we deserved. Even so, the day-to-day attack by alarm syndromes did its damage. I'm sure that years of life were cut off the hardiest of us. We're the shattered generation. And this is bad for the younger ones, who'll have no older people to lead them in the next ten years or so.

Or is it such a bad thing?

At least, those who were in their early twenties or younger when The Ball was smashed are coming along fine. Leona herself was twenty then. She became one of my students in high school. She's thirty-five physically but only fifteen in what the kids call "intage" or internal age. But since education goes faster for adults, and all those humanities courses have been eliminated, she graduated from high school last June. She still wants to be a doctor of medicine, and God knows we need M.D.'s. She'll be forty-two before she gets her degree. We're planning on having two children, the maximum allowed, and it's going to be tough raising them while she's in school. But God will see us through.

As we were leaving the cemetery, Margie Oleander, a very pretty girl of twenty-five, approached us. She asked me if she could speak privately to me. Leona didn't like that, but I told her that Margie probably wanted to talk to me about her grades in my geometry class.

Margie did talk somewhat about her troubles with her lessons. But then she began to ask some questions about the political system. Yes, I'd better erase this, and if it weren't for old habits, I'd not be doing this now.

After a few minutes, I became uneasy. She sounded as if she were trying to get me to show some resentment about the current situation.

Is she an agent provocateur or was she testing me for potential membership in the underground?

Whatever she was doing, she was in dangerous waters. So was I. I told her to ask her political philosophy teacher for answers. She said she'd read the textbook, which is provided by the government. I muttered something about, "Render unto Caesar's what is Caesar's," and walked away.

But she came after me, and asked if I could talk to her in my office tomorrow. I hesitated and then said I would.

I wonder if I would have agreed if she weren't so beautiful?

When we got home, Leona made a scene. She accused me of chasing after the younger girls because she was too old to stimulate me. I told her that I was no senile King David, which she should be well aware of, and she said she's listened to my recs and she knew what kind of man I was. I told her I'd learned from my mistakes. I've gone over the recs of the missing years many times.

"Yes," she said, "you know about them intellectually. But you don't *feel* them!"

Which is true.

I'm outside now and looking up into the night. Up there, out there, loose atoms and molecules float around, cold and alone, debris of the memory records of The Ball, atoms and molecules of what were once incredibly complex patterns, the memories of thirty-two years of the lives of four and a half billion human beings. Forever lost, except in the mind of One.

Oh, Lord, I started all over again as an eleven-year-old. Don't let me make the same mistakes again.

You've given us tomorrow again, but we've very little past to guide us.

Tomorrow I'll be very cool and very professional with Margie. Not too much, of course, since there should be a certain warmth between teacher and pupil.

If only she did not remind me of . . . whom?

But that's impossible. I can remember nothing from The Interim. Absolutely nothing.

But what if there are different kinds of memory?

After King Kong Fell

1973

THE FIRST HALF of the movie was grim and gray and somewhat tedious. Mr. Howller did not mind. That was, after all, realism. Those times had been grim and gray. Moreover, behind the tediousness was the promise of something vast and horrifying. The creeping pace and the measured ritualistic movements of the actors gave intimations of the workings of the gods. Unhurriedly, but with utmost confidence, the gods were directing events toward the climax.

Mr. Howller had felt that at the age of fifteen, and he felt it now while watching the show on TV at the age of fifty-five. Of course, when he first saw it in 1933, he had known what was coming. Hadn't he lived through some of the events only two years before that?

The old freighter, the *Wanderer*, was nosing blindly through the fog toward the surflike roar of the natives' drums. And then: the commercial. Mr. Howller rose and stepped into the hall and called down the steps loudly enough for Jill to hear him on the front porch. He thought, commercials could be a blessing. They give us time to get into the bathroom or the kitchen, or time to light up a cigarette and decide about continuing to watch this show or go on to that show.

And why couldn't real life have its commercials?

Wouldn't it be something to be grateful for if reality stopped in mid-course while the Big Salesman made His pitch? The car about to smash into you, the bullet on its way to your brain, the first cancer cell about to break loose, the boss reaching for the phone to call you in so he can fire you, the spermatozoon about to be launched toward the ovum, the final insult about to be hurled at the once, and perhaps still, beloved, the final drink of alcohol which would rupture the abused blood vessel, the decision which would lead to the light that would surely fail?

If only you could step out while the commercial interrupted these, think about it, talk about it, and then, returning to the set, switch it to another channel.

But that one is having technical difficulties, and the one after that is a talk show whose guest is the archangel Gabriel himself and after some urging by the host he agrees to blow his trumpet, and . . .

Jill entered, sat down, and began to munch the cookies and drink the lemonade he had prepared for her. Jill was six and a half years old and beautiful, but then what granddaughter wasn't beautiful? Jill was also unhappy because she had just quarreled with her best friend, Amy, who had stalked off with threats never to see Jill again. Mr. Howller reminded her that this had happened before and that Amy always came back the next day, if not sooner. To take her mind off of Amy, Mr. Howller gave her a brief outline of what had happened in the movie. Jill listened without enthusiasm, but she became excited enough once the movie had resumed. And when Kong was feeling over the edge of the abyss for John Driscoll, played by Bruce Cabot, she got into her grandfather's lap. She gave a little scream and put her hands over her eyes when Kong carried Ann Redman into the jungle (Ann played by Fay Wray).

But by the time Kong lay dead on Fifth Avenue, she was rooting for him, as millions had before her. Mr. Howller squeezed her and kissed her and said, "When your mother was about your age, I took her to see this. And when it was over, she was crying, too."

Jill sniffled and let him dry the tears with his handkerchief. When the Roadrunner cartoon came on, she got off his lap and went back to her cookie-munching. After a while she said, "Grandpa, the coyote falls off the cliff so far you can't even see him. When he hits, the whole earth shakes. But he always comes back, good as new. Why can he fall so far and not get hurt? Why couldn't King Kong fall and be just like new?"

Her grandparents and her mother had explained many times

the distinction between a "live" and a "taped" show. It did not seem to make any difference how many times they explained. Somehow, in the years of watching TV, she had gotten the fixed idea that people in "live" shows actually suffered pain, sorrow, and death. The only shows she could endure seeing were those that her elders labeled as "taped." This worried Mr. Howller more than he admitted to his wife and daughter. Jill was a very bright child, but what if too many TV shows at too early an age had done her some irreparable harm? What if, a few years from now, she could easily see, and even define, the distinction between reality and unreality on the screen but deep down in her there was a child that still could not distinguish?

"You know that the Roadrunner is a series of pictures that move. People draw pictures, and people can do anything with pictures. So the Roadrunner is drawn again and again, and he's back in the next show with his wounds all healed and he's ready to make a jackass of himself again."

"A jackass? But he's a coyote."

"Now . . ."

Mr. Howller stopped. Jill was grinning.

"O.K., now you're pulling my leg."

"But is King Kong alive or is he taped?"

"Taped. Like the Disney I took you to see last week. *Bedknobs and Broomsticks.*"

"Then *King Kong* didn't happen?"

"Oh, yes, it really happened. But this is a movie they made about King Kong after what really happened was all over. So it's not exactly like it really was, and actors took the parts of Ann Redman and Carl Denham and all the others. Except King Kong himself. He was a toy model."

Jill was silent for a minute and then she said, "You mean, there really *was* a King Kong? How do you know, Grandpa?"

"Because I was there in New York when Kong went on his rampage. I was in the theater when he broke loose, and I was in the crowd that gathered around Kong's body after he fell off the Empire State Building. I was thirteen then, just seven years older than you are now. I was with my parents, and they were visiting my Aunt Thea. She was beautiful, and she had golden hair just like Fay Wray's—I mean, Ann Redman's. She'd married a very rich man, and they had a big apartment high up in the clouds. In the Empire State Building itself."

"High up in the clouds! That must've been fun, Grandpa!"

It would have been, he thought, if there had not been so much tension in that apartment. Uncle Nate and Aunt Thea should have been happy because they were so rich and lived in such a swell place. But they weren't. No one said anything to young Tim Howller, but he felt the suppressed anger, heard the bite of tone, and saw the tightening lips. His aunt and uncle were having trouble of some sort, and his parents were upset by it. But they all tried to pretend everything was as sweet as honey when he was around.

Young Howller had been eager to accept the pretense. He didn't like to think that anybody could be mad at his tall, blonde, and beautiful aunt. He was passionately in love with her; he ached for her in the daytime; at nights he had fantasies about her of which he was ashamed when he awoke. But not for long. She was a thousand times more desirable than Fay Wray or Claudette Colbert or Elissa Landi.

But that night, when they were all going to see the première of *The Eighth Wonder of the World*, King Kong himself, young Howller had managed to ignore whatever it was that was bugging his elders. And even they seemed to be having a good time. Uncle Nate, over his parents' weak protests, had purchased orchestra seats for them. These were twenty dollars apiece, big money in Depression days, enough to feed a family for a month. Everybody got all dressed up, and Aunt Thea looked too beautiful to be real. Young Howller was so excited that he thought his heart was going to climb up and out through his throat. For days the newspapers had been full of stories about King Kong—speculations, rather, since Carl Denham wasn't telling them much. And he, Tim Howller, would be one of the lucky few to see the monster first.

Boy, wait until he got back to the kids in seventh grade in Busiris, Illinois! Would their eyes ever pop when he told them all about it!

But his happiness was too good to last. Aunt Thea suddenly said she had a headache and couldn't possibly go. Then she and

Uncle Nate went into their bedroom, and even in the front room, three rooms and a hallway distant, young Tim could hear their voices. After a while Uncle Nate, slamming doors behind him, came out. He was red-faced and scowling, but he wasn't going to call the party off. All four of them, very uncomfortable and silent, rode in a taxi to the theater on Times Square. But when they got inside, even Uncle Nate forgot the quarrel or at least he seemed to. There was the big stage with its towering silvery curtains and through the curtains came a vibration of excitement and of delicious danger. And even through the curtains the hot hairy ape-stink filled the theater.

"Did King Kong get loose just like in the movie?" Jill said.

Mr. Howller started. "What? Oh, yes, he sure did. Just like in the movie."

"Were you scared, Grandpa? Did you run away like everybody else?"

He hesitated. Jill's image of her grandfather had been cast in a heroic mold. To her he was a giant of Herculean strength and perfect courage, her defender and champion. So far he had managed to live up to the image, mainly because the demands she made were not too much for him. In time she would see the cracks and the sawdust oozing out. But she was too young to disillusion now.

"No, I didn't run," he said. "I waited until the theater was cleared of the crowd."

This was true. The big man who'd been sitting in the seat before him had leaped up yelling as Kong began tearing the bars out of his cage, had whirled and jumped over the back of his seat, and his knee had hit young Howller on the jaw. And so young Howller had been stretched out senseless on the floor under the seats while the mob screamed and tore at each other and trampled the fallen.

Later he was glad that he had been knocked out. It gave him a good excuse for not keeping cool, for not acting heroically in the situation. He knew that if he had not been unconscious, he would have been as frenzied as the others, and he would have abandoned his parents, thinking only in his terror of his own salvation. Of course, his parents had deserted him, though they claimed that they had been swept away from him by the mob. This *could* be true; maybe his folks *had* actually tried to get to him. But he had not really thought they had, and for years he had looked down on them because of their flight. When he got older, he realized that he would have done the same thing, and he knew that his contempt for them was really a disguised contempt for himself.

He had awakened with a sore jaw and a headache. The police and the ambulance men were there and starting to take care of the hurt and to haul away the dead. He staggered past them out into the lobby and, not seeing his parents there, went outside. The sidewalks and the streets were plugged with thousands of men, women, and children, on foot and in cars, fleeing northward.

He had not known where Kong was. He should have been able to figure it out, since the frantic mob was leaving the midtown part of Manhattan. But he could think of only two things. Where were his parents? And was Aunt Thea safe? And then he had a third thing to consider. He discovered that he had wet his pants. When he had seen the great ape burst loose, he had wet his pants.

Under the circumstances, he should have paid no attention to this. Certainly no one else did. But he was a very sensitive and shy boy of thirteen, and, for some reason, the need for getting dry underwear and trousers seemed even more important than finding his parents. In retrospect he would tell himself that he would have gone south anyway. But he knew deep down that if his pants had not been wet he might not have dared return to the Empire State Building.

It was impossible to buck the flow of the thousands moving like lava up Broadway. He went east on 43rd Street until he came to Fifth Avenue, where he started southward. There was a crowd to fight against here, too, but it was much smaller than that on Broadway. He was able to thread his way through it, though he often had to go out into the street and dodge the cars. These, fortunately, were not able to move faster than about three miles an hour.

"Many people got impatient because the cars wouldn't go faster," he told Jill, "and they just abandoned them and struck out on foot."

"Wasn't it noisy, Grandpa?"

"Noisy? I've never heard such noise. I think that everyone in Manhattan, except those hiding under their beds, was yelling or talking. And every driver in Manhattan was blowing his car's horn. And then there were the sirens of the fire trucks and police cars and ambulances. Yes, it was noisy."

Several times he tried to stop a fugitive so he could find out what was going on. But even when he did succeed in halting someone for a few seconds, he couldn't make himself heard. By then, as he found out later, the radio had broadcast the news. Kong had chased John Driscoll and Ann Redman out of the theater and across the street to their hotel. They had gone up to Driscoll's room, where they thought they were safe. But Kong had climbed up, using windows as ladder steps, reached into the room, knocked Driscoll out, and grabbed Ann, and had then leaped away with her. He had headed, as Carl Denham figured he would, toward the tallest structure on the island. On King Kong's own island, he lived on the highest point, Skull Mountain, where he was truly monarch of all he surveyed. Here he would climb to the top of the Empire State Building, Manhattan's Skull Mountain.

Tim Howller had not known this, but he was able to infer that Kong had traveled down Fifth Avenue from 38th Street on. He passed a dozen cars with their tops flattened down by the ape's fist or turned over on their sides or tops. He saw three sheet-covered bodies on the sidewalks, and he overheard a policeman telling a reporter that Kong had climbed up several buildings on his way south and reached into windows and pulled people out and thrown them down onto the pavement.

"But you said King Kong was carrying Ann Redman in the crook of his arm, Grandpa," Jill said. "He only had one arm to climb with, Grandpa, so . . . so wouldn't he fall off the building when he reached in to grab those poor people?"

"A very shrewd observation, my little chickadee," Mr. Howller said, using the W. C. Fields voice that usually sent her into giggles. "But his arms were long enough for him to drape Ann Redman over the arm he used to hang on with while he reached in with the other. And to forestall your next question, even if you had not thought of it, he could turn over an automobile with only one hand."

"But . . . but why'd he take time out to do that if he wanted to get to the top of the Empire State Building?"

"I don't know why *people* often do the things they do," Mr. Howller said. "So how would I know why an *ape* does the things he does?"

When he was a block away from the Empire State Building, a plane crashed onto the middle of the avenue two blocks behind him and burned furiously. Tim Howller watched it for a few minutes, then he looked upward and saw the red and green lights of the five planes and the silvery bodies slipping in and out of the searchlights.

"Five airplanes, Grandpa? But the movie . . ."

"Yes, I know. The movie showed about fourteen or fifteen. But the book says that there were six to begin with, and the book is much more accurate. The movie also shows King Kong's last stand taking place in the daylight. But it didn't; it was still nighttime."

The Army Air Force plane must have been going at least 250 mph as it dived down toward the giant ape standing on the top of the observation tower. Kong had put Ann Redman by his feet so he could hang on to the tower with one hand and grab out with the other at the planes. One had come too close, and he had seized the left biplane structure and ripped it off. Given the energy of the plane, his hand should have been torn off, too, or at least he should have been pulled loose from his hold on the tower and gone down with the plane. But he hadn't let loose, and that told something of the enormous strength of that towering body. It also told something of the relative fragility of the biplane.

Young Howller had watched the efforts of the firemen to extinguish the fire and then he had turned back toward the Empire State Building. By then it was all over. All over for King Kong, anyway. It was, in after years, one of Mr. Howller's greatest regrets that he had not seen the monstrous dark body falling through the beams of the searchlights—blackness, then the flash of blackness through the whiteness of the highest beam, blackness, the flash through the next beam, blackness, the flash through the third beam, blackness, the flash through the lowest beam. Dot, dash, dot, dash, Mr. Howller was to think afterward. A code transmitted unconsciously by the great ape and received unconsciously by those who witnessed the fall. Or by those who would hear of it and think about it. Or was he going too far in conceiving this? Wasn't he always looking for codes? And, when he found them, unable to decipher them?

Since he had been thirteen, he had been trying to equate the great falls in man's myths and legends and to find some sort of intelligence in them. The fall of the tower of Babel, of Lucifer, of Vulcan, of Icarus, and, finally, of King Kong. But he wasn't equal to the task; he didn't have the genius to perceive what the falls meant, he couldn't screen out the—to use an electronic term—the "noise." All he could come up with were folk adages. What goes up must come down. The bigger they are, the harder they fall.

"What'd you say, Grandpa?"

"I was thinking out loud, if you can call that thinking," Mr. Howller said.

Young Howller had been one of the first on the scene, and so he got a place in the front of the crowd. He had not completely forgotten his parents or Aunt Thea, but the danger was over, and he could not make himself leave to search for them. And he had even forgotten about his soaked pants. The body was only about thirty feet from him. It lay on its back on the sidewalk, just as in the movie. But the dead Kong did not look as big or as dignified as in the movie. He was spread out more like an apeskin rug than a body, and blood and bowels and their contents had splashed out around him.

After a while Carl Denham, the man responsible for capturing Kong and bringing him to New York, appeared. As in the movie, Denham spoke his classical lines by the body: "It was Beauty. As always, Beauty killed the Beast."

This was the most appropriately dramatic place for the lines to be spoken, of course, and the proper place to end the movie.

But the book had Denham speaking these lines as he leaned over the parapet of the observation tower to look down at Kong on the sidewalk. His only audience was a police sergeant.

Both the book and the movie were true. Or half true. Denham did speak those lines way up on the 102nd floor of the tower. But, showman that he was, he also spoke them when he got down to the sidewalk, where the newsmen could hear them.

Young Howller didn't hear Denham's remarks. He was too far away. Besides, at that moment he felt a tap on his shoulder and heard a man say, "Hey, kid, there's somebody trying to get your attention!"

Young Howller went into his mother's arms and wept for at least a minute. His father reached past his mother and touched him briefly on the forehead, as if blessing him, and then gave his shoulder a squeeze. When he was able to talk, Tim Howller asked his mother what had happened to them. They, as near as they could remember, had been pushed out by the crowd, though they had fought to get to him, and had run up Broadway after they found themselves in the street because King Kong had appeared. They had managed to get back to the theater, had not been able to locate Tim, and had walked back to the Empire State Building.

"What happened to Uncle Nate?" Tim said.

Uncle Nate, his mother said, had caught up with them on Fifth Avenue and just now was trying to get past the police cordon into the building so he could check on Aunt Thea.

"She must be all right!" young Howller said. "The ape climbed up her side of the building, but she could easily get away from him, her apartment's so big!"

"Well, yes," his father had said. "But if she went to bed with her headache, she would've been right next to the window. But don't worry. If she'd been hurt, we'd know it. And maybe she wasn't even home."

Young Tim had asked him what he meant by that, but his father had only shrugged.

The three of them stood in the front line of the crowd, waiting for Uncle Nate to bring news of Aunt Thea, even though they weren't really worried about her, and waiting to see what happened to Kong. Mayor Jimmy Walker showed up and conferred with the officials. Then the governor himself, Franklin Delano Roosevelt, arrived with much noise of siren and motorcycle. A minute later a big black limousine with flashing red lights and a siren pulled up. Standing on the runningboard was a giant with bronze hair and strange-looking gold-flecked eyes. He jumped off the runningboard and strode up to the mayor, governor, and police commissioner and talked briefly with them. Tim Howller asked the man next to him what the giant's name was, but the man replied that he didn't know because he was from out of town also. The giant finished talking and strode up to the crowd, which opened for him as if it were the Red Sea and he were Moses, and he had no trouble at all getting through the police cordon. Tim then asked the man on the right of his parents if he knew the yellow-eyed giant's name. This man, tall and thin, was with a beautiful woman dressed up in an evening gown and a mink coat. He turned his head when Tim called to him and presented a hawklike face and eyes that burned so brightly that Tim wondered if he took dope. Those eyes also told him that here was a man who asked questions, not one who gave answers. Tim didn't repeat his question, and a moment later the man said, in a whispering voice that still carried a long distance, "Come on, Margo. I've work to do." And the two melted into the crowd.

Mr. Howller told Jill about the two men, and she said, "What about them, Grandpa?"

"I don't really know," he said. "Often I've wondered ... Well, never mind. Whoever they were, they're irrelevant to what happened to King Kong. But I'll say one thing about New York—you sure see a lot of strange characters there."

Young Howller had expected that the mess would quickly be cleaned up. And it was true that the sanitation department had sent a big truck with a big crane and a number of men with hoses, scoop shovels, and brooms. But a dozen people at least stopped the cleanup almost before it began. Carl Denham wanted no one to touch the body except the taxidermists he had called in. If he couldn't exhibit a live Kong, he would exhibit a dead one. A colonel from Roosevelt Field claimed the body and, when asked why the Air Force wanted it, could not give an explanation. Rather, he refused to give one, and it was not until an hour later that a phone call from the White House forced him to reveal the real reason. A general wanted the skin for a trophy because Kong was the only ape ever shot down in aerial combat.

A lawyer for the owners of the Empire State Building appeared with a claim for possession of the body. His clients wanted reimbursement for the damage done to the building.

A representative of the transit system wanted Kong's body so it could be sold to help pay for the damage the ape had done to the Sixth Avenue Elevated.

The owner of the theater from which Kong had escaped arrived with his lawyer and announced he intended to sue Denham for an amount which would cover the sums he would have to pay to those who were inevitably going to sue him.

The police ordered the body seized as evidence in the trial for involuntary manslaughter and criminal negligence in which Denham and the theater owner would be defendants in due process.

The manslaughter charges were later dropped, but Denham did serve a year before being paroled. On being released, he was killed by a religious fanatic, a native brought back by the second expedition to Kong's island. He was, in fact, the witch doctor. He had murdered Denham because Denham had abducted and slain his god, Kong.

His Majesty's New York consul showed up with papers which proved that Kong's island was in British waters. Therefore, Denham had no right to anything removed from the island without permission of His Majesty's government.

Denham was in a lot of trouble. But the worst blow of all was to come next day. He would be handed notification that he was being sued by Ann Redman. She wanted compensation to the tune of ten million dollars for various physical indignities and injuries suffered during her two abductions by the ape, plus the mental anguish these had caused her. Unfortunately for her, Denham went to prison without a penny in his pocket, and she dropped the suit. Thus, the public never found out exactly what the "physical indignities and injuries" were, but this did not keep it from making many speculations. Ann Redman also sued John Driscoll, though for a different reason. She claimed breach of promise. Driscoll, interviewed by newsmen, made his famous remark that she should have been suing Kong, not him. This convinced most of the public that what it had suspected had indeed happened. Just how it could have been done was difficult to explain, but the public had never lacked wiseacres who would not only attempt the difficult but would not draw back even at the impossible.

Actually, Mr. Howller thought, the deed was not beyond possibility. Take an adult male gorilla who stood six feet high and weighed 350 pounds. According to Swiss zoo director Ernst Lang, he would have a full erection only two inches long. How did Professor Lang know this? Did he enter the cage during a mating and measure the phallus? Not very likely. Even the timid and amiable gorilla would scarcely submit to this type of handling in that kind of situation. Never mind. Professor Lang said it was so, and so it must be. Perhaps he used a telescope with gradations across the lens like those on a submarine's periscope. In any event, until someone entered the cage and slapped down a ruler during the action, Professor Lang's word would have to be taken as the last word.

By mathematical extrapolation, using the square-cube law, a gorilla twenty feet tall would have an erect penis about twenty-one inches long. What the diameter would be was another guess and perhaps a vital one, for Ann Redman anyway. Whatever anyone else thought about the possibility, Kong must have decided that he would never know unless he tried. Just how well he succeeded, only he and his victim knew, since the attempt would have taken place before Driscoll and Denham got to the observation tower and before the searchlight beams centered on their target.

But Ann Redman must have told her lover, John Driscoll, the truth, and he turned out not to be such a strong man after all.

"What're you thinking about, Grandpa?"

Mr. Howller looked at the screen. The Roadrunner had been succeeded by the Pink Panther, who was enduring as much pain and violence as the poor old coyote.

"Nothing," he said. "I'm just watching the Pink Panther with you."

"But you didn't say what happened to King Kong," she said.

"Oh," he said, "we stood around until dawn, and then the big shots finally came to some sort of agreement. The body just couldn't be left there much longer, if for no other reason than that it was blocking traffic. Blocking traffic meant that business would be held up. And lots of people would lose lots of money. And so Kong's body was taken away by the Police Department, though it used the Sanitation Department's crane, and it was kept in an icehouse until its ownership could be thrashed out."

"Poor Kong."

"No," he said, "not poor Kong. He was dead and out of it."

"He went to heaven?"

"As much as anybody," Mr. Howller said.

"But he killed a lot of people, and he carried off that nice girl. Wasn't he bad?"

"No, he wasn't bad. He was an animal, and he didn't know the difference between good and evil. Anyway, even if he'd been human, he would've been doing what any human would have done."

"What do you mean, Grandpa?"

"Well, if you were captured by people only a foot tall and carried off to a far place and put in a cage, wouldn't you try to escape? And if these people tried to put you back in, or got so scared that they tried to kill you right now, wouldn't you step on them?"

"Sure, I'd step on them, Grandpa."

"You'd be justified, too. And King Kong was justified. He was only acting according to the dictates of his instincts."

"What?"

"He was an animal, and so he can't be blamed, no matter what he did. He wasn't evil. It was what happened around Kong that was evil."

"What do you mean?" Jill said.

"He brought out the bad and the good in the people."

But mostly bad, he thought, and he encouraged Jill to forget about Kong and concentrate on the Pink Panther. And as he looked at the screen, he saw it through tears. Even after forty-two years, he thought, tears. This was what the fall of Kong had meant to him.

The crane had hooked the corpse and lifted it up. And there

were two flattened-out bodies under Kong; he must have dropped them onto the sidewalk on his way up and then fallen on them from the tower. But how explain the nakedness of the corpses of the man and the woman?

The hair of the woman was long and, in a small area not covered by blood, yellow. And part of her face was recognizable.

Young Tim had not known until then that Uncle Nate had returned from looking for Aunt Thea. Uncle Nate gave a long wailing cry that sounded as if he, too, were falling from the top of the Empire State Building.

A second later young Tim Howller was wailing. But where Uncle Nate's was the cry of betrayal, and perhaps of revenge satisfied, Tim's was both of betrayal and of grief for the death of one he had passionately loved with a thirteen-year-old's love, for one whom the thirteen-year-old in him still loved.

"Grandpa, are there any more King Kongs?"

"No," Mr. Howller said. To say yes would force him to try to explain something that she could not understand. When she got older, she would know that every dawn saw the death of the old Kong and the birth of the new